CAUGHT!

"You might as well admit it," Grady pressed. "You were following me."

"Okay," Tori snapped. "You win. I was following you."

"I knew it." His baby blues narrowed and his luscious lips thinned. He could challenge Arnold Schwarzenegger for the starring role if they ever made a movie called *The Intimidator.* "What I want to know is why."

She resisted the urge to bury her face in her hands. She'd had such high hopes that she could excel at private detecting. "There's a simple explanation," she hedged.

He crossed his arms over his chest. "I'm waiting."

One of the artificial spotlights shone down on him, adding light to his captivating features. Her eyes widened, the way they had the first time she'd seen his likeness. *That's it,* she thought. *The perfect explanation.*

"The truth is," she said, and took a breath for courage, "that I think you're hot."

Other *Love Spell* books by Darlene Gardner:

BAIT & SWITCH
THE MISCONCEPTION

snoops in the city

Darlene Gardner

LOVE SPELL NEW YORK CITY

To my sister Lynette,
a private investigator who
qualifies as the snoop in my family.

LOVE SPELL®

July 2004

Published by

Dorchester Publishing Co., Inc.
200 Madison Avenue
New York, NY 10016

ISBN 0-505-52586-0

The name "Love Spell" and its logo are trademarks of Dorchester Publishing Co., Inc.

Printed in the United States of America.

Visit us on the web at www.dorchesterpub.com.

snoops in
the city

Chapter One

Ladies!!! Earn $$$ while performing valuable public service. Telemarketers needed to spread word about erectile dysfunction products. Sexy voice a plus. Call 1-800-GET-HARD.

Tori Whitley's red pen hovered above the classified ad in the help-wanted section of the Sunday *Palm-Times*. Should she or shouldn't she?

On the plus side, she'd have the potential to make a lot of women happy. On the negative, she'd be like those annoying telemarketers who interrupted her dinner to hawk credit cards and time-shares.

Was she so desperate that she'd consider lowering her voice to a throaty purr to entice men to buy Viagra-like products?

She spotted the envelope for her past-due rent payment on top of the stack of unpaid bills on her laminated kitchen counter. By virtue of her latest extension, she had twelve days to come up with the money.

Yep. She really was that desperate.

Or maybe she wasn't.

Her key chain, perfect for occasions like this, tempted her from its usual spot on top of her microwave. She snatched it up, separated the tiny silver disco ball from her gaggle of keys, concentrated and shook. She waited a beat, turned the ball over and leaned closer to read the answer.

My sources say that would be a bummer.

She hadn't been aware she'd been holding her breath until she wasn't anymore. Good. Provocative telemarketing was out. But that didn't solve her problem. She had a maxed-out credit card, a checking-account balance of $168, and no job. Scratch that. She worked weekends at the makeup counter of Frasier's department store, but that barely qualified.

She drew in another deep breath, then released the air slowly and carefully. She would not sigh. She would not feel sorry for herself. Above all, she would not call her parents and ask for help.

Her father, a successful civil litigator, wouldn't hesitate to open his overflowing wallet. Her mother would offer advice. *Come home and repair your broken relationship with Sumner,* she'd say. *He'll take care of you.*

The upshot was that Sumner Aldridge would probably oblige even though Tori had done him a favor by breaking things off. To achieve his goal of making partner in her father's law firm, Sumner needed a corporate wife who adored him, not a girlfriend who liked him.

Besides, she had goals of her own. Turning twenty-five had made her realize it was past time she was independent, like her brother the architect and her sister the pediatrician. She wanted a career. A purpose.

No. Tori couldn't call home. Not after she'd overheard her mother tell her father that their poor, dithering youngest child wouldn't last six months on her own.

It had been late March when Tori moved across the state from her parents' sprawling Siesta Key home to her modest Seahaven apartment. It was now mid-September.

Her six months would be up at the end of the month.

The sun blazed through the kitchen windows, reminding her that she lived in Florida, with its warm climate and low unemployment rate. She had job applications all over town. Something was bound to come up.

The phone rang and she jumped to her feet, upsetting her bright yellow kitchen chair. Somebody was probably calling right now to schedule an interview. Maybe even someone other than the children's performer searching for an assistant who could learn how to make balloon animals.

Just in case it was Clara Clown, Tori reminded herself of the line she'd come up with about being long-winded and grabbed the phone.

"Hello," she said, not quite managing to keep a breathless note out of the greeting.

"Hey, gorgeous. How goes it?"

The raspy voice belonged not to a prospective employer, but to her cousin Eddie Sassenbury.

3

The youngest of her uncle Gary's four sons, Eddie stood out by being the only one without a job pulling in a six-figure income. When her family members mentioned him, they called him "that Eddie." As in, "Did you know *that Eddie* spies on cheating spouses?" Or, "Imagine anyone hiring *that Eddie.*"

"It would go better if you returned my calls." She fought to keep her tone cheerful while she righted the kitchen chair. "I haven't seen you since I moved here."

"Sorry, cuz. I've been busy, busy, busy," he said and she conjured up a mental picture of him. Leaning back in the faux leather chair in the Boca Raton storefront that housed his private-detective agency, his feet propped on a desk, a cigarette dangling from his lips. "You know how the private dick business goes."

"How does it go?"

"Beats being a security guard," Eddie said, referring to the job he'd taken after striking out at becoming a cop. Tori didn't know why he'd failed but suspected the stumbling block might have been the polygraph. "Business is picking up. I'm so busy I can't find the time to hire an associate."

"That's great, Eddie. Really great." Tori cradled the phone between her shoulder and ear, opened the refrigerator, and took out a two-quart jug of cranberry juice. "I always knew you'd make a good snoop. Like I told the other kids, hiding in the bushes with binoculars didn't mean you'd grow up to be a Peeping Tom."

"Job training, is what it was." Eddie sounded proud. "So talk to me. What's this you said on your last message about the bartending not going so well?"

Something inside Tori's chest softened. Her parents

claimed *that Eddie* only got in touch when he wanted something, but this proved them wrong.

"The bar manager fired me," she confessed as she removed a gaily colored glass from the cabinet. "He said I let too many customers run up bar tabs. But I knew they'd make good, Eddie. Just because we hadn't seen any of them in—"

"Tough luck," Eddie interrupted. "You thinking of getting another bartending gig?"

"Nobody will hire me," she said, then tried to look on the bright side of being trash-talked by her ex-boss to prospective employers. "Bartending wasn't for me anyway. All those drunk men, all those late nights. I'm looking for something else."

"Any bites?"

Tori thought of the mail-room supervisor who'd called yesterday to set up an interview that turned out to be at the county prison. She would have gone, too, if he hadn't insisted on somebody with experience.

"Not yet." She set the glass down on the counter and picked up the jug. "But something will turn up."

"Just did," he said. "I want you to work for me."

Something buoyant rose in her chest, making her realize how deflated she'd been. So what if Eddie was the black sheep of the family? He had a career, which was more than she could say for herself. She could be a sheep, too, if it meant following him into the ranks of the employed.

"I'm there," she said. "I haven't worked in an office before but I learn fast."

"Who said I need you in the office? I want you in the field."

The cranberry juice missed the glass and sloshed onto the counter. "You've got to be joking."

"No joke. I've got a client who wants a business-man in Seahaven investigated. Thought of you right off the bat."

The juice dripped off the counter and spilled onto the floor in a skinny red stream. "But, Eddie. This is Tori you're talking to. I'm not sneaky."

"Sure you are."

"Am not. Remember the night you talked me into sneaking out my bedroom window? It shattered when I slammed it shut. Then Mom came outside in her sun-flower pajamas and yelled at you for being a bad influence. Didn't that teach you anything?"

"To suppress any memory involving Aunt Pamela in sunflower pajamas," Eddie answered. "Okay. So you're not sneaky. You don't need to be for this job. You majored in library science, right?"

Tori pursed her lips. During her four degree-free years at the University of Florida, she'd also majored in psychology, sociology, English, history, and a sub-ject she couldn't recall at the moment.

"The library science major didn't take," she said.

"But it taught you how to research. That's all you gotta do. Find out stuff and write it up in a report."

"Isn't finding out stuff the hard part?"

"Usually. But this job's a snap. Access public rec-ords, maybe follow the guy and write down what you see. What do you say?"

Tori watched the cranberry juice on the floor form a red puddle vaguely in the shape of a stop sign. "I say this doesn't sound like something I can do."

6

"Look, this client has major bucks. I can't risk referring her to another agency and losing her business. And have I mentioned I'll pay you?"

Despite Tori's growing resolve to refuse him, she couldn't keep from asking, "How much?"

He named a figure high enough to cover her rent for the next three months, which would temporarily solve her cash-flow problem. But she couldn't do this. She had zero experience and about that much expectancy of being good at PI work. She didn't even need to look into her silver disco ball for advice.

"Sorry, Eddie, but my answer's still no," she said.

The door knocker sounded, giving her an excuse to cut off his protest and hang up. Two more knocks later, she pulled open her door to a warm wind and the cold stare of Helen Grumley, the female half of the married team that managed the apartment complex where she lived. The back of her neck prickled with foreboding.

With her gray hair and round figure, Mrs. Grumley looked remarkably like Tori's paternal grandmother, but the resemblance ended there. Not only did her grandmother understand that gray-haired women shouldn't wear the color olive, she actually liked Tori.

"Hello, Mrs. Grumley," Tori said politely. "What can I do for you?"

"You can pay your rent on time. You're two days late," she said flatly. Behind her, the fronds of the palmetto trees that buffered the four-story apartment building from the parking lot swayed violently in the wind.

"I certainly plan to do that next time," Tori said.

"But Morty gave me a two-week extension this month."

"Morty?" The sun at Mrs. Grumley's back threw her in stark focus. Her nostrils flared. "You call my husband 'Morty'?"

Tori clamped her lips together. Morty Grumley was sixty-five, if he were a day. "I meant, Mr. Grumley."

"Well, *Mr. Grumley* didn't consult me about this. If he had, I would have informed him it's against the policy of Seahaven Shores to grant any tenant more than two extensions in a year. This is your third in six months."

"I'm grateful you and Mr. Grumley have made an exception in my case."

Mrs. Grumley was a few inches shorter than Tori but straightened her spine until it seemed they were nearly eye to eye. "I'm revoking your exception."

"But . . . but Morty, I mean Mr. Grumley, said—"

"Mr. Grumley was mistaken. If I don't have your rent payment by the day after tomorrow, you'll have to leave Seahaven Shores."

The older woman had reached the halfway point of the long outdoor corridor that stretched in front of the row of apartments before the shock of her threat wore off.

Morty, Tori thought, would catch hell.

She closed the door and leaned heavily against it while she considered her options. Even if someone hired her today, she wouldn't get paid in time to cover her rent.

Eddie's offer seemed to be her only way out of this

mess, but could she take it? She picked up her key chain by the silver disco ball, shook it, and turned it over.

Signs point to groovy.

That decided, she went to the phone and dialed.

"Eddie, it's me," she said, ignoring the spilled cranberry juice turning the floor red. "If I agree to be a PI, what would you say to an advance?"

After all, how hard could this PI business be?

Chapter Two

Margo Lazenby drummed her fingertips on the surface of the restaurant's rustic wooden table before it occurred to her that *rat-a-tat-tatt*ing wasn't the best way to treat a French manicure.

She got her hands under control by folding them in her lap, only to start tapping the toe of her sling-back Prada shoe against the weather-beaten floor.

Displays of excitement weren't dignified but she couldn't help it. Any minute now, a real-life private eye would walk through the restaurant door.

Her expectations probably shouldn't be this high, considering her disappointment when she'd first seen Eddie Sassenbury.

She'd been at an obscure strip shopping center indulging her secret passion for George Armstrong's Custard when she spotted Sassenbury's office. She'd impulsively ducked inside, her palms sweating even

11

though the chance of running into someone she knew in that section of town was remote.

She imagined being greeted by somebody like Tom Selleck, who'd been so mouthwatering in *Magnum P.I.* Or the potently capable Robert Urich in *Spenser: For Hire.* Or possibly even, *sigh,* the debonair Pierce Brosnan from the James Bond films.

Instead she'd gotten a scaled-down version of Peter Falk, who'd played the rumpled Lieutenant Colombo in those old TV movies.

Hearing that Sassenbury had assigned a female PI to her case was almost a relief. She'd seen *Charlie's Angels.* Females could kick ass as well as, if not better than, men nowadays. But where was her ass-kicker?

The diamond-encrusted face of Margo's slim gold wristwatch showed ten minutes past the appointed meeting time. As head of the Lazenby Cosmetics empire, she wasn't used to being kept waiting.

But then nothing was usual about this rendezvous.

The Sea and Swallow didn't remotely resemble any of the dining establishments Margo typically frequented. The restaurant overlooked the vast blue beauty of the Atlantic, but its decor was rustic, its atmosphere casual, its menu pedestrian.

Margo would have liked to meet at one of her regular haunts in ritzy Palm Beach, but that was out of the question. Seahaven served as a better location for their clandestine assignation, but as a precaution she'd avoided the downtown.

The center of town gave her the willies anyway. Even though some of the original shops had been refurbished and a few new ones added, Seahaven's downtown was almost frighteningly quaint.

A scant twenty miles north of Palm Beach, Seahaven wasn't quite the place to be. Yet. But it would be. Developers were knocking on the town's door, making regular appearances at Seahaven City Council meetings, clamoring for zoning changes and special favors.

And why not? The town encompassed one of the last underdeveloped stretches of coastline in eastern Florida. Margo herself planned to build the new site for Lazenby's corporate headquarters on the fringes of Seahaven.

Owing to the lavish contribution she'd made to the city's development-mad mayor's re-election campaign, Margo wasn't entirely anonymous in downtown Seahaven. So she'd dressed in an Oscar de la Renta suit in basic please-don't-notice-me black and arranged to have the PI meet her at this unpretentious place across the bridge on Highway A1A.

She reached into her Gucci handbag and pulled out her cell phone, intending to call Eddie Sassenbury and ask where the hell her PI was, when the front door of the restaurant flew open.

It let in a stiff, salty breeze and a young woman with thick shoulder-length deep auburn hair who looked to be in her midtwenties.

Margo dropped the cell phone back into her bag and clasped her hands together as she watched the woman approach a waitress. The waitress nodded toward the table where Margo sat.

13

Yes! This stylish creature, this female version of James Bond, was her PI.

Margo had seldom seen a woman with her coloring who knew how to capitalize on it, but this woman had managed it beautifully. Her golden-hued skin was smooth and flawless, complementing her hair so well that Margo wagered she was a master of foundation choice.

If Margo had analyzed the woman's colors, she'd label her an "autumn." Women with skin and hair like hers typically looked best in warm colors that were yellow based, and she obviously knew that.

She'd chosen a blouse in a lovely shade of gold, which she'd paired with cinnamon brown slacks. Even her lipstick, with its brownish undertones, was perfect.

This was a woman with a sense of style and color, which the world had far too few of, to Margo's way of thinking.

A woman who would look good while kicking ass!

She had a feeling the young woman would do. Oh, yes, she would do very nicely.

Tori consciously slowed her momentum so she wouldn't rush over to the Woman in Black's table.

Now that she was on the case, she was eager to get started. She needed to look at this as an opportunity rather than an ordeal. Not only would the payment help prove she could make it on her own, but she might discover she had an aptitude for private detecting.

She doubted she was a natural, owing to the fact that she'd always been a bust at the board game Clue, but she was a fast learner.

After she'd read the writing on her magic disco ball, she'd headed straight for the bookstore to pick up help. She hadn't yet read *So, You Want to Be a PI* cover to cover, but she felt more secure with the reference book in her purse.

"Are you Victoria Whitley?" the Woman in Black asked in a stage whisper when Tori got to within a few feet of the table.

The woman's face was fine boned and beautiful, the lines bracketing her mouth the only giveaway that she was probably on the downside of sixty. Her dark hair was salon-perfect and her makeup was not only expensive but expertly applied to bring out her large, wide-set dark eyes.

"Y—" Tori began, but didn't get the word out.

"Quick. Sit down," the woman ordered in a quiet voice that managed to pack an authoritative punch.

Tori sat in a chair catty-corner to the woman.

"I was going to say that everybody calls me Tori," Tori whispered back. "I'm sorry, but Eddie didn't tell me your name."

"I know."

Tori waited for her to expand on her reply. She didn't. "What *is* your name?"

The Woman in Black cast a furtive glance around the room before lifting her menu and shielding her face from the diners at the next table. She peeked at Tori from around the side of the menu.

"You can call me . . . Ms. M," she said, still in that loud whisper. "Yes, I like that. It's a good name for a PI's boss. It reminds me of James Bond's boss in the movies. He goes by the one letter, too."

15

"James Bond isn't a private detective," Tori said slowly. "He's a secret agent."

"Close enough," Ms. M said.

Tori nodded, as though this weren't the oddest conversation she'd had in, oh, forever.

She leaned forward. "Why are we whispering?"

"I know how you private eyes operate. I don't want us to attract attention," Ms. M said.

Too late, Tori thought. They possibly could have gotten away with the stage whispers, but the other diners had started staring when Ms. M hid her face behind the menu. Not to mention the only other person Tori had ever seen wear an expensive black suit on a sunny day at the beach had been carrying an urn.

"I think we should stop whispering and that you should put the menu down," Tori said in her regular voice. At the woman's crestfallen expression, she added, "Sometimes you're more conspicuous when you try not to be."

Ms. M brightened. "Oooo, I didn't think of that, but it's brilliant. I knew I was doing the right thing when I hired an expert like you."

Tori's instinct was to cringe at the label, but she stopped herself. She was a PI now. She had a book. She could claim a little expertise.

"I hope you won't be disappointed," she began, then stopped. That was lame. How could she inspire confidence in her client if she didn't have any in herself? Tori tried again. "I mean, you won't be disappointed."

Ms. M leaned forward; her gorgeous eyes narrowed as they focused on Tori. "Can I ask you something?"

Oh, Lord. She'd want Tori to recite her credentials, which was within her rights. Tori managed to nod while she tried to come up with a way to make her nonexistent experience seem impressive.

"What brand of makeup do you wear?" Ms. M asked.

Makeup? O-kay.

"My foundation and powder are by Lazenby, but my eye makeup is from Revlon," Tori said slowly, wondering where Ms. M was headed with this. Would she shift into a discussion of the use of makeup in various disguises?

Ms. M sat up straighter, like she had a board at her back. "Revlon's a drugstore brand. What's wrong with Lazenby's eye makeup?"

Okay, Tori could play along.

"It's not worth the price difference. Revlon has a wider choice of colors and a smoother texture, not to mention a softer brown shade of mascara." Tori registered the woman's intent expression. "Why do you ask?"

"I was interested."

Tori waited for her to elaborate, but instead Ms. M waved off an approaching waitress and bent to lift an expensive-looking calfskin briefcase off the floor. She pulled out a piece of paper with a photograph printed on it and set it down on the table between them.

"Your mission, should you decide to accept it, is to get information on this man," Ms. M said in a dramatic voice.

Tori thought she recognized the line from *Mission: Impossible* but couldn't puzzle over it now. They'd reached the purpose of their meeting: Her assignment.

She dropped her gaze to the paper and felt her mouth gape open. She closed it quickly, before drool escaped.

She'd imagined somebody ordinary when Eddie told her she'd be trailing a businessman around town. But this man, who peered out from the piece of paper with eyes as blue as the shimmering ocean, struck her as extraordinary.

Probably in his late twenties, he wasn't handsome so much as he was striking.

He had a square, cleft chin and a no-nonsense slant to his mouth. His tan and the blond streaks in his sandy-brown hair attested to time spent outdoors. Combine those features with hollow cheekbones and a nose that appeared to have been broken at least once, and masculinity emanated off him like reflected sunlight.

He looked, in short, like Prince Charming's more rugged, more intelligent brother.

But that was ridiculous. If the mysterious Ms. M wanted him investigated, he couldn't be a modernized version of a fairy-tale prince. More likely, he was a frog in disguise.

"His name is Grady Palmer. He graduated from Florida State with a degree in business seven years ago and took over the operation of Palmer Construction a year later when his father retired. In the last nine months or so, his company's won a number of prestigious city contracts."

Tori kept her gaze on the photo, imagining the man

vying for business. She couldn't envision him being second best.

"It seems to me you already know quite a bit about him." Tori tried to sound nonchalant, like she imagined a good PI would. She couldn't let Ms. M guess she thought the man in the photo was a hunk, especially because his hunkiness was immaterial. "What would you want me to find out?"

"Anything and everything," Ms. M said. "I printed this photo off his company's Web site, where I got the other information. But I want to know more than typed words on a page. I want the measure of the man."

Tori lifted her head and met Ms. M's intent stare. If the Mysterious One was turning a PI loose on Grady Palmer, that intriguing face could be hiding something ugly.

"Why do you want him investigated?"

"Your boss and I agreed I wouldn't have to divulge my reasons," she said enigmatically. "Otherwise, I wouldn't have hired your firm."

"Is there something . . . shady you suspect him of?"

"Let's just say that if there's any dirt on him, I want you to dig it up." Ms. M smiled. "I have to confess I was a little nervous about this meeting, but I have a good feeling about you."

"You do?" Tori asked in surprise.

Ms. M nodded. "I do. You remind me of Pierce Brosnan."

"The actor who plays James Bond?"

"Exactly. Maybe I should call you Jane."

As in Bond, Jane Bond.

A fit of honesty seized Tori at the undeserved admiration in the other woman's eyes. "I can't claim to be in his league," she said.

"Nobody is, but you'll do fine," Ms. M said. "I didn't get where I am today without very good instincts."

Ms. M's clothes and mannerisms screamed *success*. Tori wondered what she did for a living but thought it a waste of breath to ask.

"If your instincts are so good, why don't you take Grady Palmer's measure yourself?" Tori asked instead.

"I have my reasons."

Reasons she obviously didn't intend to share.

"You'll keep me informed of your findings, of course," Ms. M said in a breathy, excited voice. "I'm rather anxious for the information, Jane."

Tori had a moment's misgiving about what she was getting herself into. She considered whipping her disco ball out of her purse for another consultation, but that was silly. The magic ball had already told her to take the case.

She looked down once again at the picture of Grady Palmer. He seemed to dare her to find out what kind of man he was. Her heartbeat quickened. The assignment wasn't really so hard. Ms. M wasn't the only one with good instincts about people.

Within a day or so, maybe sooner, she'd have figured out whether Palmer was one of the good guys.

"I can't wait to get started," Tori said.

She might not have any experience, but neither had

Sherlock Holmes before he embarked on his first case. And she was smart and resourceful. Some of the time.

How hard could it be to follow Mr. Blue Eyes around?

Chapter Three

The woman in the floppy hat who was keeping conspicuously behind the fat man was following him.

Grady Palmer had noticed her the instant she'd joined the gallery at the seventeenth hole of the Seahaven Golf and Country Club. Every one of the spectators in the gallery stood out, considering only five of them had showed, but none so much as the woman.

Not only wasn't she related to somebody in Grady's foursome, like the other four, but she was the kind of woman a man noticed.

He'd seen her several times in the last few days. Once at the stamp machine while he stood in line at the post office and again in a silver Volkswagen Beetle convertible parked across the street from his construction office.

Today she'd gone to some lengths to appear unobtrusive, covering her reddish brown hair with the hat and her eyes with large, dark sunglasses.

But she had that extra bit of oomph, that intangible *something*, that made her stand out in a crowd. The sun shone from a cloudless blue sky but it seemed to shimmer most brightly on the woman.

Grady noted her hat was neither black nor white but tan, which figured. His life would be less complicated if the people around him subscribed to the rules of the old Westerns.

Black hat equals bad guy. White hat equals good guy.

But who was he kidding? In Seahaven, a good man—or woman, for that matter—was hard to find because there weren't many. He didn't need John Wayne to help him figure out what a tan hat tied with a dark-green ribbon signified.

Somebody had gotten suspicious of him.

Which proved once again that nothing was exactly what it seemed.

Take this so-called charity golf tournament, in which Grady was part of a foursome that included Mayor Honoria Black. The profits were earmarked for a domestic abuse hotline, but the tournament was about increasing the mayor's chances to win re-election in November.

The woman in the hat stood off to his right, clear across the fairway, not far from Mayor Black and the city's tax assessor. If the fat man would move a little to the left, Grady might be able to—

"Hey, Palmer. You gonna hit that ball or wait for it to sprout wings?"

Grady tore his gaze from the woman in the hat and focused on the portly, chain-smoking city clerk of Seahaven. Pete Aiken stood in the rough in the shade of a giant palmetto tree. He was probably near his own ball but Grady couldn't see much through the haze of smoke surrounding him.

"The way things are going today, it'd fly into the sand trap," Grady said, keeping his smile so firmly in place that the muscles on the sides of his mouth ached.

He'd been told as a kid that his features would freeze in place if he made funny faces. He wondered if the same warning applied to insincere smiles.

Nah. If it did, he wouldn't be able to bend his lips. He'd smiled more in the fourteen months since he'd let the FBI rope him into a sting operation to weed out corruption at Seahaven City Hall than a villain in a B Western. He recognized the irony, because a black hat was exactly what he was portraying.

Grady's role in Operation Citygate consisted of amassing evidence against corrupt city officials, which he couldn't do without ingratiating himself with them.

"Don't look at me for golf tips," Aiken said. "I'm not letting you beat me."

Grady fought to keep his smile in place. Assholes like Pete Aiken made him rue the day he'd listened to the loud whispers about corruption at Seahaven City Hall and contacted a college-friend-turned-FBI-agent. He intended only to relay that his construction company's low bid to build a city office complex had been suspiciously passed over.

Instead he'd gotten sucked into an ongoing investigation that had him carrying bugs, paying bribes, and watching his back. He'd almost refused—until he'd asked himself what one of the old-West characters played by Clint Eastwood or John Wayne would have done.

The right thing, came the answer.

But doing the right thing was fraught with pitfalls. If his "friends" in city government saw through his act, he could be in danger.

The woman in the floppy hat could be a harbinger of that danger.

He selected a club from his golf bag and tried to block out everything but the ball as he positioned himself over it. He hit a serviceable shot that barely reached the green, then climbed into the golf cart. The fat man now completely obscured the woman, so he focused on Aiken.

A swing and a miss. Strike . . . who knows what number. Aiken had piled up so many air swings that Grady lost count hours ago. Even though the wind was blowing like the Big Bad Wolf on steroids, it still represented a spectacular display of ineptitude.

Aiken looked furtively around, spotted Grady watching, took his cigarette from where it dangled in his mouth, and gave a hale, hearty laugh. "You don't mind if I take a mulligan, right?"

A "mulligan" is golf parlance for a do-over, considered taboo in tournament play. At least Aiken had asked this time instead of merely shaving his score at the end of the hole.

Grady gritted his teeth but made it look like a smile. Aiken would get his due soon enough. Grady was about to bid on the construction of a multimillion-dollar community center. City bylaws required the bids be sealed but Aiken had claimed he could make sure Grady submitted the low bid—for a fee. Grady had Aiken on tape accepting the bribe.

"Go right ahead," Grady said.

His cigarette once more hanging limply from his mouth and his wide hips jiggling as he eyed the ball, Aiken took a mighty swing. A clump of dirt and grass sailed into the air along with the ball, which shot sideways across the fairway at roughly a ten-degree angle.

"I lost the sucker," Aiken complained. "Do you see it?"

Grady followed the speck of white as it veered a few feet above the ground across the immaculate green fairway, straight at . . . the mayor.

"Fore!" He bellowed a warning as Mayor Black, her back to them, lined up a shot. Behind the mayor, the people in the gallery lifted their heads.

"Fore!" Grady shouted again, louder this time.

The gallery scattered but the mayor looked around helplessly. The ball was set to bean her when the woman in the floppy hat rushed her, wrapped her arms around the mayor's waist, and knocked her to the ground.

The errant golf ball sailed over the two prone women and careened off the mayor's golf cart with a loud *ping*. It rolled to the dead center of the eighteenth fairway, about one hundred yards shy of the green.

"Aw, shit," Aiken remarked as he and Grady took off across the fairway. In a louder voice, Aiken yelled, "Sorry, Mayor. Grady didn't mean it."

Grady shot a look at Aiken over his shoulder. "*You* hit the ball."

Aiken pointed at him with his rapidly diminishing

cigarette. "The mayor doesn't know that, buddy o' mine."

Grady swallowed his protest at Aiken's descriptive phrase and focused on the scene of the incident. The mayor got to her feet, waving off everybody rushing to her aid. Grady slowed his steps to a walk. Aiken did the same.

"I'm okay," Mayor Black announced in her loud baritone. She raised her arms and shook her large, square hands for emphasis. Beside her, Wade Morrison, the tax assessor, helped the mayor's savior up from the ground.

The woman's floppy hat had come off, revealing a head of pretty red-brown hair that was parted slightly off center. Her nose was long, her lips luscious, her chin small, her features familiar. Grady had been right. It was the same woman.

"Hot damn," Aiken said. "I'd let a golf ball knock me out if it meant getting up close with a woman like that."

The woman shoved the hat Morrison held out to her back on, then turned and stared at Grady, who was fifteen yards away and closing. Her shoulders stiffened, her mouth grew pinched, and her body went still an instant before she turned and bolted.

Determined to get some answers, he gave chase and might have caught her if the mayor hadn't stepped in front of him. He stopped abruptly, barely avoiding careening into her.

He probably wouldn't have knocked her down. Tall and athletically built with short, thick hair the color of her name, Honoria Black gave the impression she could take care of herself. Her stare was direct and, owing to one eyebrow that was slightly higher than the other, disconcerting.

"Tell me, Grady, should I hire a bodyguard or give you the name of my golf pro?" she asked, swinging her index finger back and forth like a metronome.

"It was an accident," he murmured, his attention on the khaki-clad figure hurrying toward the parking lot. As he watched, she grew smaller and smaller.

"They happen," the mayor said before lowering her voice to a whisper. "But if you're not careful, I know a guy named Guido who breaks legs for a living."

Her words registered and he turned from the woman in the distance to Mayor Black. She winked at him before walking away.

Had that been a joke, Grady wondered, or a veiled threat?

Morrison, the tax assessor, sidled up next to him. A quiet, unassuming guy, he had wire-rimmed glasses and dark brown hair that fell into his face. Grady suspected his office was dirtier than a pigsty, but hadn't managed to get close enough to Morrison to determine whether the assessor accepted bribes for tax breaks.

Grady dredged up his I-want-to-be-friends smile, but Morrison failed to return it.

"If you know what's good for you, you'll stay on the mayor's good side," he advised in a soft voice.

Morrison moved away as quickly as he'd appeared, sending Grady's thoughts off to the races. What did that mean? His gaze shifted to the parking lot, but the woman was gone. He rubbed the bridge of his nose.

Was his part in the sting operation making him paranoid? Morrison could simply have been warning him that the not-so-benevolent mayor of Seahaven held grudges.

Even if Mayor Black had gotten suspicious of all the bribe money he'd handed out, concluding that her investigator had shown up at the golf course was too much of a stretch. Then again, she'd prevented him from interrogating the woman by stepping in front of him.

Grady headed for the eighteenth green, trying to put the woman in the floppy hat out of his mind. But she wouldn't go.

Neither would the thought that the mayor or some-body else in city hall had hired the woman to find out if he was as corrupt as he seemed.

Chapter Four

Careful to keep the front door of Grady Palmer's house in view, Tori crouched down low in the driver's seat of her silver Volkswagen.

Thanks to chapters 2 and 3 of *So, You Want to Be a PI*, she had a better handle on what it took to be a good snoop.

Appearing innocuous topped the list.

She'd failed on that account at the golf course, but she couldn't blame herself for emerging from the cover of the fat man to save the mayor from the golf ball.

She'd made up her mind to become a good PI, not a bad Samaritan.

She took heart that her covert operation had been successful up to that point. Stumbling across the newspaper item about Grady Palmer participating in a charity golf tournament had been a stroke of luck of which she took full advantage.

She'd thought on her feet when there had been a

handful of fans following Grady and company around the course rather than the legion she'd imagined. She hadn't joined the gallery until Grady's foursome teed off on the seventeenth hole, and then she'd kept carefully out of sight.

She'd meant to get a sense of how he conducted himself in a competitive situation, but the errant golf ball had ruined that opportunity.

So she was back to surveillance, applying the same see-but-not-seen principle she'd used since she began following him. Instead of parking in front of the subject's well-tended house, she'd set up down the block and across the street.

He lived in a modest neighborhood of older single-family homes in the southern part of Seahaven, about a dozen blocks from where the bay wound around a finger of land and merged into the intracoastal waterway.

She found it interesting that he lived here when he could afford something in one of Seahaven's pricier communities. With some digging into public records, she'd discovered that Palmer Construction was thriving. But maybe his little white house, with its surrounding ficus hedges, palmetto trees, and flowering plants, charmed him. It certainly had that effect on her.

She pulled out her notebook.

Either Grady has a gardener or a green thumb, she wrote. She frowned, crossed out *Grady* and substituted *Palmer*. *So, You Want to Be a PI* strongly advised against getting too close to a subject.

A ring sounded, startling her so much her elbow bumped the car horn. It pealed in concert with what she realized was her cell phone. She jerked her elbow back from the horn and fished the phone from her pocketbook, nervously looking up and down the still-deserted street. All clear.

"Hello," she whispered into the phone.

"Hey, doll."

"If anybody besides you called me that, I'd have to hurt them," she told her cousin Eddie.

He laughed. "How's it going?"

"I've decided to be the best PI I can be," she confided. "Who knows? Maybe I have a knack for this. Maybe this is the career I've been waiting for."

"Stranger things have happened," he said. "So, listen—"

"Want to know where I am?" she interrupted. "On the subject's street. I have him under surveillance."

"As long as you're driving a rental car instead of that conspicuous Beetle of yours, sounds like you've got it covered," he said. "Now, as I was saying . . ."

Tori barely listened as she took stock of the Volkswagen Beetle her father had bought her six months ago. He'd done it over her protests, insisting he'd sleep easier knowing she had a car in good working condition. Surely Eddie was wrong. Yeah, it sported a yellow smiley face as an antenna topper, but the car was silver, not red or yellow.

". . . so don't be surprised if you get a call," Eddie finished.

The front door to Grady Palmer's house opened and the man himself stepped out. He'd changed into khakis and a cream-colored shirt that complemented his coloring better than the yellow one he'd worn on the golf course.

33

He strolled rather than strutted, like nothing was so important that it couldn't wait. He seemed to look in her direction as he walked to the black SUV parked in his driveway. She sank lower behind the steering wheel.

"A call from who?" Tori asked.

"The client. She's going to call you for an update."

"But I told her I'd call her," Tori protested.

Grady—no, Palmer—had disappeared inside the SUV. She heard the engine turn over and the vehicle roar to life.

"She says she can't wait," Eddie claimed.

The SUV pulled away from the curb. Tori cradled the phone against her shoulder and started her car. "I can't—"

"Gotta go. Busy, busy, busy," Eddie said.

"Eddie, don't you dare hang up on me!" she shouted into the phone, but he'd already hung up.

No sooner had she disconnected than the phone rang again. Tori answered while being careful not to follow too closely behind Palmer's SUV. Her paperback advocated keeping two cars behind the subject and herself but hadn't said where to find said cars when none were present.

"Hello, Jane. Ms. M here," the caller announced after Tori said hello.

"Who's 'Jane'?" Tori asked.

"You are. You told me I could call you that," Ms. M said, and Tori remembered with an internal groan the older woman's likening her to "Jane" Bond. "What have you found out?"

She'd found out quite a lot. She knew that Grady Palmer was twenty-eight years old and that he'd never been married. He'd grown up in Seahaven the son of Paul and Beth Ann Palmer and had a 21-year-old sister, Lorelei.

He'd gotten a traffic ticket for going sixty in a forty-five-mile-per-hour zone five years ago, and purchased his home for nearly two hundred thousand dollars three years ago. As far as Tori could determine, he lived alone in that home.

But she didn't know anything pertinent except that Grady Palmer's life centered on work. He'd gone back to the office today after the golf tournament even though it was Friday. In the five days she'd followed him, this marked the first time he'd stepped out for the evening.

"This isn't the best time for me to talk," she said as Palmer took a left turn down another residential street that featured more swaying palmetto trees and unpretentious but well-kept homes.

She turned too, trying to keep her distance.

"Why not?" Ms. M asked.

An ambulance siren blared in the distance, growing louder, then fainter.

"You're following him, aren't you?" Ms. M asked excitedly. "You're following him right now!"

Palmer turned left and so did Tori. Where was the man headed? They'd probably traveled a mile and he'd yet to leave the neighborhood.

"That ambulance you heard, that was the television," Tori fibbed. "I'm watching . . . *E.R.*"

"You are not," Ms. M said indignantly. "*E.R.*'s not on Friday nights."

"Okay. You're right." Tori followed suit as her subject made another right turn. "I didn't want to tell you

I was following him because the investigation is in the preliminary stages. It's better if I wait until I can give you a full report."

Ms. M ignored her rational plea to be left alone. "What's he doing?"

He was stopping his SUV and getting out. Tori slammed on her brakes, which squeaked in protest. Only then did she realize that the last road they'd turned down ended at a seawall.

"I've got to go," she told Ms. M.

"But—"

Tori hung up, desperately trying to figure out what to do. Leave. Yes, she should hightail it out of there. She was about to put the car in reverse when Grady Palmer tapped on the glass of the driver's-side window.

For a man who looked like he never hurried, he sure moved fast.

Her hand gripped the automatic gear shift, and she positioned her foot to stomp down on the gas pedal. What should she do? Stay and face the subject of her surveillance or make like the wind? She simply couldn't decide.

When he settled one hand on the roof of the car and tapped more insistently on the window, he made the decision for her. If she pulled away now, she might run over his foot.

Swallowing her nervousness, she hit the button that automatically lowered the window. He leaned down so that his face was only a foot or so from hers.

The follower being confronted by the followee could not be a good thing, but then not many followees looked like Grady Palmer.

His photographic image didn't do the flesh-and-blood item justice. His hair was a more interesting shade of brown, his eyes a richer blue, and his mouth was to kiss for. Really, the man had a ridiculously sensuous mouth. His upper lip bowed in the center and his lower lip was plump and lush.

She tore her gaze from his mouth before her own started salivating, reminded herself she'd never been a sucker for a handsome face, even if it did contain a killer mouth, and forced herself to concentrate on getting out of her predicament.

"May I help you?" she asked good-naturedly, the way she used to at the bar before she'd been fired.

"You'll want this," he said in a voice so low and rich it could have belonged to a late-night disc jockey. He handed her a piece of thick white card stock.

She automatically took it, turning it over to see embossed printing and a flowery script her nerves prevented her from reading.

"It's an invitation to Mayor Black's party," he supplied. "It's a thank-you for participating in the golf tournament. The directions to her place are on the back."

She examined the card more closely, finding that it was indeed a party invitation. She felt her brows knit. She couldn't think clearly. Not with him so close. It wasn't yet full dark but felt that way with him positioned by the window, blocking what little light remained of the day.

"I don't understand why you gave me this," she said.

"Because that's where I'm going."

Tori's heart hammered but she concentrated on

sounding blasé. "Why would I care where you're going?"

His dark eyebrows, which were of an ideal shape and thickness, rose.

"I'm trying to be considerate," he said. "You're not very good at following. Sooner or later, you were going to lose me."

That could be true, she thought, but he didn't have to rub it in. Couldn't he see that she was trying here?

"What makes you think I would have lost you?" she asked indignantly. He cocked an eyebrow. *Whoops.* "I mean, why would I be following you?"

"You can explain at the party. No reason we shouldn't go together since we're both headed to the same place."

Her mouth gaped open. This was bad. Very, very bad. Private detectives did not attend parties on the muscular arms of their subjects.

"I can't go with you," she protested. "We're strangers."

"Then maybe you should tell me your name."

"Tori Whitley," she said before it occurred to her that she should have exercised her right to remain silent. Or at least used an alias.

"I'm Grady Palmer, but you already knew that."

Even if her denial hadn't stuck in her throat, she doubted he'd believe it. He'd gotten six feet from her car when he called over his shoulder, "I'll see you at the party. If you lose me, you have the directions."

Chapter Five

Tori spent the drive to Mayor Honoria Black's house trying to dream up a legitimate excuse for following Grady Palmer, and coming up with a big blank.

Okay, then. An excuse might not be the way to go. Outright denial sounded like a better strategy.

"Me, follow you?" She placed her hand on her breastbone and affected a fluttering laugh. "You're sadly mistaken, sir."

Like that would work, she thought with a roll of her eyes.

She hadn't come up with anything better by the time cars parked on the street and in the paver-block circular driveway of a sprawling contemporary alerted her they'd arrived at their destination.

Located in a pricey enclave of homes that hugged the intracoastal waterway, the Mediterranean-style house had a multilevel stucco exterior in pale coral and a barrel-tile roof in a slightly darker shade.

Dramatic ground-level spotlights highlighted the forty-foot-tall giant palmettos in the front yard and shone on the covered, double-door entry. Every arched window was illuminated from within, attesting to a party going on.

Tori had heard homeowners in this part of Seahaven acquired older waterfront houses, demolished them, and replaced them with pricier versions.

Although she thought it a shame to tear down history, she couldn't help admiring the dynamic, resourceful, self-made mayor.

A recent profile in the *Seahaven Gazette* told of the killing she'd made investing commissions she earned as a realtor into property she later resold at a substantial profit.

If private investigation didn't work, Tori thought as she parked behind Grady's SUV, maybe she should consider a career in real estate.

She wiped her damp palms on her slacks. She needed to stop this nonsense about taking up an alternative career and concentrate on convincing Grady he had it wrong.

She might even manage to turn a negative into a positive. Taking a man's measure had to be easier face-to-face instead of in the shadows, observing from afar.

Besides, by process of elimination, she had to be good at something. Why not PI work?

"You're full of surprises," he said when she joined him in front of the house. He'd jammed his hands in the pockets of his khakis, lending him a deceptively casual air. "I didn't think you'd come."

Not coming had been an option? She'd been so rattled, that hadn't occurred to her. But fleeing would only have made him more suspicious.

"I'm not exactly dressed for a party." Her slacks and blouse were of good quality but were both brown. She would have worn the more correct black, the better to blend into the surroundings, but the color made her look washed out.

"You look great to me." His eyes skimmed over her, and her pulse skittered. "But that's not what I meant. I wasn't sure you'd come now that you know that I know you've been following me."

Her time of reckoning had come.

"I wanted to set you straight about that." She only had to tilt her head back slightly to meet his eyes, which surprised her. He seemed like a giant but probably fell just shy of six feet. "I wasn't following you."

"So that's why you took off at the golf course when you saw me coming?"

Oh, no. She'd thought the floppy hat and sunglasses had kept him from recognizing her. *Start bluffing,* a shrill voice inside her head screamed. *Now.*

"That had nothing to do with you," she said, airily waving a hand. "I left because the event was almost over."

He didn't reply. She nervously chewed her bottom lip, thinking she should elaborate to make her story more believable.

"There wasn't much more to see," she said.

Still no response.

"And I remembered something else I had to do."

Was that suspicion she saw in his beautiful eyes?

"Something vitally important," she clarified. There.

41

That should allay his distrust. Except he still looked puzzled. "I needed . . . to feed my cat."

Oh, great. Had she really said that?

"She gets hungry if she's home alone too long."

He tilted his head quizzically. "Why don't you leave food out for her?"

"Because . . . I don't want her to stuff herself. You know what they say about a number of small meals a day being better than one large meal."

"I thought cats stopped eating when they were full."

"Not this cat." She spread her hands wide. "This is one fat cat."

"As interesting as all this is," he said slowly, "we were talking about you following me."

Adrenaline rushed through her like a river after a storm, and she recognized it as the flight-or-fight instinct. Flee! her mind screamed.

She nodded toward the etched-glass front doors. The muffled laughter and music behind them sounded like salvation. "We should go inside so we don't miss out on the fun."

"Not until we straighten this out," he said, and she looked wildly about for help. A car door slammed somewhere down the block, but they were alone on the front lawn. "I want to know why I've seen you four times in the past few days."

"You couldn't have," she cried. She'd adhered to the instructions in the paperback to a T, donning dark glasses, being careful not to get within twenty yards of him, sticking to the shadows.

"Let's count them." He held up one hand, then raised his thumb before unfolding his fingers one by one. "At the post office, across the street from Palmer Construction, at the golf course, and in my neighborhood. How do you explain that?"

"It sounds like a coincidence," she ventured.

He snorted. "You obviously don't watch crime shows on TV."

"Why's that?"

"The cops never believe in coincidence."

"That's silly," Tori said lightly. "If there were no such thing as coincidence, there wouldn't be a word for it, now would there?"

"If this is all a big coincidence," he said, taking a step toward her, "why are you so nervous?"

Her sweating palms, fast-beating heart, and shallow breathing made denying it pointless. She'd never perfected the art of lying anyway. She doubted she could convince a three-year-old that there was a Santa Claus.

"You might as well admit it," he pressed. "You were following me."

"Okay," she snapped. "You win. I was following you."

"I knew it." His baby blues narrowed and his luscious lips thinned. He could challenge Arnold Schwarzenegger for the starring role if they ever made a movie called *The Intimidator*. "What I want to know is why."

She resisted the urge to bury her face in her hands. She'd had such high hopes that she could excel at private detecting. Yet here she was on the brink of failing not only herself but Eddie and Ms. M as well. The thought of it made her feel like weeping.

"There's a simple explanation," Tori hedged as she desperately cast about for one.

He crossed his arms over his chest. "I'm waiting."

One of the artificial spotlights shone down on him, adding light to his captivating features. Her eyes widened, the way they had the first time she'd seen his likeness. *That's it,* she thought. *The perfect explanation.*

"The truth is," she said, taking a breath for courage, "that I think you're hot."

Chapter Six

Grady carried a strawberry daiquiri and a Scotch and water past a mostly decorative coral-and-marble fireplace in Honoria Black's great room fifteen minutes later, one phrase echoing in his mind.

Yeah, right.

Tori Whitley, if that was her real name, hadn't fooled him. He knew some females found him attractive, but Tori was hardly the type of woman who trailed guys around town.

Besides, if Tori thought he was so hot, wouldn't she touch him the way she casually touched everyone else she talked to?

Not that he wanted her to touch him. Much. Okay, strike that. He might crave the feel of her hands on his skin, but he was smart enough to know he shouldn't.

She'd probably been hired by one of the people at this party to spy on him. Maybe, as he'd originally suspected, she worked for the mayor herself.

He might have figured it out by now if a city councilman and his wife hadn't strolled up to them seconds after she'd uttered the I'm-so-hot-for-you whopper.

After he'd introduced Tori, she'd chatted and laughed with the couple as though they'd known each other forever. She'd told them she worked part time at the makeup counter at Frasier's department store while she looked for steadier work. That had prompted the councilman to tell her of a secretarial opening at city hall.

Grady had followed the three of them into the mayor's stunning home, forced to bide his time until he could get Tori alone.

But now she talked to Honoria Black by the glass doors that led to the patio, her face rapt with interest as she gazed up at the mayor. Honoria, nearly six feet tall in her stocking feet, should have drawn his eye in her bold red pantsuit. But Tori, dressed in sparrow brown, upstaged her with her laughing face and sparkling eyes.

"Opportunity is everywhere," he heard Honoria say as he approached. "The trick is recognizing it when you see it. I think that's my true talent."

"You're too modest," Tori replied. "From what I read, you're talented at everything you do."

"Here's my secret. I never do anything I know I won't be good at," Honoria said and laughed so loudly heads all over the room turned.

At this juncture in her life, Grady suspected the mayor excelled at profiting at the expense of the citizens she'd been elected to serve.

If Honoria were a character in a Western, she'd be the smooth heavy—the big, rich boss who did the conniving before sending stooges out to do the dirty work.

Given some time and a little luck, Grady might even be able to prove it.

"So now I know why you hosted a golf tournament, Honoria," Grady said when he joined them, handing the daiquiri to Tori. She took it with a smile of thanks that did something odd to his gut. Please God, he prayed, let it be indigestion. "You knew you were a ringer."

"Absolutely." The mayor commandeered the Scotch and water he'd intended for himself and toasted him. "Tori tells me I've you to thank for bringing her to the party. How long have you two been dating?"

Grady checked his watch. "For about twenty minutes."

The mayor turned back to Tori. "I thought you said you were at the golf course because of him."

Tori brought a slender index finger to her mouth and laid it against her lips. "Shhh. We don't want him getting a big head."

The retort was nothing more than meaningless party banter, at which Tori was amazingly adept. The mayor let out her loud, boisterous laugh, no doubt as Tori had intended.

Grady narrowed his eyes as he watched the two women. Were they in on this together? Was the buddy act part of a plan to make him think they didn't know each other?

"We've got to be careful not to let him get too full of himself," the mayor said in a teasing voice. "Our Grady, he's a real lady-killer. You saw how he almost clouted me today with that ball."

Tori's brows knitted. "But Grady wasn't the one who—"

Oh, damn.

"You'll never let me forget that, will you, Mayor?" Grady interrupted. If Pete Aiken thought Grady had ratted on him, he'd be less likely to hook him up with other dirty officials. Grady couldn't risk that—not with Aiken hip-deep in the corruption plaguing city hall.

"One of the reasons I've gotten to where I am today is because I'm careful." The mayor considered him over the lip of the glass as she sipped the stolen Scotch and water. "I look out for people who might want to hurt me."

Did she keep making comments like that because she knew Grady was one of those people? Was she aware that he'd love to bring her down along with her administration?

"Even if Grady *had* hit that ball," Tori said, cutting her eyes at him to show she knew otherwise, "he didn't do it deliberately."

The mayor clapped her hands. "The way Tori leaps to your defense is precious, Grady. Why, you could probably convince her you're here tonight to have a good time."

"That *is* why he's here," Tori said.

"Like I said, she's precious." The mayor winked at Grady. To Tori, she said, "I meant what I said about repaying the favor you did me today. Call if I can ever do anything for you. But now you'll have to excuse me. I need to say hello to Wade."

"What did she mean?" Tori asked after the mayor left them to greet the late-arriving tax assessor. She caught her lower lip with her upper teeth. "Why else would you come to the party if not to have a good time?"

"She thinks I'm here because I want the city to award Palmer Construction the contract to build the new community center."

The alternative, that the mayor knew he cozied up to city officials so he could eventually double-cross them, was more hazardous for his peace of mind.

"Palmer Construction? Is that the company you work for?"

"It's the company I run," he answered. "But you already know that."

"How would I know that?"

"Because for some reason you were following me."

"I already told you why I was following you. Why can't you accept that?"

"Because every silver lining has a cloud."

"That's a pessimistic thing to say."

"It's the truth. You're a beautiful woman." He indicated her with a sweep of his hand. "Men are supposed to follow you."

She folded her arms, stretching the material of her brown shirt across her chest. Her breasts were small, he noticed, but nicely shaped. Big, dark, angry eyes dominated her oval face.

"This is the twenty-first century. If we women want to follow men around, nobody can stop us." She glanced around the room and pointed to Ned Weimer, who was moving toward the outside patio. "There's a man in motion. He seems to be alone, too. I think I'll follow him."

She pivoted and headed for Weimer, leaving Grady to wonder what the hell had happened. He watched in amazement as she caught up to the mayor's chief of staff. Weimer was divorced, fortyish, and as slick as the dyed black hair he gelled back from his angular face.

Unfortunately, Weimer was no dummy. The FBI believed the corruption in city hall reached all the way to the top but had nothing on either Weimer or the mayor.

Tori laid a hand on Weimer's arm, walking with him out the glass doors to the patio. Something unpleasant slithered through Grady but he refused to characterize it as jealousy.

He couldn't be jealous of Ned Weimer. The man was phonier than a six-dollar bill. As for Tori, he hadn't invested enough in her emotionally to get proprietary.

He didn't even trust her, he thought as he hurried across the room, deftly avoiding saying more than hello to passing acquaintances. If Tori decided in mid-date that she preferred Ned Weimer, he told himself as he stepped into the fresh air, he'd have one fewer worry.

Tori stood with Weimer on the terra-cotta tile under a palm tree illuminated by a string of tiny white lights, sandwiched between the beauty of the mayor's teardrop-shaped pool and the intracoastal waterway. Ned laughed at something she said and his teeth flashed white in the night.

The chief of staff probably had them professionally brightened to complement his professionally darkened black hair. He hooked his thumbs in the pockets of the trendy white slacks he wore with a short-sleeved black silk shirt. *Oh, please.*

Grady wouldn't be able to stand it if Tori thought Ned Weimer was hot, too.

"Hey, Ned," he said as he approached the two of them. "I see you've met my date."

"Your date?" Weimer focused his too-small eyes on Tori. "I got the impression you were here by yourself."

"I drove here by myself," Tori said.

"Only because she followed me." Grady slid closer to her, captured her left hand and deliberately rubbed his thumb over her palm. "Isn't that right, Tori?"

She didn't pull away, but then she couldn't. Not if she still expected him to buy her story. But if she had the hots for him, why had her body gone as tense as a tuning fork? Then again, why had his?

"Yes," she admitted, not looking at him. "I am here with Grady."

"Well, hell." Ned shook his perfectly immobile head of hair. "I should have known you approaching me like that was too good to be true."

"My thoughts exactly," Grady murmured.

"No offense," Ned said, targeting his comment at Tori, "but I see a woman over there who actually may be here by herself."

Before he sauntered away, Ned took a business card from his wallet and handed it to Tori. She pulled her hand from Grady's to take it.

"What's this for?" she asked.

Ned slapped Grady on the back as he moved away.

"Insurance," he said. "If you get tired of Palmer, you know where to find me."

She laughed. Grady didn't.

"First me, then Weimer," he said. "Is accosting strange men a habit of yours?"

Her chin lifted. It had a tiny cleft in its center that made him want to dip his finger into it. Not that he would.

"Of course not," she said. "Besides, you're the one who accosted me. I never would have approached you."

"Why not?" he asked grumpily. "You approached Weimer."

"Ned's more approachable," she said.

He let out a frustrated breath. "Trust me on this. Ned Weimer is not a good guy."

She raised eyebrows a few shades darker than her hair. Her auburn curls rustled in the gentle breeze. "And you are?"

A painful awareness hit him that his presence at the party gave the appearance he supported Honoria Black in her bid to win re-election. In truth, Grady had already made an anonymous donation to the campaign of slow-growth advocate Forest Richardson. The local lawyer probably wouldn't turn out to be much of an improvement over Mayor Black, but he couldn't be worse.

"Hell, yeah, I'm a good guy," he said, and moodily

looked around at the collection of hobnobbers and phonies on the patio.

His gaze drifted across the pool and snagged on Wade Morrison, the city tax assessor he felt sure was as crooked as the Leaning Tower of Pisa. He'd suggested to his FBI contact that they offer him a bribe, but had been told to concentrate instead on the officials who approached him.

Morrison talked to a bleached blonde in a black leather miniskirt and scandalously high heels.

The blonde tossed her long, straight hair in a gesture he recognized. His body stilled. She turned slightly, giving him a clear view of her familiar, overly made-up face as she bestowed a dazzling smile on the undeserving tax assessor.

Laying a slender, long-fingered hand on Morrison's arm, she batted her heavily mascaraed lashes at him. Grady sucked in a breath, ready to rush across the room and rip away her hand. But then Morrison nodded and left her side, probably because she'd charmed him into bringing her a drink.

"Grady, is something wrong?"

Tori's question snapped him out of his momentary paralysis. "Yeah, something's wrong," he ground out. "I see somebody over there I need to talk to."

"The blonde?" Her voice spiked with curiosity. "Who is she?"

"My sister."

Chapter Seven

Lorelei Palmer loved a party.

She loved the way everybody dressed to the nines, the buzz of conversation, the flowing alcohol, the delectable finger food. But most of all, she loved the excitement that swirled in the air.

The air of *possibility*.

Her gaze swept over the pool area, where guests mingled in the shadow of the intracoastal, looking for one guest in particular.

She got an eyeful of her brother, leaving the side of an attractive woman with amazing auburn hair. His jaw was set, the corners of his mouth slanted downward.

She resisted the urge to stick out her tongue, reminding herself that she loved him, too. Despite his ongoing mission to make sure she never had any fun.

"Grady!" She went to meet him, taking very small steps so she didn't fall off her heels. With the three-inch lifts, she still reached only five foot five, which made it difficult for her to do more than kiss the air on either side of his cheeks. "How wonderful to see you."

"You should have seen me this afternoon at the office." He didn't crack a smile. "But I hear you didn't come back after lunch."

She ignored the censure in his voice. What a stick-in-the-mud. So she hadn't come back to work. How was she to know he'd drop in after the golf tournament? Besides, he had a secretary. There was only so much answering the phone and paperwork to go around.

"I bought new clothes for the party." She twirled to exhibit the leather skirt and midriff-baring top she'd picked up at the mall. She'd put them on credit because she didn't have the money to pay for them, but, hey, you only lived once. "Why do you think I'm working, if not to fund my social life?"

He ignored her question. "I wasn't aware you were invited."

"I wasn't." She beamed up at him. She thought about giving his cheek an affectionate pat but now didn't seem to be the right time. "But you know how much I love a party. If you expected me to stay away, you shouldn't have told me about it."

He screwed up his forehead. "I didn't mention the party to anyone besides Frankie," he said, referring to his business manager.

She gave a theatrical laugh. "If you think I couldn't hear you and Frankie talking, you seriously underestimated me."

Grady's lips thinned and he lowered his voice the

way he did when he was trying to hold on to his temper. "You shouldn't be here."

"Oh, don't get your Jockey shorts in a twist, Duke." She used the nickname primarily because she knew it annoyed him. She tossed her head, enjoying the way the blond strands swung. The money she'd spent at the beauty salon had definitely been worth it. "Nobody cares that I crashed the party."

Nobody except Grady. Oh, she knew he loved her, but she was tired of him playing the heavy. Only seven years older than her twenty-one, he acted more like her father than her brother.

She had a father, thank you very much. Grady did, too. Along with a mother who had cried over him for the past month. Lorelei had cried, too. At night with her door closed where nobody could see how the growing chasm between her parents and her brother hurt her, too.

"Would you leave if I asked you to go?" he asked.

She put her hands on her leather-clad hips. "Would you drop this ridiculous grudge against Mom and Dad and visit them if I asked you to?"

His face became a mask, more unreadable than granite, but she sensed her words had hit a nerve.

"We're not talking about me," Grady said. "We're talking about you."

"Yeah? Well, I think it's time we did talk about what's wrong between you and them. Every time I ask, you change the subject. And they're no better."

He rubbed a hand over his face. "Lorelei, now is not the right time to discuss this."

"When will the time be right, Grady?" she asked urgently.

"Not now. You shouldn't even be here."

The stubborn set to his chin made her firm her own jaw. "Well, I am here. And I'm not going anywhere."

He sighed. "I'll accept that if you promise me something."

She made a noncommittal noise, not in the mood to concede anything. But she couldn't stay angry, either. It simply wasn't in her nature.

"What?" she asked.

"Stay away from Wade Morrison."

"Who's Wade Morrison?"

He cocked a dark eyebrow. "The tax assessor. The guy who was hitting on you."

The possibility that somebody had been trying to score with her temporarily drove away her worries about the rift between Grady and their parents. What did he mean? She'd arrived at the party five minutes ago and hadn't yet talked to anyone besides Grady. Wait. She'd asked the tall geeky guy with the dark, wavy hair where she could get a drink.

"Are you talking about the stealth hunk?"

Grady looked exasperated but nodded toward the man who'd directed her to the bar. "I'm talking about him."

"That *is* the stealth hunk."

"Okay. I'll bite. What's a stealth hunk?"

She gave him a devilish smile. "A hunk dressed like a geek. Take off his glasses, get him out of those horrible clothes, and you've got yourself one fine naked man."

"You say things like that to shock me, don't you?"

"Not really. Shocking you's a bonus," Lorelei said, laughing. She rubbed a finger against her lower lip as she stared at Wade Morrison. He'd be really yummy without clothes. "You truly think he was hitting on me?"

"You've still got a lot to learn about men, Lorelei," Grady said in that lecturing big-brother tone of his. "They always have a hidden agenda."

"And you think Wade Morrison's hidden agenda is to get into my pants?"

She watched him cringe at her blunt language. "He's bad news. He hits on all the girls. Breaks hearts all over the place."

"Is he married?"

"I don't think so," Grady said, seeming disappointed he couldn't add infidelity to the list of Wade Morrison's sins, "but he's a real player."

"Hmmmm," Lorelei said.

"So you stay away from him, okay?"

Lying to her brother violated Lorelei's moral code, so she gave him a dazzling smile and tried a bit of misdirection.

"What's the name of the city's planning director? The one with the beard, the long gray ponytail, and the bald head?"

"Larry Schlichter. Why?"

"Isn't that him with the woman you were talking to?" she asked, nodding toward the couple. Grady's head turned so fast she felt a breeze. "Looks to me like he's trying to make time with her."

"Damn," he muttered under his breath but not so

softly she couldn't hear. Now this was getting interesting.

"Who is she?"

"My date," he said shortly.

"Maybe you better rescue her. He's invading her personal space. If she backs up any farther, she'll hit a wall."

Grady took off without a backward glance, which freed her to head across the patio straight for the very man he'd warned her against.

Wade Morrison had his back to her. It was, she decided, a very nice back. The material of his dress shirt, white with skinny blue pinstripes, stretched across surprisingly broad shoulders as he bent to take an hors d'oeuvre from the tray of a much-shorter waiter. Too bad the shirt was so ugly.

She tapped him on the shoulder. He turned, his expression puzzled but not especially welcoming. His jaw worked while he finished chewing the hors d'oeuvre. She guessed it had been a miniature egg roll, considering he held another one.

"Couldn't you find the bar?" he asked with raised eyebrows. His wire-rimmed glasses slipped, and he pushed them back up his long, straight nose.

With his regular features and long, aesthetic face, he really was a cutie, she decided. The best part was he didn't seem to know it.

His hair was such a dark brown that it was almost black, and a lock of it hung nearly to his eyes. He could have dressed to accentuate his tall, lean frame, but his pants were baggy and his shirt a half size too big. And he had on, *ugh,* a tie.

"I could have found the bar," she said, smiling straight into pretty brown eyes covered by glasses instead of accentuated by contacts, "but I see something I'd rather have instead of a drink."

Wade turned his head as though checking if someone stood behind him. But the only thing in sight was the pier that led to the mayor's luxury motorboat.

"How old are you?" he asked, his eyes narrowing suspiciously.

Lorelei laughed. He really was too cute. "Twenty-one."

"I'm thirty."

"Then you're past the age of consent." She made her brows dance. "Just like me."

His Adam's apple bobbed as he swallowed. Was this for real? Had she actually made him nervous? The notion charmed her and she silently thanked her brother for pointing Wade Morrison out in the crowd. Grady had his information wrong about this guy being a player, but Wade definitely merited a second look. And maybe many more.

He cleared his throat. "You're making a mistake."

"No mistake." She took a step closer and he stepped back. Good thing she hadn't touched him. He might take a running leap into the intracoastal. "I like you."

"You don't know me."

"I'd like to get to know you," she said. "I'm Lorelei Palmer. What do you say we leave the party and go somewhere more private?"

His head shook back and forth so fast his features blurred. The eggroll in his hand plopped onto the tile at his feet. "No."

"Relax," Lorelei said. "I didn't mean we should go somewhere to have sex. I meant somewhere to talk. I promise I won't ravish you."

At the mention of sex, his eyes took a quick dip down her body. Was that a sheen of perspiration on his upper lip? Good, she thought smugly.

He picked up the eggroll with a cocktail napkin and shoved his hand behind his back. She hoped it was because he didn't trust himself not to grab her.

"I can't," he said.

She smiled, enjoying his discomfort. "Why not?"

"Because"—he looked about, almost wildly—"Because I have social obligations. I see one over there. Excuse me."

And then he was gone, leaving Lorelei to stare after the beautiful retreating back encased in the ugly shirt. She put her hands on her hips. *Well, damn.*

She shrugged. Wade Morrison was too skittish to withstand another approach from her tonight. She'd leave him alone but not for long.

Because whatever Lorelei wanted, Lorelei got.

Somewhere between her brother's warning and Wade's delightfully disconcerted reaction to her, she'd decided she wanted Wade Morrison.

Chapter Eight

Telling Grady Palmer she'd been following him because she thought he was hot was a stroke of brilliance.

Tori took in the wide set of his shoulders, the proud lift of his chin, and the interesting cast of his profile and congratulated herself on her quick thinking.

He was between the punch bowl and the far wall, immersed in conversation with the overweight man he'd partnered at the golf tournament. Pete Aiken, the city clerk who was never without a cigarette. Tori knew enough not to let her own head get turned by Grady, but that didn't change one irrefutable fact.

Grady Palmer was one hot hunk.

"Let me see if I've got this straight. You saw Grady and, zap, just like that you had to have him?"

Tori reluctantly focused on the woman asking the question. Putting herself in a position to be grilled by the hunky subject's sister had not been brilliant.

Lorelei Palmer popped the olive from the end of her

martini straw into her mouth, chewing it with obvious pleasure as she waited for an answer.

Tori cast another glance at Grady, fruitlessly wishing he'd rescue her from this predicament, but his full attention was on Pete Aiken.

"You can't stop looking at him, can you?" Lorelei asked, making Tori's head snap back around.

"Yes, I can," she retorted, then frowned. How close were Grady and Lorelei? How much of this conversation would she report back to him?

"I mean, no I can't," she said. "He does it for me."

Amusement filled Lorelei's face. Her makeup was expensive, maybe even top-of-the-line Lazenby products, but she'd applied it with such a heavy touch that it was difficult to tell what she looked like under it. Her eye makeup was wrong, too. She should have used a deep blue to make her sky blue eyes stand out, but she'd gone with a light shade. Still, her eyes glowed with intelligence.

"Of course he does it for you," Lorelei said smugly. "A blind woman could see that."

"How so?" Tori asked, even though she had a premonition she shouldn't.

"Sense of smell," Lorelei said. "The pheromones coming off you two are aromatic."

When Lorelei threw back her head and giggled, the sound was so lighthearted that Tori had to like her. Not that Lorelei was right.

Yes, Tori kept looking at Grady. But not because he was the most attractive man at the party or even because the man could fill out a pair of khakis.

She needed to figure out what was going on between him and Pete Aiken. She'd clearly seen Pete strike the golf ball that had nearly hit Mayor Black, yet Grady claimed responsibility. Why?

And why were the two men whispering, their heads close enough together that nobody could overhear? Grady didn't seem happy about the discussion. His brow was knotted and his hand gestures seemed angry.

What would a real private detective make of the situation? She frowned. She kept forgetting that she was a real PI, entrusted with a case and determined to succeed.

It seemed to her that she needed to investigate the people with whom Grady associated to find out what sort of man he was. Pete Aiken would be a good place to start.

"Grady hasn't had a girlfriend in ages," Lorelei continued, "but don't worry that there's something funny about him. He dated a couple of my friends in high school and they assured me he has all the normal male urges. Not that I particularly wanted to hear about it. But you know how a group of girls can be when they start talking about sex. Sometimes they forget who's related to who."

Sex? Tori worked to keep her expression impassive but inside she frowned. She didn't want to think about Grady and sex.

"Then why hasn't he had a girlfriend lately?" Tori asked like a good PI should.

"The last one lied about being pregnant so he'd propose, but I don't think that's it. It's not like he fell for it or anything. I think it's because he's a frigging workaholic." Lorelei threw up one of her hands.

Aside from her blue eyes, she didn't look like her brother, but Tori recognized the gesture as one of Grady's. "With the schedule he keeps, he doesn't have time for anything. Except nagging me, of course."

"What does he nag you about?"

"You name it, he's nagged about it. It's worse since I went to work for him. He has this thing about punctuality and responsibility."

"That's understandable," Tori said, then backtracked when Lorelei made a face. "I mean, considering he is your boss."

"Yeah, but he doesn't have to be so anal about it. I mean, what's the big deal if I sleep in every now and then after partying late? I expect you to get the Duke to lighten up."

The Duke? Tori wondered at the nickname but a more pressing agenda was setting Lorelei straight. "I can't get Grady to do anything he doesn't want to do."

Lorelei let out a bark of laughter, which still sounded feminine. "You must be kidding. We're women. We have the power."

"I'm not so sure about that," Tori hedged.

"I am. See that tall guy over there in the awful shirt?"

She indicated a dark-haired man leaning against a far wall, letting the party pass him by. Because he'd been part of Grady's foursome at the golf tournament, Tori had made it her business to find out his name. Wade something or other.

"I see him." Tori noticed he kept glancing their way for a couple of seconds at a time, as though he either didn't want to be obvious or couldn't help himself.

"Watch this," Lorelei said.

She puckered her lipstick-caked mouth—Tori would bet money the shade was Lazenby's Scarlet Woman—before touching two fingertips to her lips and blowing him a kiss.

Wade had been in the process of bringing a drink to his lips. He tipped the glass but its contents missed his mouth and dribbled down the front of his shirt.

He looked down at himself, set the drink on the nearest flat surface, and disappeared. Probably in search of a towel.

"See?" Lorelei said smugly.

Tori couldn't help but laugh.

"Now you try it with Grady," she said with an impish grin.

Tori shook her head. "I couldn't."

"Sure, you can. He respects people who are upfront about what they want and need. Go ahead. Blow him a kiss. Let him know you want to get busy with him tonight."

Lorelei made the declaration matter-of-factly, as though it was a given that Tori wanted her brother in bed.

The possibility that Grady had reached the same conclusion hit Tori like a lightning bolt.

Could he really believe she wanted to sleep with him just because she'd admitted to following him all over town because she thought he was hot?

She closed her eyes.

Of course he could.

Her gaze zoomed to him, and her mouth went dry at the virile picture he made. But just because she thought he was hot didn't mean she wanted him in her bed. She needed to get to know a man before she slept with him. Fear that he'd discover she had him under investigation didn't constitute a strong enough reason.

As she watched, Grady's body went rigid. He squared his shoulders and threw up his hands, alerting her that he hadn't liked what Pete said.

"He looks like he's busy," Tori said, relieved to have an excuse not to blow him kisses.

"Yeah, he does," Lorelei agreed. "Although I can't imagine why he's letting Pete Aiken bend his ear. The air over there is positively putrid. That man smokes so much somebody should hook him to the end of a train. I swear, it boggles my mind, the people Grady's been hanging out with lately."

"Is that right?" Tori muttered, her attention still on Grady. His head bobbed as he directed a few more choice words at Pete before heading toward her and Lorelei with long, purposeful strides.

"Speak of the devil," Lorelei said. "Hey, Grady, we were just talking about you. There's so much Tori hasn't told me yet."

"She'll have to take a raincheck," Grady said, taking firm hold of her arm. "We've got to be going."

"It's not even ten o'clock," Lorelei protested.

"I know," Grady said, sliding Tori a long look. "But we want to be alone."

Tori's pulse did a mad dance as her stomach pitched to the floor. Her moment of reckoning had come.

So much for her brilliant strategy.

* * *

Tori freed herself of Grady's arm when they reached the covered walkway and tried to disappear into the night, but he matched her brisk pace.

She needed to think of a way to bluff herself out of this one. Quick. But how could she reject the man she was supposedly hot for? Especially when he'd made it clear he doubted her story.

"I thought we could go somewhere more private," he said in a silky voice when she reached her Volkswagen.

She fought an inclination to jump into the car and drive away and bravely turned around. Moonlight cast a soft glow on his strong, ultramasculine face, and her heart beat a quick tattoo.

She nervously licked her lips, watched his eyes dip, and nearly swallowed her tongue. Bad move. Lip licking would not convince him she didn't yearn to go to bed with him.

"It's been a long day for you, with the golf tournament and all," she said. "I'd understand if you want to call it a night."

"I'm not tired," he said.

The heat of Grady's body seemed to wrap around her, like a wool blanket on a chilly night. Even though Pete Aiken had all but blown smoke in his face as they talked inside the party, the scent didn't cling to him. His eyelids grew heavy, making her think of bedrooms and satin sheets.

A pulse beat deep inside her body as she imagined the things they could do on those sheets. *Oh, dear.* Why couldn't Ms. M want an ugly man investigated?

Then the too-hot-to-handle cover story wouldn't have occurred to her, and she wouldn't be in this predicament.

"In fact, I'm feeling more wide awake by the moment."

His eyes, which looked more violet than blue in the darkness, held a promise of pleasure. She hadn't slept with a man in the six months she'd lived in Seahaven, and her body suddenly craved what it had been missing.

Hey, wait a minute, her brain screamed. Grady Palmer had it going on in the sex-appeal department, but tangling with him was strictly taboo. Her job was to dig up dirt on him. Under no circumstances could she sleep with him.

"Why don't we—" he began.

"I can't," she cried. "I mean, we can't. Because I'm not going home."

He frowned. "Where are you going?"

Where could she be headed so late at night? Tori looked away from the suspicion written on his face and tried to come up with a feasible explanation.

The night wasn't especially bright, with cloud cover obscuring the moon, but Mayor Black's outside lights gave off enough voltage for Tori to make out some of the surroundings.

Her gaze fell on the garish orange-and-black lettering on the window sticker of the BMW parked in front of her Volkswagen. That's it, she thought.

"I'm going to *Grim Tales from the Reaper*," she said, reading from the window sticker.

"What's that?"

She squinted, unsuccessfully trying to make out the window sticker's small print. Time to improvise.

"It's a play. A musical sci-fi spoof. Dancing. Singing. Screaming in horror."

He ran a hand through his hair. "I didn't think plays started this late at night."

"Not in Seahaven, they don't. But *Grim Tales* is showing in Miami Beach. At midnight."

"Why midnight?"

"It's a cult thing. Sort of like *The Rocky Horror Picture Show* back in the 1970s. The midnight showing's part of its allure."

"Sounds interesting," he said, although she doubted he thought so. "Mind if I come along?"

"You can't," she quickly interjected. "It's sold out, and you don't have a ticket. My friends and I got them way in advance. Oh, my gosh. What time is it?"

He checked his watch. "A quarter past ten."

"I was supposed to pick up my friends fifteen minutes ago." She remotely unlocked the driver's-side door of her Volkswagen and scooted around the vehicle. "Sorry, but I've got to go."

"Okay," he said mildly. "Then maybe we can have that cup of coffee another time."

"Coffee." She peered at him over the roof of her car. "What coffee?"

"The coffee I was going to suggest we get at this place I know on Route One that's open until midnight."

"You were talking about coffee?"

"Yep," he said.

She cast her mind back over the evening, realizing

71

he hadn't done anything to indicate he wanted sex with her. He'd suggested he wanted to talk, specifically about how a woman like her found herself following a man like him.

But why was he so suspicious of her motives? Unless men had something to hide, most of them wouldn't object to being followed by an attractive woman. But maybe Grady didn't consider her attractive. Maybe he'd asked her to coffee to make sure she wasn't looney tunes.

Accepting his invitation would be the smart move, both to assure him of her sanity and to discover more about him. But if she reversed her position, he might really think she was nuts.

"My friends are waiting," she said. "I've got to go."

"Who'll feed your cat?" he asked before she could escape.

"My what?"

"Your fat cat," he supplied, and she remembered the lame story she'd invented. "You've been away from home for a while. Won't she get hungry?"

"I left plenty of food out this time," Tori said before she ducked into her car, intent on getting away from his questions.

She drove off thinking it hadn't been a bad debut. If you didn't count the moment she'd lusted after him in the darkness and his skepticism about her nonexistent cat, that is.

On the positive side, she'd invented a plausible reason for following him and came up with a believable excuse not to have sex with him. Never mind that he hadn't wanted sex in the first place.

If she had the foggiest idea how to proceed with the investigation, the PI thing might work out after all.

She did know one thing. After she finished her shift at the Frasier's makeup counter tomorrow, she needed to visit the pound.

She hadn't read very far into *So, You Want to Be a PI,* but she knew enough to cover her tracks.

Chapter Nine

Grady consciously slowed his momentum so he didn't burst through the back entrance of Frasier's department store like an old-West sheriff on the lookout for an outlaw. Technically, Tori qualified as more of a liar than a bandit.

Hadn't she realized he'd check out her story? He'd booted up his computer the moment he'd gotten home the night before, and typed "Grim Tales from the Reaper" into a search engine.

He'd gotten a hit on the current events page of the Eleanor J. Reaper High School Web site.

It seemed the drama department at Reaper High, which was up the road from Seahaven, was putting on a series of vignettes for children based on Grimm's fairy tales.

Hence the clever title *Grimm Tales from the Reaper*.

If Grady weren't mistaken, the city councilman he

and Tori had walked into the party with last night had a teenage daughter who attended Reaper High.

His inclination was to hunt Tori down and demand to know why she'd lied, but the confrontational approach hadn't worked very well last night.

Better to bide his time and go along with her you're-so-hot fiction while he figured out what she was up to.

He had doubts that he'd find her at Frasier's. She'd mentioned she worked weekends at the store, but that could have been another lie. "Tori Whitley" might not even be her real name. Directory assistance listed a number of Whitleys, but none with *T* as a first initial.

He looked around for a salesperson who wasn't helping another customer and found one in the petite, pimply faced teenager manning the cash register in the juniors' department.

"Can you tell me if there's a Tori Whitley working here?" he asked her.

"Sure is." The teen smiled at him through her braces. "Go through jewelry and you can't miss her. Sometimes she even has a line."

"Then I'd better get over there before someone gets in front of me."

The teenager's eyebrows rounded like the arches of a bridge. "You mean you'd get in line?"

"Sure," he said.

"I wouldn't have figured you for the sort, but I'm cool with it," the teen said. "I think it's true what they say about it taking all kinds."

Puzzled by her comment, Grady threaded his way past glass cases of glittering gold and silver jewelry before Tori's fall of auburn hair caught his attention.

76

She was focused intently on a woman sitting on a raised stool in front of her. The woman had her eyes closed, as though in some kind of trance. Then Tori picked up a brush and dabbed something powdery on the woman's nose.

The teen's comment suddenly made sense.

He felt an uncomfortable sensation prick the back of his neck and slowly turned to see a middle-aged woman with pockmarked skin and a cane closing in on him. He'd noticed her shuffling through the racks in the juniors' department while he questioned the clerk.

Had she heard him say he'd wait in line for Tori? Had she trailed him to watch the show?

"I'm not here for a makeover," he told the woman, who looked at him curiously. He felt compelled to add, "I don't wear makeup. Not that I think there's anything wrong with men wearing makeup if that's their thing. Except it's not my thing, because I don't wear it."

His voice trailed off when he realized he was protesting too much. She extended a business card holder to him.

"I don't care what you do, buddy," she said. "I just wanted to tell you that you dropped this."

He took his business cards with as much dignity as he could muster. "Thank you," he said.

She walked away and he gladly returned his attention to Tori, who was putting the finishing touches on the woman's makeup with a sure and steady hand.

If this had been his first glimpse of her, he realized with startling clarity, he would have found a way to introduce himself. Her unusual coloring, big eyes, and slightly upturned nose made her pleasing to the eye, but that was only part of the reason. She worked with a one-track absorption that made her even more attractive.

But that was dangerous thinking. Grady, more than anybody, knew appearances could deceive.

Tori might not look like anybody's flunky but she couldn't be trusted. She'd lied about the play and, most likely, her reason for following him. No doubt she'd told him other whoppers, too. The fat cat came to mind.

She must have sensed somebody approaching, because she raised a finger without taking her eyes from the woman. "I'll be with you in a minute," she said.

"Take your time," he replied, and those big eyes flew to him.

"Grady." Surprise and anxiety clouded her features. The absence of pleasure didn't surprise him, but he found that it bothered him. "What are you doing here?"

"I'm here to see you," he said. "I would have called but directory assistance didn't have a listing for you."

"I'm listed under 'V. Whitley,'" she said. "'Tori' is short for 'Victoria.'"

Likely story, he thought, although he had to admit her explanation sounded plausible.

"Didn't you say you drive a VW bug, Tori?" interjected her dark-haired customer, who was pretty enough to be a model. "That's how you should tell the men you meet to remember how you're listed. It won't backfire on you the way it used to on me. Before I got married, my name was Zedney. My first name's Elaine, so my initials were E.Z. Which I wasn't."

The chatty customer didn't give either of them a

chance to reply, instead asking Tori, "You are done, right?"

Tori had barely nodded in reply before her customer got out of her seat and marched up to Grady. "I need a man's opinion." She tilted up her face. "How do I look?"

Tori had applied her makeup with a light touch, a smart choice considering the woman's natural beauty.

"Great," he answered truthfully. "You should buy everything."

"I was thinking the same thing, but it's good to hear you second that." To Tori, she said, "Ring me up."

He stood silently by while Tori completed the sale, patiently enduring Elaine's incessant chatter. Tori didn't look at him until her customer had finally gone. Her dark eyes locked on his and he felt the heat, the same way he had the night before.

She quickly lowered her lashes before he could determine whether she felt it, too. "You didn't have to talk her into buying all those products," she said.

"It didn't take much persuasion," he said, resting his hands on the glass counter. "Besides, I wanted you to get the commission."

She backed away from the counter and busied herself straightening jars of makeup on a shelf behind her that already looked perfectly in order. "Nobody at Frasier's works on commission," she said.

"Then you should find a place where you can," he said. "You did a good job."

She shrugged her slim shoulders. "It's just something I do to earn extra money. There's not much to it."

Judging by the number of makeup-impaired women

in the world, Grady didn't agree. Lorelei, who applied her makeup with a paint roller, could certainly use Tori's expertise. But he hadn't come to Frasier's to talk about his sister.

"How was the play last night?" he asked abruptly, hoping to get a reaction from her.

He succeeded, but he hadn't counted on bewilderment. "The play?" she asked, a blank look on her face.

"*Grimm Tales from the Reaper*," he supplied, and saw the light of remembrance enter her eyes. She'd told so many lies, she probably had a hard time keeping them all straight.

One of her hands kneaded the other. "Really, really scary," she answered.

"I thought you said it was a spoof," he said, his gaze dropping to her hands to show he'd noticed her edginess.

She abruptly stopped rubbing them together and hid them behind her back. "You must have heard me wrong," she said, biting her bottom lip. "I said the play was spooky. Not spoofy."

The bottom seemed to fall out of his stomach, causing him to feel vaguely nauseous. And disappointed in himself for hoping she'd come clean about the play. But now that he'd reestablished that she was lying, he needed to get to the purpose of his visit.

"You probably wonder what I'm doing here." He gave her his most charming smile. "I came to apologize."

She shuffled her feet. "You don't have anything to apologize for."

"Yes, I do," he said. "Instead of cross-examining

you about why you were following me, I should have gotten down on my knees and given thanks that a woman as beautiful and interesting as you is attracted to me."

Her lips parted. "Are you serious?"

He might have laid the compliments on too thick, but there was no turning back now. "Dead serious," Grady said. "Let me make it up to you by taking you out tomorrow night."

She hesitated in giving her answer. "I sort of have plans tomorrow night."

Grady swallowed his disappointment. Was she refusing him again? "Don't tell me you're going to another play," he said mildly.

Her auburn hair swayed when she shook her head, catching the fluorescent lights overhead so that it shone. "I promised my neighbor I'd go to her church carnival. It's for charity." She paused, then seemed to fight an internal battle before she added, "I don't suppose you'd like to go with me?"

"I'd love to," Grady said quickly, even as the irony of the setting registered with him.

A carnival, bound to be full of wide-eyed, excited children, represented innocence. The term didn't apply to Tori, no matter how angelic she looked.

"Good," she said, but her smile wavered.

"I'll look forward to it," he said.

Much later, after he called the FBI agent working on Operation Citygate and asked him to run a background check on one Victoria Whitley, Grady realized at least part of his conversation with Tori had been truthful.

He did look forward to their date.

He didn't intend to probe his subconscious to discover the truth of why that was, because he had a feeling he wouldn't like the answer.

Chapter Ten

The bundle in the oversized canvas bag she passed off as a purse squirmed, diverting Tori's anxiety over her imminent return to the Roseate Spoonbill.

Careful to support the bottom of the bag with the flat of her palm, she opened the drawstring top and peered inside.

"Shhh," she told the scrawny white cat that stared back at her. "I was already fired once. I don't want to get kicked out a second time."

The cat—she hadn't named it yet—gave her the same plaintive look that had wormed its way into Tori's heart at the pound.

She'd been all set to take home a plump feline named Big Bertha when the white cat, which she'd been trying to ignore, let loose with a pitiful meow that seemed to say, "Pick me."

She'd met those sad, blue eyes and reluctantly given up on her quest for a fat cat. Adopting her hadn't been easy, either, not when the county pound required apartment dwellers to provide a copy of a lease showing their place of residence had no pet restrictions.

Since Tori was relatively sure Seahaven Shores had a no-pets clause, she'd given her cousin Eddie's address as her own. He deserved nothing less for convincing her that investigating Grady would be a cinch. *Ha!*

"You better not cry. You need to remember I wasn't heartless enough to leave you home alone on your first night with me," she told the cat in the bag before she pulled the drawstring loosely closed.

The bartending job she'd had and lost at the Roseate Spoonbill hadn't been her first as a Seahaven resident. After striking out as a bank teller and a waitress, she'd taken a six-week course in mixing drinks.

She'd applied at the Roseate Spoonbill, an establishment a few miles south of Seahaven, because the logo on the front of the building had amused her. A rose-colored cartoon bird lilted drunkenly to one side, a whiskey bottle dangling from its spoon-shaped beak.

Now she saw the bird as an adequate metaphor for her professional life. Tori drank only moderately. But if she didn't get help soon, she was in danger of falling flat on her face. Again.

"Here goes," she said under her breath and walked into the bar. Joey Girdano, the bar manager, noticed her immediately.

"Hey, Whitley. Didn't I fire you?" he asked as he chewed energetically on a wad of gum. A small man with coarse, wavy hair and a thick mustache he never thought to trim, Joey was a recovering alcoholic whose jaws never stopped moving. He claimed the gum helped him keep from reaching for whiskey.

"Don't worry," Tori said, "I'm not here to ask for my job back."

"You wouldn't get it back if you did," Joey said.

The cat in her bag made a loud noise, causing the assortment of men and women bellying up to the bar to stare at her. Tori duplicated the noise the best she could, which hurt her throat.

"You don't have to get hissy about it," Joey said. "You were a lousy bartender, not to mention gullible as hell. Those people you let run up tabs still haven't paid."

"You're joking."

"I never joke about money." He blew a bubble, popped it. "As long as you spend yours, you're welcome here anytime."

"Crystal's working tonight, right?"

"Station three," Joey said. "If you buy a drink, I won't even hassle her about talking to you."

"She's your best waitress. You won't hassle her even if I don't buy a drink."

Joey laughed, showing off crooked teeth. "You might be right, but I will hassle you."

Five minutes later, Tori sipped a glass of Chablis at a back table while she waited for her red-haired, freckled friend to finish serving a nearby table.

"No more noises out of you," she whispered to the cat, soothingly stroking the outside of the bag.

She used the downtime to pat herself on the back for finishing another chapter of *So, You Want to Be a*

PI. The book had given her the idea for an Internet search of local newspaper archives, which had paid off handsomely.

Palmer Construction had been mentioned repeatedly, mostly in conjunction with city construction projects. In the past nine months, the city had awarded Grady's company contracts to build an addition to the city police station and to renovate the main library branch.

But those black-and-white facts on a page still told her little about the man himself. For that, she needed a different strategy, which is why she'd sought out Crystal.

"Hey, girlfriend, I've missed having you around." Crystal sat down across from her, radiating the energy and life that earned her more tips than better-looking waitresses. "I . . . Did you know your purse is moving?"

The bag on her lap wiggled furiously, refusing to be ignored.

"Oh, no. I think she needs air," Tori said, frantically loosening the drawstring at the top. The cat stuck out its miniature white head and breathed.

Crystal recoiled. "What are you doing carrying around an ugly white rat?"

"It's a cat, not a rat. I agree she's undersized, but she's not ugly."

"She's more than undersized. She's a runt. And she is, too, ugly," Crystal said.

Tori might have protested if the cat's not-quite-white fur, close-set blue eyes, and weird pink area around the eyes had not made credibility difficult.

"Since when do you have a cat, anyway?" Crystal asked.

"Since a couple of hours ago." Tori stroked the pitiful little thing's head. "I was in the market for something bigger but she kind of picked me."

"Good thing for the cat, because nobody was going to pick her," Crystal said, then cast a glance over her shoulder. "It doesn't look like Joey's seen her yet, but don't bet against him. Usually rats can sniff out cats."

"Joey's not a rat," Tori said.

"That's what I love about you. You're always ready to give people the benefit of the doubt, even the guy who fired you."

Tori saw her opening and took it. "That's sort of why I'm here. I've been thinking lately that I might be too gullible."

"Ya think?"

"So I need some tips on how to take a man's measure. You know, find out what kind of person he is."

Crystal snorted. "And you think *I* know?"

"You're surrounded by men, Crystal. Three brothers. A husband. Two little boys. If you don't know men, who does?"

"Maybe nobody."

"You must have learned something from hanging out with all those men."

"Does checking to see if the toilet seat's up before sitting down count?"

Tori made a face, and Crystal rolled her eyes. "Okay, okay. Let me think about it. Are you talking about any man in particular?"

"Nobody you know. Just this guy I'm going out with tomorrow night."

Crystal put her elbows on the table and leaned forward. "Where's this coming from, Tor? Why are you going out with this guy if you're not sure about him? It's not like you to have doubts about people."

She wouldn't have doubts about Grady, either, if Ms. M hadn't put them there with her comment about dirt digging.

"Like I said, I figure it's time I stopped being gullible, is all," she said. "So do you have any tips?"

"Yeah," Crystal said. "Date him for a year or two, paying particular attention to how he acts around old people and kids. That should do it."

"I don't have a year or two," Tori complained.

Crystal rubbed the back of her neck. "The only way you'll get an instant answer is if you give him a pop quiz. Like one of those personality tests that run in *Cosmo*."

"That's an idea," Tori said thoughtfully. "But a morality quiz would be better."

"Oh, honey. That was a joke."

"Still, it could work. I've taken a couple of those quizzes, and they're pretty revealing."

Crystal shook her head. "So what are you gonna do, whip out the magazine and a pen and have him fill in his answers?"

"No," Tori said. "That would be too strange."

"Now you're talking."

"I'll have a bunch of questions in mind that I can tailor to a particular situation. Then I'll wait for opportunities to work them into our conversation."

88

"And now you're talking crazy again. Listen to me, there's a far better way to figure out what kind of guy he is."

Tori put her elbows on the table. "I'm all ears."

"Listen to your gut."

Tori bit her bottom lip, turning that piece of advice over in her mind. She intended to follow it, just not exclusively.

While they were talking, the cat had worked the drawstring loose. By the time Tori noticed, she'd squiggled out of the bag onto her lap. Then she perched her tiny paws on the table and peered at Crystal.

"Are you gonna keep that thing?" Crystal asked.

A wave of unexpected tenderness hit Tori when she looked down at the helpless, previously unloved creature. She guessed she'd have to give her a name. "Yes, I am."

"Then if you go the multiple-choice route," Crystal said wryly, "you should ask this guy something that'll give you an idea about how he feels about cats disguising themselves as scrawny white rats."

Chapter Eleven

The smell of French fries mingled with the sweet scent of cotton candy in the heavy night air, filling Grady with nostalgia.

He'd forgotten how much he loved carnivals until Tori had brought him here to the western outreaches of Seahaven where a small parcel of land had temporarily been transformed into a playground.

Walking the midway, with loud-mouthed carnies urging them to try their luck at carnival games, Operation Citygate and Pete Aiken's claim that somebody else wanted in on the action seemed far away.

In jeans, tennis shoes, and a yellow cropped shirt that made her hair look even more burnished, Tori Whitley didn't seem like she had an ulterior motive for being with him.

If she'd acted this way at the party, he wouldn't have had his FBI contact run the background check.

The agent wouldn't have the results for a few days, but at the moment Grady was in no hurry.

Tori hadn't done a single suspicious thing since they'd arrived at the carnival, although her conversation had been a bit strange.

She nodded toward a skinny man with a mallet who was poised to test his strength on the high striker.

"If that guy dropped a hundred-dollar bill, would you pocket it, give it back to him, or donate it to the church, which probably needs it more than he does?" she asked.

He grinned down at her, wondering how she came up with these questions. On the drive to the carnival, she'd asked under which circumstances he'd contest a traffic ticket if he knew he was guilty. When they'd passed a pair of nuns, she'd wanted to know what he'd do if he saw one of them pocketing money from the collection plate. Always, she gave him three or four answers from which to choose.

"If that guy dropped a hundred, you'd better believe one of the kids around here would get to it before I did," he said.

"Then would you turn the other way, follow the kid and convince him to return the money, or tell the skinny guy what had happened and let him handle it by himself?"

He laughed, not sure he could keep the choices straight. "What's with all these questions?"

"Nothing," she said quickly, then expanded on her answer before he could press. "I guess I'm trying to get to know you better."

Her eyes radiated sincerity as she gazed up at him,

Snoops in the City

and he realized he believed her. He'd been inspired by
that old saying about keeping your friends close and
your enemies closer when he asked her out, but she
didn't seem like an enemy at the moment.

"Hey, buddy, come over here and impress your
lady," called a man from a nearby ring-toss booth.
"Two out of three wins a prize."

The prize was a giant stuffed replica of SpongeBob
SquarePants.

"If you win me one of those things," Tori told him,
"I might have to hurt you."

He laughed again, something he hadn't done nearly
enough of since he'd gotten involved with Operation
Citygate. He reached for her hand, which she gave
him without hesitation, and realized he was enjoying
himself.

Except having a good time hadn't been on his
agenda. This was a fishing expedition, designed to reel
in information. He hadn't learned anything new about
her, except her cheeks dimpled charmingly when she
smiled.

"Where to?" Grady asked.

"Where else?" she answered. "The merry-go-
round."

She directed him toward a medium-sized carousel
surrounded by excited children. Nobody in line
looked older than twelve except the young father
carrying a cute little girl who probably couldn't walk
on her own.

"You really want to ride the carousel?" Grady
asked.

"I do. And I want you to come with me." She raised

93

shining eyes to him. "Get on one of those horses for me, Grady. Please."

He pictured himself on the carousel, his long legs dangling from one of the painted horses as the people surrounding the ride laughed and pointed. Then he envisioned Tori's disappointment if he said no.

"I'm game," he said, visually locating the ticket stand and then reaching in his back pocket for his wallet. Laughter bubbled from her in a merry burst, and his hand stilled.

He'd been had.

"Forgive me, but I wanted to know what you'd do if your very silly date begged you to go on a totally inappropriate ride." The brown of her eyes seemed to grow warmer as she gazed at him. "And now I do."

"That was a dirty trick," he said, but found himself grinning. "It'd serve you right if I went back there and won you a SpongeBob."

A high, nasal voice coming from behind him interrupted whatever she'd been about to say. "Grady? Is that you?"

He recognized Helen Tribecka's voice even before he pasted on a smile and turned to greet her. What were the odds, he thought, of running into his mother's best friend at a carnival?

A small, dark-haired woman with rounded shoulders and an intimidating glare, she had flashing eyes that missed nothing. Such as the misfired baseball that dented her husband's car when Grady was ten and the curbside lilies he'd flattened while learning to drive.

She held the hand of a dark-haired, chubby-cheeked

child whose head didn't quite reach her waist. Of course. She'd come with her grandson.

"Hello, Mrs. Tribecka," he said, then drew Tori closer to his side. "This is Tori Whitley. Tori, Mrs. Tribecka lives a few doors down from my parents. This is her daughter Anna's son."

Mrs. Tribecka greeted Tori, then addressed Grady. "Your mother didn't say anything about you having a girlfriend."

His mother told Mrs. Tribecka everything. "Tori and I just met," Grady explained.

"That explains it then," she said, making use of her patented glare. "Your mother can't know what's going on in your life when you don't call."

"I'm Tommy," the little boy interjected into the resulting silence. "I ride fish."

Glad of the distraction, Grady bent down to the little boy's level. "Hey, Tommy, I'm Grady. That's sort of, um, fishy."

"I ride big fish," the boy said, spreading his arms wide.

"We've talked about this, Tommy. You rode a boat, not a fish." Mrs. Tribecka's voice gentled when she talked to the boy, who giggled and pointed to a nearby ride. Tiny boats connected by spokes circled a shallow moat.

"No boat," he insisted. "Fish. I tell Mommy and Daddy I ride fish."

"Speaking of parents," Mrs. Tribecka said, returning her attention to Grady, "you should call yours."

Grady stiffened and raised to his full height. "I heard you the first time."

Grady tugged on Tori's hand, not so subtly backing away from his former neighbor, who thought she knew what she was talking about but didn't.

"It was good seeing you, Mrs. Tribecka, Tommy," he said politely while he searched for an opening in the stream of people walking by. As Tori murmured how nice it was to have met them, he saw the opportunity for their getaway. He took it, pulling Tori along with him.

"Call your parents," Mrs. Tribecka called after them.

"Fish is fun," Tommy added.

"What was all that about?" Tori asked as he ushered her away from them.

"The kid thinks boats are fish."

"Not that," she said, sounding worried. "Why did Mrs. Tribecka keep telling you to call your parents? Is something wrong?"

"Nothing's wrong," he said, "and it seems to me we were talking about something vitally important before we ran into her. Ah, yes. SpongeBob Square-Pants."

"But, why—"

"Because she's a busybody, that's why," he said, closing the subject. "Now my question is, since when do sponges wear pants? Do you think it's when they came to life and realized they were naked?"

She smirked at him. "Very funny."

"Now what do you want to do next?" he asked. "I'm game for anything but the carousel."

She chose the Ferris wheel and waited beside him

with obvious impatience until the ride attendant ushered them onto a bright blue seat and pulled down the safety bar.

"The Ferris wheel is my favorite carnival ride," she confided when they were settled. Their car moved up a notch, and the attendant below waited for another pair of riders to alight so he could seat the people next in line.

"Do you know that's one of the first personal things you've told me about yourself?"

"What else do you want to know?" she asked, her expression open and unguarded, like a woman with nothing to hide.

The question paramount in his mind was why she'd lied to him about the play last night, but he asked, "Does your family live in Seahaven?"

"Nope, it's just me," she answered. "Everybody else lives on the west coast. My parents are in Siesta Key, which is near Sarasota, where my dad practices law. My sister Susan's in Bradenton, and my brother David's in Tampa."

"When did you move here?"

"Almost six months ago. I turned twenty-five and figured it was about time I struck out on my own."

"Why Seahaven?" he asked.

"I guess because it didn't seem as daunting as some other parts of Florida. I love the little downtown and the sense you get of living in a small town even though you're really not. I thought I could succeed here."

"At what?"

"That's the problem," she said as their car moved another notch closer to the Ferris wheel's peak. "Did I mention that my sister's a pediatrician and my brother's an architect? I keep thinking there's a career out there for me, but I can't seem to find anything I'm good at."

"You're good at giving makeovers."

"That's a job, not a career," she said, then clutched at his arm when their car made the final ascent to the peak of the Ferris wheel. "Oh, look."

The carnival spread out before them like a miniature feast for the eyes. He could pick out the gaily colored canopy of the carousel, which appeared to be about the size of a nickel, but he was more interested in looking at her.

The lights illuminating the Ferris wheel captured her in their reflection, and her auburn hair appeared streaked with flames. Her shirt was golden, but the color wasn't the reason she seemed to glow. The light came from within, shining out of her big, dark eyes.

Their car stayed at the peak for precious seconds, then rapidly descended. Tori squealed and squeezed his arm. It seemed the most natural thing in the world to put an arm around her and draw her close.

He could feel excitement vibrating inside her as the Ferris wheel made its wide, sweeping circles.

"This is wonderful," she said, then leaned close and met his eyes. Hers were smiling. "Thanks for coming to the carnival with me."

The sentiment seemed to come from her heart, touching Grady. "You're welcome," he said.

The carnival faded away until the world consisted of only the two of them. He felt her breath on his face along with the wind, a soft flutter that caressed his skin and made him feel even more alive than the ride.

"Let me ask you another question, but you've got to listen to all the choices before you answer," he said, and she nodded.

"If a man on a Ferris wheel kissed you, would you, (a) push him off at the top of the ride, (b) suffer silently through it, (c) close your eyes and enjoy the experience, or (d) kiss him back?"

She didn't answer for long seconds, and he had a vivid glimpse of the woman from the other night. The one who had claimed he attracted her, then surrounded herself with people so he couldn't make a move.

He waited for her to rebuff him by answering "(e) none of the above," because she had no intention of letting him kiss her.

But then she parted her lips, blinked her big eyes, and invited in a soft voice, "Why don't you try it and find out?"

Meaning to take things slowly, he buried one hand in her hair, enjoying the silky feel of the strands against his fingers. He lowered his head, she raised hers, and he captured her mouth.

He intended to press gentle kisses across the length of it, cajoling her to open to him so he could deepen the kiss. But at the first hot, tangy taste of her, he threw out his script.

She had a mouth made to be kissed, he thought as he gathered her close. Even with the safety bar in the way, her soft, womanly body fit perfectly against his.

The scent of cotton candy clung to her hair, making her seem even sweeter. She rested a hand along his jaw, moaning a little as she leaned into him and returned the kiss.

His willpower snapped, and he took advantage of her open mouth to slip his tongue between her lips. She gasped and he took advantage, stroking and circling her tongue with his as he kissed her deeply, wetly. The way a man kissed a woman he wanted to take to bed.

He angled her head to give him better access to her mouth as his free hand caught at her waist, pulling her more firmly against him. The softness of her breasts touched his chest, and he was instantly hard.

His heart lunged but it might have been due to the revolutions of the Ferris wheel. Or because of the soft sounds Tori made in the back of her throat.

When she moaned, he took it as a request, thrusting his tongue into her mouth again and again. Her hands were at the back of his head, her fingers tangled in his hair.

The Ferris wheel jarred to a stop, and their car swayed, not recklessly but enough to remind them of where they were. Tori tore her mouth from his and placed her hands against his chest.

"Grady, stop," she said.

He desperately tried to regain his equilibrium, but his breathing came in ragged gasps. His heart drummed so fast it hurt his chest.

He looked into her eyes, finding them glazed and unfocused in her pale face. The kiss had felt real and wild and out of control. He still felt that way.

"Next time we'll have to try that on solid ground," he said, laughing a little while he strove to get his body under control. "I actually forgot we were on the Ferris wheel."

"It's not that," she rasped, turning her head to the side so he couldn't see her eyes. "It's just that things are moving too fast."

He frowned. "You have to know I'd never force you to do anything you didn't want to do."

"I know," she said, still not looking at him.

The night went downhill after that. Their banter dried up, and she seemed determined to keep at least a foot between them at all times. Within an hour, they were at her apartment door.

"Goodnight, Grady," she said, slipping inside before he could touch her.

Not that he meant to. Not after that disaster of a kiss. Except, at the time, the kiss had seemed more like a beginning than an ending.

He could have sworn she'd responded to him, but then why had she reverted to her previous touch-me-not incarnation?

Could it be because she hadn't wanted him to get the wrong idea about how the night would end?

If she were on a job, she could be willing to go so far but no further. She'd kiss him, but she wouldn't sleep with him.

His doubts about her, which had nearly vanished earlier in the evening, rose once again.

Chapter Twelve

Tori kept her foot steady on the gas pedal as she drew relentlessly nearer to Boca Raton and her cousin's PI office. Dark sunglasses shielded her bleary eyes from the midday sun.

After the way she'd bungled things the night before, she hadn't even needed her silver disco ball to tell her to get off the case before she did something incredibly stupid. Like have wild, I-don't-care-that-you're-off-limits sex with the man she was investigating.

"I knew he was hot, Gordo," she told the newly named cat, which was perched on the passenger seat watching her intently. "But I didn't know he was scorching until he kissed me."

She'd never considered herself a passionate person, but last night on the Ferris wheel she'd been in favor of skipping the foreplay and going directly to the sex.

Good thing the safety bar had prevented her from tearing his clothes off.

After the Ferris wheel had jarred to a halt and she'd found the strength to tell him to stop, she hadn't trusted herself to get within touching distance.

If he'd kissed her at the door, she'd probably have dragged him inside. By now, she'd know exactly how much he measured. But she was pretty sure that's not what Ms. M had in mind when she asked her to take the measure of the man.

The dreams she'd had involving his slick, naked flesh surfaced, and a flush of heat hit Tori hard. She reached over, turned the air conditioner up a couple of notches, and stomped down harder on the gas pedal.

How will you ever be good at anything if you quit when the going gets tough? a little voice inside her head asked, but she shut it out.

"I'm not quitting," she told the cat. "I'm . . . exercising an option to finish up the job early."

Any illusions she had about private investigation as the right career for her were gone. She'd cut her losses and try something else.

As for Grady, he seemed like a good enough guy to her.

He'd provided all the right responses to her multiple-choice morality quiz. He also opened doors for women, overprotected his younger sister, and had the most delectable mouth God ever gave a man. Most tellingly, he could have pressed her to sleep with him last night but hadn't.

She still didn't know why Ms. M wanted him investigated, but she was ready to give him a favorable report and move on. Maybe then she'd be able to get some sleep.

She pressed her foot down harder on the gas pedal.

A siren sounded somewhere behind her, and she checked her rearview mirror. Blue and white lights whirled atop a police cruiser directly behind her.

She swore, noticed a forty-five mile-per-hour speed-limit sign, and glanced down at her speedometer.

Sixty-seven.

She pulled over to the shoulder of the road, wondering if she could talk herself out of getting a ticket she could ill afford to pay.

When a tall, well-built cop with mirrored sunglasses appeared beside the car, she hit the automatic-power button that lowered the window.

She tried a smile. "You're not going to believe this, but I never speed."

His mouth remained set in a grim line. *Okay, bad opening.* Obviously he didn't believe that.

"I had a lot on my mind."

Silence.

"But I know that's no excuse."

Why had she said that? It *was* her excuse.

"I've never gotten a ticket before." She grimaced and felt an urge to come clean. "Except when I was eighteen, but that doesn't count because almost everybody drives too fast in their teens."

No change of expression.

"So, I hoped, maybe, you might, you know, go a little easy on me."

Cars whizzed by, some, she was sure, driving faster than she had been. The cop finally spoke, his voice a tough-guy baritone. "Is that a guinea pig on the seat beside you?"

105

Gordo didn't take offense, so she did. "It's a cat," she informed him.

"Ugliest damn cat I've ever seen," he remarked.

She sighed, removed her license and registration from her wallet, and wondered if the cop would have cut her a break had Gordo been a cute little puppy.

He paid particular attention to her driver's license, making her suspect she shared the name Tori Sassenbury Whitley with an escaped criminal.

"Sassenbury. That's a name you don't hear every day. You any relation to the Sassenbury runs a PI office a mile or so from here?" he asked.

The tension seeped out of her and hope broke free. The cop knew Eddie. Maybe she'd drive away from this without a ticket after all.

"Yes," she said eagerly. "Eddie's my cousin."

"He's also a prick," the cop said before getting out his pad and writing her a ticket.

A one-hundred-dollar speeding ticket burned a hole in her purse by the time she pulled into the parking lot adjacent to Eddie's office.

It amazed her that nothing in Boca Raton was ugly, not even its strip malls. A grocery store for the fruits-and-grains crowd shared space with a gourmet frozen custard shop, a Radio Shack, a drugstore, a Chinese restaurant, and an assortment of small businesses.

The stores boasted matching pale orange exteriors and architecturally interesting rooftops, but Tori was not in the mood to admire the scenery.

The sooner she discharged her obligation to Eddie, the sooner she could find a job that would enable her to pay the speeding ticket. She couldn't in good conscience take the entire amount Eddie had quoted her, not when she'd been on the job for barely a week.

The words SASSENBURY INVESTIGATIONS flowed across the glass window of Eddie's office in bold black lettering. Tori shook her head at the string of numbers under the name.

"Why include a phone number," she muttered as she put Gordo into her canvas bag, "when Eddie never answers the phone?"

She half expected the office to be locked, but the door swung open, and she mentally reviewed her speech as she came through it.

"I am not a bimbo."

That wasn't Tori's opening line.

"I am not a woman to be trifled with."

That wasn't bad, but it wasn't part of Tori's speech, either.

"And I demand to know where Eddie Sassenbury is this instant."

Tori screwed up her forehead. Eddie Sassenbury, in all his rumpled glory, sat behind what looked to be a secretary's desk. Stubble blackened his jaw, dark smudges shadowed his eyes, and he looked like he'd slept in his clothes, which wasn't unusual.

"Afraid I can't tell you that, lady," Eddie said. "I only work for the man."

The nonbimbo was a beauty. She had long, straight hair in a lustrous ebony that was a striking contrast to her alabaster complexion. A wraparound summer dress that was surely a designer original showcased her tall, willowy figure. It was lilac, the perfect shade for her.

"Don't you dare underestimate me." The beauty shook an index finger at Eddie. "I can tell when somebody's lying. I know you know where he is."

Eddie pasted on the I'm-innocent look Tori knew well. Her cousin used to call upon it at family gatherings when somebody asked who put the Tabasco sauce in the fruit punch.

"Can I help with something?" Tori asked loudly.

Both Eddie and the beauty seemed surprised to see her, probably because the decibel level of the woman's tirade had masked the sound of Tori's arrival.

"Who are you?" the beauty demanded.

"Tori Whitley," she said.

"Hey, don't you work for the guy?" Eddie piped up. "Maybe you can help this lady out."

Tori shot an optical dagger at Eddie when the beauty advanced on her sling-back sandals. Her face was white with anger, revealing that her raspberry rouge and lipstick were blue-based, the perfect choices for a woman with her coloring.

"Where can I find the snake?" she demanded.

"I haven't seen him slithering around recently. I came here looking for him myself." Tori sent Eddie a pointed look over the woman's shoulder. "I need to talk to him, too."

The beauty's raspberry lips twisted. "If you work for him, maybe it's you I need to talk to. Maybe you're the one who took those photos of me and Brock."

From the set of her mouth, Tori deduced Brock wasn't the woman's husband. "I'm not much of a photographer," Tori said.

"Whoever took the photos wasn't, either. He didn't

get my face. Only these babies." She pointed to her chest. Thirty-eight double-Ds, Tori guessed. "Jefferson said he'd know them anywhere."

"Jefferson?"

"My husband. And now he's threatening to divorce me!" She stomped one high-heeled foot. "All because of that yellow-bellied snake Eddie Sassenbury."

The pitch of the woman's voice rose even higher. Behind them, Eddie interjected, "It's a little harsh calling a guy who's only doing his job a snake."

Both women ignored him.

"It doesn't sound to me like it was the snake's fault," Tori said. "It sounds like this happened because you were cheating on Jefferson."

"Like that's not justifiable. My husband's seventy-three years old and wrinkled as a prune."

"Is he rich?"

"Of course he's rich," she snapped.

"Then he was probably trying to find out if you married him for his money."

"Of course I did," she retorted.

"Then why are you so angry at Eddie? If you blame anybody, it should be your husband."

"Because?"

"Jefferson's the one who didn't trust you," Tori finished.

Some of the defiance left the beauty's face. The space between her lovely blue eyes grew closer as she thought. "You're right," she said.

"You should give him a piece of your mind."

"I should," the beauty agreed, nodding vigorously. She strode from the office without another word.

Tori moved toward Eddie with the same sense of purpose but he spoke first. "That was brilliant." He clapped his hands in applause.

"It wasn't that brilliant," Tori hissed. "By the time she gets home, she'll realize her husband was right not to trust her. Then she'll come looking for you again."

"Hopefully I'll have a secretary by then." Eddie sounded spectacularly unconcerned by the prospect of the beauty's return. "Then my secretary can tell her she doesn't know where I am."

"You *are* a snake," Tori said.

Eddie's features contorted in mock pain. "How can you say that about your own cousin? I gave you a job when nobody else would."

"You talked me into taking a job I wasn't suited for when I was desperate!"

Eddie put his hands behind his neck and his feet up on his desk. His white tennis shoes didn't fit with his rumpled image. They were always immaculate, as though he bought a new pair every few weeks. "Same thing."

Gordo meowed loudly, as if in protest. Why was she hiding her anyway? What did she care if Eddie saw her? She put the bag on the table, opened it, and took out the cat.

Eddie visibly recoiled. "What the hell is that?"

"It's my cat," Tori said. "And you better not say anything disparaging about her, because I am not in a good mood."

"So the job's not going so great?"

Tori rolled her eyes, then figured she could make

better use of her time than arguing with him. "The job's not going. It already went."

His dark eyebrows rose. "What do you mean, 'went'?"

"I found out what the client wants to know," Tori said. "Grady Palmer is a good guy. End of story."

Cradling Gordo in one hand, she used the other to thrust at Eddie the few pages of the report she'd composed after she got home the night before. He took them, his brows drawing together as he read.

"Good stuff, Tor, but premature. The client's paying major bucks to have this guy investigated. We've got to give it more time."

"How much more time?"

"Three weeks," he said. "I told the client we needed a month to do a thorough job."

"You didn't tell *me*!"

"Like that would have been smart."

Eddie swung his legs down from the desk and tossed Tori's report on the surface. He stood up, trying to smooth the wrinkles from his pants. It didn't work. He withdrew a card from his wallet and scribbled something on the back of it.

"Here's my cell number. If you need me, call. Now if we're done, I got a workman's comp case needs my attention. Bus driver claims back problems but he's putting an addition on his house."

"We're not done," Tori said. "You didn't listen to me."

"Sure did," Eddie said. "You said you'd take the job. I gave it to you. You got a problem making decisions, but you never go back on your word once you do."

Tori paced from one side of the office to the other. Eddie was right. She fulfilled her commitments. If she said she'd do something, she did it.

She expected Eddie to walk out of the office, leaving her alone to stew. And possibly to lock up. But when she pivoted to start another round of pacing, she nearly bumped into him, which would have squashed Gordo for sure.

"You okay?" he asked.

She was about to nod but then he gently rubbed her shoulders and she couldn't be anything but honest.

"No, I'm not okay," she said. "There's more to this than I'm telling you. Grady noticed me following him and confronted me. So I told him I was attracted to him and he asked me to the mayor's party."

Eddie's tired eyes lit up like a flashlight.

"You made contact? But that's great. Much better than following him around and compiling information."

"It doesn't feel great to me. It feels . . . sneaky."

"PIs are supposed to be sneaky."

"But what if Grady doesn't deserve to have somebody snooping around in his business? What if he really is a good guy?"

"Then you'll prove it." Eddie scratched his chin. "Look at it this way. You'll be doing him a favor. Proving he's a good guy."

She sighed, knowing she couldn't tell her cousin everything. "Why do I get the feeling you know exactly what to say to get me to do what you want?"

"Because I do. And because you're way too good a person to leave me in the lurch."

"You don't understand, Eddie." Tears welled in her eyes and she wiped one away. "I'm afraid I'll make a mess of this."

"Hey, didn't you pay attention when you got rid of that client so you could have it out with me yourself? I know what you can do."

She sniffed. "What's that?"

"Anything you put your mind to." He kissed her on the forehead. "All you've got to decide is what to put it to."

Chapter Thirteen

The ladies' room on the first floor of Seahaven City Hall smelled of antiseptic cleaner and hand soap.

Lorelei wrinkled her nose and sprayed a cloud of perfume into the air, then walked with her arms outstretched through the fragrant mist.

There. Now all she needed was for the perfume to live up to its name.

Eau de Vixen.

Just in case perfume alone wouldn't do the trick, she crossed to the mirror above the sink, puckered her lips, and applied another layer of hot-pink gloss.

She ran a brush through her professionally tinted blond hair, pinched her cheeks, and powdered her nose. Then she inched down her already low-cut blouse.

The mirror didn't provide a view of the lower half of her body but she already knew she had exceptional legs. Long and lean with good calf definition. She'd showcased them by wearing a bright pink miniskirt.

She smacked her shimmering pink lips together and grinned at her reflection.

"You better be ready, Wade Morrison, because here I come," she said aloud.

A few minutes later, finding the tax assessor clerk's desk vacant, she sashayed through the open door of his office.

Wade Morrison sat slumped over his desk, so engrossed in his paperwork that he didn't look up. He held up a finger to indicate he'd be with her in a minute, and a corner of Lorelei's mouth twitched with amusement.

His pale yellow dress shirt wasn't so much ugly this time as boring. She couldn't say the same for his tie, a yellow-and-blue abomination that he wore loose around his neck.

With his glasses perched on his nose and his dark-brown hair a disheveled mess, he looked like a first-class nerd. Especially because the calculator at his fingertips and those creases in his forehead probably meant he was puzzling over some math problem.

She shuddered at the very thought. Thank goodness high school graduation had delivered her from the evil of math.

Wade didn't seem to feel the same. His complete and unqualified concentration made her wonder what it would be like to be the recipient of his full attention.

She vowed to find out.

Before she could do that, she needed him to notice her. Especially since he seemed to have forgotten he'd heard somebody arrive.

"Hey, there, handsome," she said into the silence.

His head jerked up, causing his glasses to slip even farther down his nose. She read slack-jawed shock on his face and had to clamp her lips to keep from laughing. He was too cute.

"Remember me? Lorelei Palmer from the mayor's party."

"I thought . . ." He pushed his glasses up his nose, cleared his throat, and tried again. "I thought you were my clerk."

"Do I look like your clerk?"

He cleared his throat again. "Not hardly."

He folded his hands on his desk and clenched them, seeming to strive to get himself under control. "What can I do for you?"

She thought about using a throaty voice to answer that she surely could think of something, but feared he might go into apoplexy.

"I was in the vicinity and thought you could take me to lunch," she said, which was true only because she'd made it her point to be in the vicinity. She put some oomph into her steps as she moved toward him, enjoying the way his jaw loosened even further. "I'll let you pick the place."

He started shaking his head before she finished speaking. "I can't."

"Don't tell me you're one of those guys who eats lunch at his desk."

He hesitated, causing her to peer at him more closely. Behind his glasses, his right eye looked red and watery. Moisture glistened on his cheek.

"What happened to your eye?"

"Nothing," he said, shaking his head.

"Something happened."

"I got poked, that's all. It's not a big deal."

"It is, too, a big deal." She came around the desk, not stopping until she could reach out and touch him. "Take off your glasses," she ordered.

"That's not necessary."

"I say it is. Now take them off so I can see what you did."

"It was only a finger—"

"Take them off," she repeated with even more authority. This time, he complied.

He squinted, obviously sensitive to the overhead fluorescent light. She leaned close. She loved a man who wore cologne but couldn't smell any on his skin, which had a clean, appealing scent nevertheless. Breathing it in, she gently pried his eye open with her thumb and forefinger.

The color of his iris reminded her of the cherry-wood dining-room furniture at her parents' house, but the white of his eye was red and inflamed.

Excessive tearing made it difficult for her to get a good look at the injury.

"I think your cornea is scratched," she said after a moment. "You need to see an eye doctor. He'll give you some medicated drops and it'll heal in a couple of days."

"Are you a nurse?"

"Me? A nurse?" She took her hand from his face and straightened. "Why would you ask such a silly question?"

He wiped the moisture from under his eye with a fingertip and put his glasses back on. "Because you seem to know what you're talking about."

"I was a candy striper for a summer when I was in high school," she confessed, "but it was so not me."

"I don't know about that. You have a nice bedside manner," he said, not quite meeting her eyes.

The guy was so shy he'd probably hide under his desk if she informed him she was better in bed than beside it. Okay. That was too forward. But she was making inroads here.

"Does that mean you'll go to lunch with me?"

He stared down at his desk, not a good sign. Before he could refuse, she continued, "No, of course you can't go. What was I thinking? You need to have that eye looked at."

He nodded, obviously relieved.

"So how about dinner?" she asked.

"Dinner's not a good idea," he said quickly.

"Why not?" she asked, before a terrible possibility occurred to her. "Oh, no. Grady was wrong, wasn't he? You *are* married."

His brows knitted, and she braced herself to hear that he was off limits. Despite the free-and-easy act she sometimes put on to get Grady's goat, she wouldn't date a married man.

"Are you related to Grady Palmer of Palmer Construction?" He phrased it as a question but it sounded like an accusation.

"He's my brother," she said, "and you didn't answer my question."

His reluctance either meant he didn't want her to know he was available or he was already taken. She suspected it was the former.

"For the record," she continued, "I asked if you were married."

"I'm not married," he finally said.

"Engaged?"

"No."

"Gay?"

"No!"

"Seeing somebody exclusively?"

"Well, no."

"Then what's the problem? Don't you find me attractive?"

If he denied it, she'd know he was lying. He didn't even try. "That's not it."

Lorelei threw up her hands. "What then?"

His shoulders rose, then fell. "You're twenty-one years old, and—"

"We've already been over how my age is so not a big deal," Lorelei interrupted.

"You didn't let me finish."

She swept her hand through the air with a flourish. "By all means, finish."

"And I have responsibilities that leave me no time for a woman like you."

"You can't possibly know what kind of woman I am," she said indignantly. "You don't know anything about me."

"I know you like to have fun."

"And I know you have too little of it," she shot back.

120

He ran a hand over his forehead. "You don't understand."

"Then have dinner with me and explain."

She held her breath, sure he'd refuse, but then she sensed that he arrived at a decision.

"You said I could pick the place, right?"

She nodded eagerly. "Right."

"Mario's Pizzeria. Six o'clock."

She started to object to both the place and the early hour but thought better of it. She'd envisioned a romantic dinner at a French restaurant, but she could compromise.

"Deal," she said. "But I have one caveat."

"What?" He looked suspicious.

"You have to get that eye checked out first." She'd spent the last ten minutes silently empathizing with him for the pain she knew it caused. "Promise?"

"Promise," he said on a sigh.

She smiled at him, glad her impromptu visit to his office had paid off in more ways than one.

"Good," she said, walking away before calling over her shoulder. "Because when I come into that pizza parlor tonight, I want you to see that you're about to become one lucky man."

Mario's Pizzeria was unremittingly red.

Red booths, red carpet, red doors.

Plastic red-and-white tableclothes covered the tables, and the young employees behind the crimson counter spread red tomato sauce on pizzas they fed into an industrial-sized oven.

Five minutes after the waitress had seated Wade Morrison at a booth for four, his eyes still had trouble adjusting to the sea of red, especially his right one.

The pain had significantly lessened, thanks to the antibiotic drops the ophthalmologist had prescribed.

Lorelei had been right. He had a scratched cornea.

But she'd been wrong, too. No doubt she'd be wearing some crazy, skin-baring outfit when she entered the pizza parlor. But she was the one who would get an eyeful.

"Daddy, watch this."

The tiny blond girl across from him rose to her full height of three feet one inch and jumped up and down on the booth's cushioned seat.

"Stop that, Mary Kate," he said sternly, but the giggles of a second, equally blond girl drowned him out.

"Ashley wants to be kangaroo, too," she said gleefully, scrambling to her feet and joining her sister up, then down.

Both of the girls had messy, lopsided ponytails, but Mary Kate's listed to the right while Ashley's veered left. Other than that and their T-shirts of different colors, they could have been carbon copies.

"Girls," Wade said sternly. "Stop that right now."

" 'S fun," Mary Kate said.

"Kangaroo roo," Ashley cried.

"Roo roo," Mary Kate added.

The place was nearly full, mostly with families. But even the diners with young children turned disapproving looks toward Wade.

"Girls," he repeated, but their giggles didn't ease.

Aware of the murmurs getting increasingly louder, he quickly came around the booth. He caught and lifted a giggling Mary Kate, scooted into the booth with her on his lap, and managed to gather Ashley to him on her way down from one of the jumps. He held the twins close while they giggled helplessly.

He didn't smile. He needed to make them understand they couldn't act like marsupials in restaurants.

"Listen to me, girls," he said.

After a few more laughing gulps, they did, each one gazing up at him with big green eyes.

Wade wished their mother hadn't named them after the Olsen twins who starred in all those silly look-alike movies, but had to admit the girls resembled the actresses. Up to a point. He thought his Mary Kate and Ashley much cuter.

"No more jumping in restaurants," he said.

Ashley screwed up her tiny forehead. "Why not, Daddy?"

"Restaurants are places for eating, not jumping."

Mary Kate reached out a pudgy hand and tapped him on the mouth. "Daddy, smile."

"I'll smile if you promise not to jump anymore."

"Promise," Mary Kate said happily.

"Promise," Ashley said.

After that, he did smile. Although the little girls were a constant trial—as this morning's poke in the eye proved—they were also his biggest joy. Because he never regretted having them, he'd even be able to withstand Lorelei Palmer's look of horror when she came into the restaurant.

He didn't have any illusions. The beautiful, vivacious young woman would be horrified at the thought of dating a man with three-year-old twins.

Just as he was horrified at getting involved with a woman whose main objective was to have fun. But he couldn't blame Lorelei for her joie de vivre. Chronologically she was a woman, but emotionally she seemed little more than a vibrant, spirited child.

Wade didn't know why she'd latched onto him, but they were clearly at different stages of their lives.

He had responsibilities, as he'd started to explain when she stopped by his office. Because she was an uncommonly determined young woman, he'd decided it would be best to show her exactly how daunting those responsibilities were.

"Want pizza, Daddy," Mary Kate said.

"We'll have pizza in a little while, honey. We have to wait for Lorelei."

"Is she a mommy?"

Wade tried hard not to sigh. If they were lucky, the twins saw their mother twice a month. Obviously that wasn't enough.

"No. Lorelei is not a mommy."

Lorelei was a fantasy. A fantasy that wouldn't last the night after she saw the twins. A fantasy he never should have had in the first place.

"She's . . . a friend."

"Like Kristen?" Ashley asked.

Kristen was the latest in a long line of teenagers who babysat for the twins when Wade had an after-hours event he couldn't get out of, like the mayor's party. The twins spent their days at a church-run day-care near their home. The overwhelming majority of their nights, they spent with Wade.

"Yes. Like Kristen," Wade said, hoping they hadn't gotten attached to her. Like the other babysitters before her, she'd told him she wouldn't babysit again.

"Need to pee, Daddy," Ashley said, standing up in the booth and squeezing her short legs together.

The moment Wade had feared most was here. Taking one little girl into the men's room was bad enough, but he had to do double duty. Mary Kate was too young to be left alone.

"But I told you to go before we left home," he said. "You did go, didn't you?"

"Need to pee," Ashley repeated.

Mary Kate busily colored on the paper placemat the waitress had provided. She reached across the table for a fat blue crayon, bumping his water glass in the process.

He grabbed for it but wasn't fast enough. The glass tipped and water spilled over the table.

"Oops," Mary Kate said, covering her mouth with both hands.

"Need to pee," Ashley said.

"Wade?" asked another feminine voice.

Wade looked up, and there she was. Lorelei Palmer. Her sleeveless denim dress was short and tight, leaving little to the imagination. Her eyes, which were so pretty under the heavy mascara, were round and surprised.

"Hi, Lorelei," he said while he ineffectually wiped at the spill with a napkin that was already soaked. "Meet Mary Kate and Ashley. My daughters."

125

She stared transfixed at the twins, speechless for the first time since he'd met her.

Mary Kate patted her hands in the spilled water on the table, laughing as she splashed.

"Need to pee," Ashley said.

Wade expected Lorelei to suddenly remember she had another engagement and flee, but instead she flagged down a passing waitress.

"We've had a spill," she told her.

The waitress bustled off, presumably to get something with which to wipe up the water. Wade waited for Lorelei to sprint after her on her way out the door, but she held her ground.

"Hi, Ash. Hi, M.K.," she said. "I'm Lorelei."

Mary Kate splashed.

"Need to pee," Ashley told her.

Lorelei's face creased in a smile.

"Then, by all means, let's go pee," she told his daughter before reaching for her hand. The little girl gladly gave it to her, and they hurried off to the bathroom.

"I need to pee, too," Mary Kate said, crawling over Wade's lap and running to catch up.

Wade stared after them, realizing Lorelei Palmer was made of sterner stuff than he'd thought. Or maybe she was merely more polite than he'd given her credit for.

She hadn't run scared at the sight of Ashley and Mary Kate, but she would. He knew her type.

He'd not only dated it, he'd married it.

Chapter Fourteen

Lorelei Palmer surprised Wade by making it through dinner with her megawatt smile still intact.

"I never knew little kids could be so much fun," she said.

Wade wiped a piece of mozzarella cheese from Ashley's chin and tossed the soiled napkin onto the growing pile to his left.

The other side of the table didn't have a discard pile. Mary Kate, seated next to Lorelei, wore so much tomato sauce she was nearly as red as the rest of the restaurant.

"I never babysat growing up," Lorelei continued. "Nobody ever asked me for some strange reason, so I haven't been around kids much."

No big surprise there, Wade thought.

"But your two are absolute dolls. Maybe they'd like to go shopping with me sometime. It would be fun. We could try on some clothes, maybe do lunch."

"They're a little young for that," Wade said.

"Get out of here. All females love to shop. It's a biological fact." She bent down so her pretty face was close to Mary Kate's. "You like shopping, right, M.K.?"

"Like to chop," she said, bringing her hand down on the edge of the table. Mary Kate had been chopping since Wade had watched a Jackie Chan movie on television a few nights before.

"Chop, chop," Ashley said, imitating her sister.

"See? I told you," Lorelei said brightly. She really was beautiful, Wade thought. He didn't usually gravitate toward bottle blondes, but Lorelei would be stunning no matter what her hair color. She had a great face, with huge eyes and well-defined cheekbones. She definitely didn't need all the makeup she wore. Her natural effervescence was adornment enough.

She winked, telling him she knew he was staring. "So where should we go now?"

Half afraid she'd suggest a department store, Wade quickly replied, "Home. It's getting late."

"Seven o'clock's not late," she said like a woman who'd never had kids. "Let's do something while the night's still young."

Wade needed to get the girls home and to bed, but that wouldn't solve his Lorelei problem. And that's what she presented: a problem.

If she had been a different woman, he might have gotten past their nine-year age difference.

But he'd figured out fairly quickly that she was a free-wheeling party girl. Despite the way she cooed at his daughters, she clearly hadn't yet figured out what dating a man with three-year-old twins entailed.

"What do you suggest we do?" he asked.

She leaned forward slightly, and he had a clear view of the tops of her breasts peeking out above the snug-fitting bodice of her denim dress. If the twins hadn't been along, he wondered, would she have suggested they go back to her place?

Her breasts were lovely, large enough to fill a man's hand and . . . *Splat!* A wet spot on his glasses suddenly distorted his view of her cleavage.

Mary Kate took a striped plastic straw from her mouth. "Bill's eye!" she cried.

"Bull's eye," he corrected, taking off his glasses and wiping them on the edge of his shirt. "But we've gone over this before. My glasses are not a target."

He reached across the table and took the straw from her resisting hand. He didn't have to wonder how he'd missed her lining up the shot. He knew.

He put his glasses back on, and then Lorelei distracted him again. Appearing to be deep in thought, she absently licked a lower lip she'd slathered with pink gloss right there at the table after finishing her pizza.

Wade shouldn't wonder what her lips would taste like, shouldn't be willing to find out even if he had to endure the pink goo to do it.

But he did wonder. God help him, he did.

"Why don't we all go . . . bowling?" Lorelei seemed absurdly pleased by her very bad suggestion.

Intending to let her down gently, Wade said, "Mary Kate and Ashley don't bowl."

"Maybe not yet, but I bet they want to learn. What do you say, M.K. and Ash? What'll it be? Go bowling or go home?"

"No go home," Mary Kate said. Her blond hair shook as her head swiveled.

"No, no," Ashley added.

"See," Lorelei said smugly. "They want to go bowling."

"Do you realize how old they are?"

"How old are you and M.K., hon?" she asked Ashley. "Four? Five?"

Ashley giggled and held up three fat fingers.

"One, two, three," Lorelei counted. To Wade, she said, "They're three."

She'd completely missed the point that three-year-olds didn't belong in bowling alleys.

Wade thought about explaining to her the realities of life with small children but doubted it would do any good. A more hard-headed woman he'd yet to meet.

What Lorelei needed was a demonstration.

That would make her stop thinking of the twins as pretty little dolls. That would make her stop slanting him those flirtatious smiles of which nothing could ever come.

"So what do you say?" she asked Wade. "Are we on?"

Wade shrugged. "Sure. Why not? Let's go bowling."

M.K. and Ash are monsters, Lorelei thought.

No, scratch that. The twins weren't big enough to be monsters. Gnomes, maybe. Gnomes are tiny, except nowhere near as attractive as the diminutive blond girls.

What was itty bitty, cute, and monstrous to boot? Gremlins?

Yes. M.K. and Ash were gremlins.

"No, Ashley," Wade said with infinite patience as he plucked his daughter off the circular ball-return tray. "That's dangerous."

The little girl kicked her legs and waved her arms.

"Let go, Daddy," Ash cried. "Let go."

Lorelei sat at the scorekeeper's table, waiting her turn at the lanes. M.K. was up. Except the little girl was no longer lining up her shot.

She was halfway down the lane, merrily chasing her hot-pink bowling ball. It bounced crazily off the fat blue bumpers in the gutters before slowing down to a near stop. She bent down to give it another shove.

"Oh, hell." Lorelei jumped to her feet and rushed toward the lane. "Wade, M.K.'s loose."

"Darn," he said, which Lorelei figured was a G-rated version of what he really wanted to say.

He cut off Lorelei at the head of the lane, shoving a still-squirming Ash at her before taking off in pursuit of his other daughter.

"Watch out," Lorelei called over a bobbing blond head. "The lane's oiled."

The thundering sound of bowling balls in the adjacent lanes plus a booming voice over the loudspeaker drowned out her warning.

"Evacuate lane five immediately," the loudspeaker

131

voice said. "Only bowling balls are allowed on the lanes."

Didn't he think Wade knew that, for cripe's sake?

He was surprisingly fleet for a geeky man, as though he could have been an athlete had he chosen. He most definitely would have caught the little gremlin without incident if the slick soles of his rented red-white-and-blue shoes hadn't failed him.

His feet slipped out from under him and his perfect derriere hit the lane with a painful-looking bang.

Lorelei winced.

"Ouch," Ash said from the circle of her arms.

M.K. had finished knocking over the bowling pins. She turned around, spotted her father, and ran toward him, somehow keeping her balance. When she reached him, she patted him on the head in sympathy.

In Lorelei's arms, Ash stopped squirming.

"Daddy needs ice cream," she told Lorelei solemnly.

Ten minutes later, Lorelei sat with Wade, Ash, and M.K. at a cheap Formica table-for-four in the snack bar adjacent to the lanes.

Considering the lecture the manager of the bowling alley had given them after Wade and M.K. returned from their wild trip, Lorelei supposed they were lucky they hadn't been kicked out of the place.

Although that would have been okay. The whole bowling scene had worn thin. Personally, she could have used a drink. And she wasn't talking lemonade or, so help her, Kool-Aid.

Wade needed something at least as strong as a beer.

Lines of strain etched his forehead and he kept glancing at the gremlins, as though he expected them to dump the contents of their ice cream cups on their heads or some similar horror.

"I didn't figure you for a family man," she said while she dug her spoon into a mound of double-chocolate-fudge ice cream.

He stopped in the process of bringing his French vanilla cone to his mouth. Of the snack bar's twelve flavors of ice cream, it hadn't surprised her that he'd chosen vanilla.

"I didn't figure you did. That's why I wanted you to meet the girls."

She watched them happily shoveling ice cream into their miniature mouths, oblivious to anything but the cool, sweet treat. They looked precious and angelic, which they probably were. Most of the time.

"I like your girls," she said. "So how often do you have them? A couple of nights a week? Every other weekend?"

"All the time," Wade said. "I have primary custody."

"But what about their . . ." She lowered her voice to a whisper in case the girls were listening. ". . . mother? When does she see them?"

"Seldom," Wade whispered back. "Once or twice a month tops."

There was a story here, one Lorelei wouldn't pry from him with M.K. and Ash within hearing range. But the bottom line was that Wade Morrison wasn't only a single father, he was a single father with a lot more than occasional visitation rights.

She'd been truthful when she claimed she liked his daughters. M.K. and Ash might be gremlins, but they were joyful and sweet and cute as can be.

But she'd learned in a few short hours they were also demanding and time-consuming and a huge part of Wade's life.

Wade took a couple of licks of his ice cream, then bit into the cone. He ate with gusto, making her wonder about his other appetites, making her lose track of what she'd been thinking.

"Don't worry about letting me down easy." Wade's deep, resonant voice broke into her thoughts. "I understand you don't want to see me again."

What was he talking about? She'd been dying to find out exactly what was under those nerdy clothes since the mayor's party.

"You're twenty-one years old," he continued. "I know you don't want to date a man with kids."

Kids. That's right. He had kids.

"I never said that," she countered.

"Maybe not aloud, but you're thinking it. Why do you think I took your suggestion to go bowling?"

"You knew it would be a fiasco," she accused.

"Heck, yeah."

"Then why did you agree to it?"

"So neither one of us would make a mistake. But like I said, it's okay. I know your type and kids don't exactly mix."

Her back went ramrod straight. "My type? That's the second time you've said that. What type exactly do you think I am?"

"The party-girl type," he said, "like my ex-wife."

He added the second part of the sentence in a low voice, maybe not even deliberately, and suddenly Lorelei understood. His ex-wife preferred being out on the town to raising her girls.

And Wade thought Lorelei was cut from the same party clothes. Lorelei frowned, not liking that depiction of herself. Not wanting to believe it even if he were right.

"You're wrong," she said.

The girls had finished their ice cream. M.K. got down from her seat and started running for who knows where. Wade stood up and deftly caught her with one long arm. He polished off the rest of his ice cream cone and scooped up Ash in his other arm before the second twin could think about escape.

"I'm right. But don't worry about it. You don't have kids. It makes complete sense for you to be a little self-absorbed."

Self-absorbed?

"Like I said, no hard feelings." His soft gaze touched on her for a few seconds, making her think of what might have been. "Have a nice life, Lorelei."

He left her there like that, sitting alone in the too-bright snack bar with a cup of melting ice cream. Lorelei gazed down at the chocolate mess.

Eating ice cream, especially chocolate ice cream, was supposed to improve your spirits. She shoved a spoonful into her mouth but didn't feel one bit better.

Chapter Fifteen

Grady stopped at his sister's desk on his way out of the office, mostly because Lorelei occupied it.

"Do you know what time it is?" he asked.

She glanced up from a stack of papers that appeared to be invoices—had she actually been working?—and glanced at the wall clock.

"Six fifteen," she said.

"But don't you turn into a pumpkin if you're not out of the office by four?"

"Not funny." She stuck out her tongue but the gesture didn't have her usual verve. Tearing off the top sheet of a pink message pad, she handed it to him, exactly as a good secretary should.

"How did I miss this call?" he asked. "I've been in the office for hours."

"I'm not saying this is so, but I might have forgotten to give it to you earlier."

"Damn it, Lorelei. I've been waiting for some important calls."

The message didn't fit the description. His mother wanted to do something special for his birthday the following Tuesday. She asked him to let her know if he could make it. He crumpled the note into a ball and tossed it into the trashcan.

"You are going to call Mom, aren't you?" Lorelei asked.

"Nope."

"I can't believe you." Lorelei sounded disgusted. "What am I supposed to say when she asks if you're coming?"

"Say no," he replied, refusing to be swayed by his sister's bewildered, indignant expression. When his mother discovered the snub, she'd probably just be sad. Tough, he thought, hardening his heart. She and his father had brought this on themselves.

"I don't know what's going on between you and Mom and Dad, but maybe I could help if someone told me."

"I don't want to talk about it," Grady said, his eyes scanning her desk for a pink message slip she may have forgotten to give him.

He'd gotten the results that morning of the background check his FBI contact had conducted on Tori, and it backed up everything she'd told him. It also brought up the possibility that her claim that she'd wanted to take things slowly was true.

He'd called her that afternoon, got her answering machine, and left a message apologizing for coming on

138

too strong. He'd offered to make it up to her by taking her to dinner, but she hadn't called back. Or had she?

"Is that message for me, too?" he asked Lorelei, pointing to a pink slip at the edge of her desk.

"Probably," she said airily, leaving him to pick it up. He fought disappointment when he recognized the name of one of his subcontractors. Grady inspected the message more closely. Something about it seemed odd. It didn't take long to figure out what.

"You included the time of the call and a return phone number," he said to Lorelei. "And you spelled Frank Czapiewski's name right."

"So?" She lifted her chin, obviously still angry at him over his rift with their parents. But it couldn't be helped. She hadn't been the child they'd betrayed.

"So, you've never done that before," he said. Her outfit—a leopard-print top paired with a short brown skirt—was as wild as ever. So was her generously applied makeup and flamboyant blond hair. But her eyes looked . . . cheerless. "Is something wrong?"

He expected her to shrug off the question with a quip, but her expression grew troubled.

"Let me ask you something," she said. "Do you think I'm self-absorbed?"

"Whoa. What kind of question is that? Who said you were self-absorbed?"

"Nobody," she said too quickly. "I'm just wondering."

"Self-absorbed, huh? Let me think about that," he said even as he noticed the mirror propped on her desk in a spot others allotted to photos of family members.

"Answer the question," she ordered.

He'd rather dive off a cliff into a rocky, foaming sea, but Lorelei wouldn't let up until he complied.

"Maybe a little," he finally replied, a tactful way of saying she was as shallow as his backyard birdbath.

Her lower lip drooped, a sight so rare it tugged at him. Hadn't she realized before now how others perceived her? He reached down to ruffle the top of her head, the way he used to when they were kids.

"If it makes you feel better, you're the most caring self-absorbed person I know."

Her eyes were suspiciously dewy but her voice sounded tough when she asked, "Weren't you leaving?"

He hesitated, wishing he could take back his answer. But his sister had never been stupid. She'd know he was lying if he backtracked now. "I'm on my way out."

"Then go," she snapped. Her mutinous expression invited no argument, but he paused at the door anyway. It wouldn't hurt to ask, just in case.

"Lorelei?"

"What?" She bit out the word.

"Is it possible you forgot to tell me about another phone call? From, oh, say, Tori?"

She grimaced, never a good sign. "This isn't fair. I didn't even get a minute to be mad at you. And now you'll be mad at me."

His chest felt lighter, as though whatever had been pressing down on it had lifted. "Then Tori did call?"

"I think it was at about three. I can't believe I didn't write it down, but we got to chatting and I guess it slipped my mind."

Grady clamped his back teeth together so he

wouldn't yell at her for being irresponsible. He knew her faults better than anybody, and he'd hired her anyway. "What did she say?"

"Something about not being able to go out to dinner," she said and his spirits fell, "but that she'd be perfectly happy to cook for you."

His mood brightened, but then he remembered the time. "Damn, Lorelei. You could have told me this sooner. I'll give her a call but I'm probably too late."

"Don't bother calling. I told her you'd be there at six thirty."

"Have I told you lately that I love you?" he asked.

"Don't try to butter me up," she muttered. "I'm still mad at you."

Tori put a brass candlestick on her kitchen table between the two place settings she'd spent the last ten minutes fussing over, checked the floor so she wouldn't step on Gordo, and stood back to survey her work.

"Do you think the candle's too much?" she asked the cat, who had taken to silently following her around the house.

She removed the candlestick and surveyed the table without it. If she hadn't expected Grady at any minute, she might hunt up her disco ball keychain. But she didn't want to overdo it. She'd already consulted the silver ball as to whether to invite Grady to dinner.

Right on, it had said, which she took as a yes.

She figured she couldn't go wrong with pasta and green salad. Spaghetti sauce simmered on the stove,

French rolls were ready to warm in the oven, and wine breathed on the table. Once Grady arrived, she'd cook the pasta and dinner would be ready in fifteen minutes.

"This is all your fault," she told Gordo. "If you hadn't torn up the apartment when we were at the carnival, I could have trusted you. And if I trusted you, Grady and I could have gone out to dinner."

She frowned, silently admitting that wouldn't have made much difference. She'd still be breathlessly anticipating Grady's arrival.

Her nerve endings did a lively jig. She'd gone on a handful of dates since moving to Seahaven, but she didn't remember this breathless anticipation. She hadn't felt it in the two years she'd dated Sumner Aldridge, either. In truth, she couldn't remember ever being this anxious over the prospect of spending time with a man, not even back in high school.

"I think I may have lost my mind," she told Gordo. "This isn't a date. It's a job. Grady's not my boyfriend."

Except he felt like her boyfriend after that kiss on the Ferris wheel.

Not only was Grady an exceptional kisser, but she liked him. Underneath that sometimes gruff exterior beat the heart of a good man.

"Prove he's a good man," Eddie had advised.

An excellent idea in theory, but she wasn't sure how to go about it. The multiple-choice test at the carnival had been a start, but his answers sounded silly when she'd written them in her report.

"Willing to ride painted horses" wasn't as impressive when taken out of context.

The doorbell rang, and her heart leaped. She put the candlestick back down, rushed to the door, and counted slowly to three to give herself time to get under control before letting him in.

The tactic didn't work.

One look at his slightly cockeyed smile and her heart tilted. The wind had tousled his hair, he needed a shave, and he was dressed in the blue jeans and short-sleeved gray shirt he'd probably worn to work. It didn't matter. She hadn't seen him in almost forty-eight hours, and he looked wonderful.

Their eyes locked.

"Hi," she said, feeling the air grow thick around them.

"Hi," he answered.

"I'm glad you called."

"Me, too." He took a step toward her, as though he might kiss her, but just as suddenly stopped. His eyes dropped. "What is that crawling up my leg?"

Tori blinked the daze from her eyes and gazed down at his pant leg. Gordo had managed to climb nearly to his knees.

"Bad cat," she said, stooping down and detangling Gordo's claws from the material of his jeans.

"That's a cat?" Grady asked incredulously.

She picked up Gordo, surprised that the little cat's body trembled. The cat made a sound in the back of her throat and glared at Grady.

"When you moved toward me like that, she must

have gotten worried," Tori said in wonder. "I didn't think cats were protective. Maybe you should pet her and try to make friends."

"Wait a minute." His eyes grew round and suspicious. "*This* is your fat cat?"

Tori mentally scolded herself for not thinking this through. She'd known Gordo was ill equipped for the role but hadn't been able to abandon her at the pound.

"I didn't say I had a fat cat," she said. "I said I had a cat whose name meant fat. It's Spanish."

"That's not how I remember it. And besides, if the cat's a she, her name would be Gorda, not Gordo."

He was right. She remembered from high school that the endings of Spanish adjectives depended upon whether they were describing nouns that were masculine or feminine, but she couldn't admit that now.

"That doesn't make sense. Next you'll tell me I should have named her Fatsa instead of Fatso."

She waited nervously while Grady scratched his jaw and swept his gaze around the apartment. He paused at Gordo's brand-new water bowl and the flimsy cardboard cat carrier the pound had supplied. Why hadn't she thought to put it out of sight?

The guarded look that had been missing when he arrived at her apartment returned. "Why don't you give it up and admit you just got this cat?"

"Gordo is a beloved pet," she bluffed, feigning outrage. "How can you suggest such a thing?"

A heavy pounding interrupted his response. Glad of the reprieve, Tori hurried to the door, still with Gordo in her arms. Her heart sank when she saw her visitor was Mrs. Grumley.

"Aha! I thought you had a . . ." her voice trailed off and her head tilted as she inspected Gordo. "Is that a mouse?"

"No, it's not a mouse. It's a cat," Tori said, dooming herself and Gordo along with her.

"Whatever it is, it spells trouble for you," Mrs. Grumley said. "I'm here to inform you that violating the clause prohibiting pets in the Seahaven Shores lease is grounds for eviction."

Tori turned her back on Mrs. Grumley, met Grady's unfriendly stare, and prayed he wouldn't abandon her in her time of need.

"Help me," she silently mouthed before facing her landlady. "She isn't my cat, Mrs. Grumley. She's Grady's."

At that, Tori walked over to Grady and shoved Gordo at him. The cat bared her claws and made her strange growling noise. In self-defense, Grady held on to her by her torso and extended her from his body so that her legs dangled like sticks.

Mrs. Grumley's already small eyes narrowed. "That cat doesn't even like him."

"She's persnickety," Tori said.

"He doesn't look like a cat owner to me," Mrs. Grumley declared.

Before Grady could agree, Tori implored him with her eyes not to contradict her. His mouth twisted slightly as he seemed to decide what to say. Tori held her breath.

"She's my cat, all right." He petted Gordo awkwardly with the hand not attached to her torso. "I'm a cat lover. Gordo and I came for a visit."

The glint in Mrs. Grumley's eyes said she didn't believe him, but she couldn't prove it. "When you leave, make sure you take that thing with you," she said, before pivoting and stalking away.

Tori closed the door on the retreating landlady, filled her lungs with air, then slowly turned. Gordo had sheathed her claws and was now emitting harmless meows, but Grady still held her extended from his body. He didn't trust the cat any more than he trusted her, Tori realized.

"Thanks," she said. "I owe you."

"What you owe me is the truth," he said harshly.

She closed her eyes, wondering what to do. The solution came to her in a flash, like it had the other night when he'd questioned her about why she was following him. She'd tell the truth.

"Okay," she said. "I admit it. I lied."

Chapter Sixteen

Grady's stomach pitched to the floor at her admission of deceit, making him feel disgusted with himself.

If this were an old Western, he wouldn't be playing the part of the hero. The hero was never a sap.

He'd known when he came to her apartment tonight that she'd lied to him about the play, but he'd been eager to overlook not only that tall tale but also his fear that she was playing him for a fool.

But he couldn't close his eyes to the multitude of lies. He was involved in some serious FBI business. If someone at city hall had caught on to him, it could spell danger.

"I knew you didn't believe me when I said I had a fat cat so I went to the pound this weekend to get one," Tori began. "Instead, I came home with Gordo."

He remained silent, waiting for her to damn herself even further than she already had.

147

"I lied about the play, too. I didn't go to Miami Beach on Friday night. I went home."

He hadn't expected her to own up to that, but she might have figured out he already knew *Grimm Tales from the Reaper* was a high school production for the fairy-tale set.

"I did it all because . . ." She paused, her chest heaving up and down in a silent sigh. Now they were finally getting somewhere. Now she'd tell him who had hired her to keep tabs on him. ". . . I didn't want you to think I was easy."

"What?" The word exploded from him.

Gordo meowed, causing Grady to realize he still held her. He put the cat down on a nearby sofa and she scrambled to the edge, her entire body on alert as she stared him down. The cat looked poised to leap if he made one false move.

"Look at it from my point of view, Grady." Tori's brown eyes seemed earnest. "I didn't want you to think I'd jump into bed with a guy I just met. That's why I made up the excuse about bolting from the golf course because of the fat cat. I didn't want to admit I was afraid you'd find out I was following you."

"But you admitted you were following me, so getting the cat wasn't necessary," he said, keeping his voice soft because of the cat's suspected kamikaze tendencies.

"It was to me. I didn't want you to think I was a liar."

"You are a liar. First about the cat, then about the play."

"Only because you told Lorelei we wanted to be alone and I thought you intended to take me up on what you thought I was offering."

"So you're saying you told both of those lies to get out of going to bed with me?"

"Exactly," she said, nodding.

Grady felt as though she'd stabbed him in the gut with a knife. "So the story about thinking I was hot was just that? A story?"

"Oh, no," she denied. "That's the truth."

He let out a breath and shook his head. "Come on, Tori. I was there on the Ferris wheel Sunday night."

"You mean you thought I told you to stop because I'm not attracted to you?" she asked with wide, rounded eyes.

His head started to pound. "You just said you don't want to sleep with me."

"I said I didn't want to sleep with you when we first met, but only because it was too soon." She paused, giving her next sentence more weight. "All I've thought about since Sunday night is how much I want to make love to you."

He ignored the heat that arrowed to his groin, reminding himself that he didn't believe a word she said. "You're not making sense. You don't want to go to bed with me."

"I do, too," she said indignantly.

He took a step closer to her, expecting her to back away, but she held her ground. Her eyes glittered with determination. A pulse beat fast in her throat when she looked him directly in the eye.

"I happen to think you're very sexy," she said.

"Oh, yeah?" he said skeptically.

"Oh, yeah," she said, her voice rising. "Just try me and see."

The gentleman inside him warned him to back off, but the man who didn't appreciate being made a fool kissed her.

Not gently, the way their first kiss had begun on the Ferris wheel. But enthusiastically, the way it had ended.

The moment her lips parted, he deepened the kiss, tracing the roof of her mouth and the sides of her cheeks before tangling his tongue with hers.

He kept a firm hand at the small of her back and another buried in the hair of her nape to keep her stationary, but she showed no sign of wanting to escape.

She threaded her fingers through the short strands of his hair, holding his head in place while she angled her mouth to better fit his.

The blood rushed through his veins, settling in his crotch. He vaguely remembered that he had some purpose for kissing her but could hardly think over the galloping of his heart. It thundered, like hoofs flying over track.

Focus, he told himself sharply as he continued to search his mind for the reason he'd kissed her. Oh, yeah. He'd intended to prove she wasn't attracted to him.

He forced himself to pay attention to her body language for an indication that she wanted him to stop. She sucked lightly on his tongue and rubbed her lower body against his growing erection.

Nope, neither of those was the sign.

But the loud, guttural moan that didn't sound quite human might be. She tore her mouth from his, looked at him quizzically, and asked, "What was that noise?"

The moan sounded again and they turned toward the sofa and a cat with one amazing larynx. Gordo appeared ready to spring, her watchfulness reminding Grady more of a hawk than a cat.

"Maybe you should rename her Simba," he said, his voice husky and out of breath. "You know, after the lion in the Disney movie."

"It's okay, Gordo." Tori sounded as breathless as he did. "Nothing to worry about."

"Tori probably would have stopped me soon anyway," Grady added.

"I would not have!" Tori said indignantly. She didn't try to move from the circle of his arms, but leaned back slightly to look him in the eye. "Did you know that you're a very negative person?"

He kept his arms around her, mostly because he liked having them there. "I prefer to think of myself as a skeptic."

"Don't you ever take a leap of faith?"

"If you leap without looking, you could get flattened by a bus."

"Then look at me. Do I look like a woman who wanted you to stop?" she asked.

He took in her disheveled hair, mussed clothing, and lips that were full and ripe from his kisses.

She grasped his hand and placed it over her breast, underneath which her heart hammered. "Does that feel like the heartbeat of a woman who wanted you to stop?"

He swallowed the sudden thickness in his throat, afraid to accept what stared him in the face. At the same time, he longed to believe it as much as he wanted to take his next breath.

"You're telling the truth, aren't you?" he asked, hearing the awe in his voice. "You really want to do this?"

"Yes, I do," she said indignantly. "But I'll change my mind soon if you don't get with the program."

The corner of his mouth quirked at her spirited reply even as his heart soared. "We still have a problem."

She rolled her eyes. "What is it now?"

"I think Gordo might be a voyeur. Did you ever notice how she's always staring?"

She cut her eyes at the cat. "Gordo's asleep."

It was true. Obviously weary of their discussion, the little cat had backed into a corner of the sofa, laid herself down, and tucked her head under a paw. She opened one eye, which seemed to glare at him.

"She still can't be trusted," he said.

Tori skimmed her fingers over the line of his jaw and smiled. He detected none of the forced brightness he'd noticed when they first met.

"Last I checked," she said, nodding toward the open door of her bedroom, "Gordo can't pick a lock."

Blood swirled through him in a heated rush, making him ignore his long-held belief about things that seemed too good to be true. If Tori were one of those things, he didn't want to know.

"If she tries it," he said, "I could probably put on a deadbolt."

Laughing, she grabbed his hand and pulled him into the bedroom. He spun her around when they'd barely cleared the threshold, and she came willingly into his arms.

The passion ignited again, but maybe it had never extinguished. How long had it been, he wondered, since he'd felt this powerful connection when he kissed a woman? Months? Years? Never?

That bond, he realized, was why he'd pursued her in the face of his doubts. Since their kiss on the Ferris wheel, his thoughts had been consumed with making love to her.

She clung to him, her hands braced on his shoulders, her soft body rubbing against him as her tongue swirled inside his mouth.

She wore another cropped top that gave tantalizing peeks at her smooth, flat stomach. He reached under it, smoothing his hand over her abdomen and venturing higher to her breast. She gasped into his mouth as he kneaded the soft flesh through the flimsy material of her bra, touching and teasing until her nipple pebbled.

"Wait," she said.

He drew back, his body growing taut. He braced himself for a last-minute retreat, unprepared for the feel of her hand at the waistband of his jeans, tugging his shirt free.

"You're wearing too many clothes," she told him before she pulled the shirt over his head and smoothed her hands over the hair-sprinkled contours of his chest.

After that, there was no turning back.

They left a trail of clothes to the bed and then came together in a fast, furious explosion of feeling in the darkness. She gasped and convulsed a moment before he reached a plateau higher than he'd ever reached before.

He leaned his forehead weakly against hers as their heartbeats slowed and they caught their breath.

"We forgot to close the door," he said.

"Doesn't matter." She ran a hand over the faint stubble on his jaw. "Gordo has to find herself her own stud."

"Stud, huh? You shouldn't say things like that to a man who's still inside you."

"Why not?" she asked, then wriggled her hips, making him grow harder. She smiled a vixen's smile. "Never mind. I think I figured it out."

Much later, after they'd finally eaten the pasta dinner and made love another time, he slipped out of her bed in the weak light of predawn.

She tossed and flung out an arm, as though reaching for him, and made a soft sound of protest. But then she turned over and fell back into a deep sleep.

Exhaustion had obviously claimed her. Grady's eyes felt gritty from lack of sleep, too, but he had an early meeting with the FBI agent coordinating Operation Citygate. Grady hadn't set an alarm but the meeting weighed on his mind, signaling an internal one.

He glanced at the illuminated numbers of Tori's bedside clock. He had barely enough time to go home, shower and grab a bite of breakfast.

He pulled on his pants and shrugged into his shirt before picking up his shoes. Sighing in resignation, he went in search of Gordo and herded the sleepy cat into the cardboard carrier. She meowed in protest.

"It's only until we get to my place," he assured her.

Memories of the night intruded when he was about to let himself out of the apartment, making it impossible for him to leave without one more look at her. He walked back to the mouth of Tori's bedroom and peered inside.

She lay on her side, her hair spilled over the pillow, her lips curved upward as though she were having a happy dream. Let it be of me, he thought. The covers bunched around her waist left one beautiful breast bare.

Merely looking at her made him want her all over again, and it seemed suddenly silly that he'd suspected her of spying on him. Something buoyant rose inside him.

After a moment, he realized it was hope.

Chapter Seventeen

Tori flipped to the index page of *So, You Want to Be a PI* and skimmed the tip of her pointer finger down the columns of topics, but none addressed what she'd done last night.

She went back to the letter *P*, just to make sure the book didn't contain a top ten list of private-eye pitfalls. She couldn't find one, but common sense dictated that sleeping with a subject would command a lofty position on such a list. Maybe even higher than wearing dark sunglasses at midnight or asking the guy you're tailing where he's going.

Yep. Having wild, mind-blowing sex with the subject under investigation was definitely wrong with a silent *W*.

So why had it felt so right?

She walked into her bedroom and tossed the book on her nightstand, glad it hadn't been there last night. She wouldn't have noticed the book in time to hide it because all she'd been able to think about was Grady.

She ran her hand over the pillow where his head had rested and drew in a deep breath. She could still smell his clean, woodsy scent, which could be why she hadn't made the bed.

He and Gordo had been gone when she awaked that morning, the meaning of which she might have obsessed over if not for the note on her kitchen table.

Hated to leave but had an early meeting, it read. *Will call later. G.*

As far as love notes went, it was lacking. But the inferred meaning was clear. He'd left because he had to, not because he wanted to. And he'd done as Mrs. Grumley had demanded and taken Gordo, which said more than his note.

The thought of hearing his voice made her whole body tingle, though not nearly as violently as it had last night when he'd whispered in her ear what he intended to do to her.

Yes, it had probably been wrong to sleep with the man she had under investigation. But the case wouldn't last forever. If things worked out between them, he needn't ever know she'd been hired to follow him.

As a precaution, she picked up the paperback and put it under her bed. No sense in taking any unnecessary chances.

The phone rang. The cordless receiver that belonged on her bedside nightstand was off the cradle again so she dashed for the phone in the kitchen.

"Hello," she said, not bothering to hide her eagerness. She hadn't hid it last night, either.

A whispery voice came over the line. A female voice. Definitely not Grady's but familiar. Of course. Her client.

"Ms. M? Is that you?"

The caller said something unintelligible in response.

"If that's you, Ms. M, please speak up. I can't hear you."

"This is Ms. M." Her voice, louder now, still sounded furtive. "Can you talk, Jane?"

Tori closed her eyes but didn't try to convince Ms. M she was no Jane Bond. It wouldn't work anyway.

"You're calling my home number," Tori said, sure that Eddie had provided it. "Nobody's here but me."

Silence came over the line. "Aren't you going to ask if I can talk?"

The question hadn't occurred to Tori but now she had to voice it. "Are you someplace you can't be overheard?"

"Yes." Ms. M had dispensed with the whisper in favor of the murmur. "I'm in my office. It's private."

And where, Tori wondered, might her office be?

"I'm sure it's not bugged," Ms. M added, another thing that hadn't occurred to Tori. "So let me have it."

"Let you have what?"

"The skinny. The dope. The lowdown."

"Excuse me?"

Tori heard Ms. M sigh. "What did you find out about the subject?"

That he likes to make love with the woman on top, Tori thought. *That he goes crazy when you nibble his earlobe.*

"Not much," Tori said. "It's only been a few days since I talked to you."

Ms. M's disappointment traveled across the phone line like a living thing when she said, "but Detective Sassenbury said you made contact with the subject."

Had she ever.

"That's true," she said. "I, um, met him the night of Mayor Black's party, and I've seen him a couple times since, but the investigation is still in the preliminary stages."

"Surely you've formed some impressions," Ms. M said. "Tell me this. Do you think he's an honest man?"

Yes, her heart screamed. But that constituted opinion, not fact, so she kept it to herself.

"Particularly in his business dealings," Ms. M specified. "It's important I know whether he can be trusted."

"I don't have a good handle on his business yet," Tori said. "I do know he seems to be a favorite with city officials and that his company's in contention to get the contract to build the new community center."

"That's interesting," Ms. M said, "especially in light of the gossip surrounding Seahaven City Hall."

What gossip? Tori wondered, but she couldn't risk sounding out of the loop.

"True," she said. "True."

"Gossip is all it is at this point. Nobody knows for certain that anybody is taking payoffs."

Tori's jaw dropped. This area of investigation hadn't occurred to her but should have, considering Ms. M had hired Eddie's detective agency to discover what kind of man Grady was.

"Of course, there's no reason for anybody to bribe the subject. He'd be on the other side of the transaction."

Tori mutely shook her head, refusing to believe

Grady doled out bribe money to secure contracts. "He doesn't seem the sort," she told Ms. M.

"That's opinion," she said curtly. "I learned long ago not to put stock in anything but fact. You need to investigate his dealings with city officials and find out whether they're on the up-and-up."

The heated talk she'd witnessed Grady having with Pete Aiken at the mayor's party came back to her. Combined with Grady's willingness to take the blame for the golf ball that had nearly felled the mayor, something about it had bothered her.

"That's what I was planning to do next," Tori said, although the thought hadn't occurred to her.

"Oh, goody. Tell me how you'll go about it. I just love stuff like this." Ms. M sounded as though she were rubbing her hands together in glee.

Think, Tori exhorted herself.

"I may have to infiltrate city hall," she said. *There.* That sounded suitably impressive.

"How?" Ms. M asked.

Tori rolled her eyes. How did she know?

"No, wait. Don't tell me. Let me guess." Ms. M's voice grew excited. "Oh, oh, I've got it. You're going to get a job at city hall so you can work there undercover."

A job? It wasn't a bad idea, especially because the chatty city councilman at the mayor's party had informed her an opening existed in secretarial. But the lack of a job is what had landed Tori in this mess, so it was a stretch to imagine she'd be able to get one now. Unless . . .

"That's exactly what I'm going to do," she told Ms. M.

From the noises on the other end of the line, it sounded as though the other woman was clapping.

After Tori hung up, she pulled out a phone book and looked up the phone numbers for city hall.

She didn't seriously believe Grady was involved in illegal dealings but needed to rule out the possibility now that Ms. M had raised it.

She ignored the nagging, internal voice that claimed Ms. M wouldn't have paid to have Grady investigated if there were nothing to find.

Ms. M was obviously a businesswoman. She dressed as if she had money and had placed her last call from a private office. Maybe Ms. M needed a builder and didn't want to commit to hiring Palmer Construction until she was sure the company's dealings were aboveboard.

Then she would have hired Sassenbury Investigations to look into the company, not the man, the little voice said.

"Shut up," she told the little voice.

Grady was a good man. She felt it. She *knew* it. And now she might be able to prove it.

She dialed the mayor's office and identified herself. Within a moment, Honoria Black came on the line.

"Mayor Black, it's Tori Whitley. Remember when you said I should call if you could ever do anything for me? I hope you were serious, because I need a job."

Chapter Eighteen

Lorelei held the bag of Lazenby products she'd bought at the Macy's cosmetics counter with her left hand as she strode through the store. Over her right arm was the requisite little black dress she'd found in the women's department.

She had other black dresses. What fashion-conscious young woman didn't? But none of them were backless, which had made this dress a must-have.

Her high heels clicking on the shiny white floor and her mind full of the sexy way she'd looked in the dress, she strode through the store with the confidence that came from familiarity.

Her head swiveled from side to side, checking for new merchandise, forever on the lookout for that certain something she couldn't do without.

Thanks to corporate America's greatest consumer tool—the credit card—she seldom denied herself.

Count her as grateful that the banks never asked for more than a minimum monthly payment.

The children's department occupied the rear of the store, next to the exit that led to the parking garage. The racks of tiny clothing usually served as Lorelei's signal to pick up the pace.

She accelerated, glancing toward the clothes only out of sheer habit. A darling green dress, its hem and neckline decorated with tiny daisies, halted her forward progress.

She veered, not stopping until she got to the miniature dress. She set down her bag of cosmetics and fingered the material, a soft cotton that would feel luxurious against the skin. The dress also came in a pale yellow that reminded her of hot buttered popcorn.

"Have you ever seen anything more precious than that dress? It's a bit pricey, I know, but well worth the cost."

Lorelei hadn't been aware of the saleslady's approach until she stood next to her. She looked to be in her thirties, with a practiced smile and a killer dress Lorelei remembered seeing on sale last month in career clothing.

The cloth of the child's dress slid through Lorelei's fingers, along with the price tag at which she hadn't glanced.

"Who is it for?" the saleslady asked.

"Oh, no," Lorelei said. "You don't understand. I was just . . . It's not for . . ."

She clamped her mouth shut, mildly surprised she couldn't communicate to the saleslady that she didn't have anyone in mind.

She started to explain again, only to be stopped by

a mental vision of two tiny green-eyed blond girls wearing the dresses.

"They're for my boyfriend's twin daughters. They're three and about the same size as that little girl over there." She indicated a small girl clutching onto her mother's skirt. "Help me decide on a size, and I'll take two of them. One in green, one in yellow."

Lorelei added tiny white purses, frilly white socks, and pretty green-and-yellow barrettes to her purchases.

She felt quite smug by the time she pulled up to the immaculate ranch-style house where Wade Morrison lived with his adorable daughters.

If she were as self-absorbed as he claimed, she thought as she gathered up the packages and slammed the car door, she never would have bought gifts for his girls.

She imagined the way he'd look when he opened the door and saw her. Surprise. Pleasure. Apprehension. She was ready for it all.

He'd probably be adorably confused as to how she knew he lived in this charming, older Seahaven neighborhood, even though anyone with Internet access could find these things out with the click of a mouse.

She gazed down at herself before ringing the doorbell. Her khaki miniskirt wasn't knock-your-socks-off sexy, but her red top clung quite nicely to her ample breasts. The heels of her sandals were high enough to show off her calf definition, and she was enjoying a good hair day.

All in all, not a bad showing considering she hadn't planned to come calling on Wade Morrison today.

She stepped over a plastic Barbie car in bubblegum pink and a Ken doll who'd not only been stripped naked but decapitated, and rang the doorbell.

The flirtatious smile died on her lips at the sight of a brown-skinned, frazzled-looking girl who was probably still in high school. Her short dark hair, unbecomingly styled to begin with, stuck out in three or four directions. A large brown spot that smelled like chocolate milk stained the dolphins that leapt on the front of her white T-shirt.

"Hi, is Wade home?" Lorelei ventured, afraid she might have the wrong house. The girl was too young to be romantically involved with Wade, and her darker coloring made it unlikely that she was a relative.

"No," the girl snapped. "But I'll give you twenty dollars if you can tell me where he went."

Ah, the babysitter.

"He didn't leave a number?" Lorelei asked.

"He left his cell phone number, but he's not answering."

A thunderous booming came from the stairs, sounding like the front end of a stampede. Whatever was coming down the steps had to be powerful, large, or . . . a pair of teeny three-year-olds.

Lorelei peeked into the house. M.K. had written on herself with pink Magic Marker. She'd probably sucked on the end of the marker, too, because pink rimmed her mouth. Ash didn't have a mark on her. Neither did she have on panties.

When the twins saw Lorelei, they picked up the pace and ran toward her full tilt.

"Chop, chop," M.K. said, jumping up and down

with what looked like glee before taking Lorelei's hand and pulling her into the house.

"Hey, M.K.," Lorelei said, bending over to put down her Macy's bags and rustle the hair on the top of her blond head.

"You can tell them apart?" the babysitter asked incredulously.

"Sure, it's easy. M.K.'s eyes are more mischievous, aren't they, sweetie?" She turned to the little girl's sister. "Ash, what happened to your underwear?"

"Had an accident," the little girl announced cheerfully. Lorelei got a whiff of something and noticed the back of Ash's shirt was soaked.

"Whoa," she said, backing up a step.

"It wasn't an accident," the babysitter said. "She did it on purpose."

"Hey," Lorelei said. "That's a nasty thing to say."

"They're nasty children," the babysitter said.

"They are not! You take that back this instant."

"I take it you've never babysat them, then. They don't listen to a word I say."

"They're three!"

"They're impossible. And once Mr. Morrison gets home, I'm never babysitting them again."

"Why wait until he gets home?" Lorelei shot back at her. "I'm here now. Just go if that's the way you feel."

Resignation instantly replaced the leap of hope that had entered the girl's dark eyes at her offer. She ruffled her already messy hair and suddenly looked about sixteen, which was probably her age. She also looked miserable.

"I can't. I know you think I'm terrible because of what I just said, but I'm not a bad person. Really I'm not. I can't leave the twins here with a stranger."

Just like that, Lorelei's anger at the girl faded. She'd obviously gotten herself into a situation she couldn't handle, which had certainly happened enough times to Lorelei.

"Want Lei Lei," M.K. said.

"Lei Lei," Ash echoed, jumping up and down and stomping her size-nothing feet.

"I'm not a stranger," Lorelei assured the girl. "I'm . . . Wade's girlfriend. You can leave them with me. I could tell them apart, couldn't I?"

"That's true," the girl said slowly. "You don't think Mr. Morrison will be mad?"

"He won't be mad," Lorelei said with more assurance than she felt. "Don't worry. I can handle the girls no problem."

The babysitter didn't have to be told again. She picked up her keys from a table in the foyer and dashed out the door.

"Thanks," she called.

When she was gone, Lorelei smiled down at the two little girls and tamped down abject terror.

Why had she said she could handle M.K. and Ash? Nobody had ever trusted her enough to leave her alone with any child before, let alone two little blond gremlins.

"Okay, Ash," she said with false bravado, "I guess the first thing we do is clean you up."

"Me, too," M.K. piped up.

"You can wait," Lorelei said, taking Ash by the hand.

"Can't," M.K. said.

"Why not?" Lorelei asked.

M.K. pointed to the carpet, which had a purple spot on it that was slowly spreading outward. The lid was off her now-empty sippy cup, and grape juice streamed down her legs.

"I spill," she said.

The streetlight turned from green to yellow but the rear lights on the car in front of Wade's Volvo didn't glow red. Wade stepped on his brakes, cursing at himself under his breath for not being able to follow the car through the intersection.

He didn't have the girls along, but the curse word he used was "darn." That's what being a father did to you, he thought. He used to at least let loose the occasional "damn."

But, heck, swearing set a bad example.

He tapped the steering wheel, impatiently waiting for the light to turn green.

The meeting with Ned Weimer, the mayor's chief of staff, had gone better than expected even though finding a babysitter had been dicey as usual.

The girls gave babysitters such a hard time that he'd yet to come across one who would agree to a repeat performance. Tonight he had a new guinea pig, the daughter of one of his neighbor's friends.

"Don't worry," the new girl had told him before he'd left. "Mary Kate and Ashley will be fine with me."

He'd worried anyway, his mind as much on what might be happening at home as it had been on the chief of staff's proposition.

The new babysitter came with a solid recommendation but she'd seemed awfully young. On the few occasions he needed to be away from the girls in the evening, he preferred leaving them with a more mature caregiver.

But everything at home was probably fine. The babysitter would have rung his cell phone if it weren't.

Even though the phone had been quiet all night, he unfastened it from the clip on his belt to reassure himself that he had no messages. The screen was blank. He pressed the power button but nothing happened.

The infernal thing acted as though it had lost its charge, which was impossible. He religiously put it on the charger each night to prevent this kind of thing from happening. That could only mean one thing: it needed a new battery.

A car horn blared behind him, alerting him that the light had turned green. He checked in both directions for traffic before pressing his foot to the accelerator. Kicking himself for not keeping a spare cell-phone battery on hand for situations like this, he did the maximum speed limit all the way home.

A sporty red Miata he'd never seen before sat at a cockeyed angle in the driveway. The personalized license plate read 2HOT4U. He stroked his chin worriedly. Hadn't the babysitter come in a battered green Chevy?

He scrambled out of his Volvo and instantly knew something wasn't right by the muted sound of rap music. He listened closer. It seemed to be coming from his house.

A lump of fear clogged his throat. He broke into a

run, burst through the door and stepped on something. His right leg shot forward. He stiffened his left arm like a clothesline so he wouldn't do a full-body slam against the wall.

Breathing hard, he glanced down at his feet. The wooden dalmatian from the movie with 101 of them perched on its side. He recognized it as the pull toy Mary Kate pulled around the house with a red string.

The dalmatian had plenty of company. Ready to trip the unexpecting was a shabby, one-eyed teddy bear; a Nerf ball with a bite taken out of it; and a half-bald Raggedy Ann doll.

Not far from the balding doll, part of the beige carpet was purple. Grape juice, if he wasn't mistaken.

Now that he was inside the house, the music was louder, with an occasional blip signaling the radio station had edited the lyrics. He heard something in addition to the rap music and the blips. Voices. Three of them singing along with the lyrics.

The first two sounded more noisy than musical, especially since the singers knew none of the words. Mary Kate and Ashley.

The third voice was rich and beautiful, managing to sound in key even though in Wade's opinion rap music had no melody.

He straightened from the wall, stepped over the toys, and followed the beauty of the woman's voice.

He spotted Mary Kate and Ashley first. Mary Kate was curiously dressed in a fancy green dress he'd never seen before but Ashley wore only underwear and a T-shirt. Their tiny feet were bare.

They ran circles around a bleached blonde with a

killer body who knew how to gyrate. Her eyes were closed, her arms raised above her head as she rapped along with the music.

Lorelei Palmer.

None of the three females heard his approach over the loud music, leaving him free to watch.

His panic had vanished but he had a hard time controlling his breathing. The material of one of those tight shirts Lorelei liked to wear strained against her breasts, instantly making him picture her naked.

He hadn't taken a woman to bed since his divorce nearly two years before. He'd been too busy with the twins to make the time. She did a sinuous bump and grind that sent his blood pressure into the stratosphere. He wanted to make the time now.

The music ended. Her eyes blinked open and locked with his before he could pull a shutter over his desire. She smiled long and slow. The tip of her tongue appeared between her ruby lips, moistening the lower one.

Heat shot straight to his groin. She shook out her hair, thrust forth her breasts, arched her eyebrows, and silently told him she knew exactly what effect she had on him.

Chapter Nineteen

"Daddy!" Mary Kate's shrill voice broke the sensual mood. She ran at him full tilt, followed by her sister.

Mary Kate took a flying leap when she'd almost reached him. He caught her easily, swinging her up in his arms. Ashley clutched at his leg.

"Me want Daddy, too," she said.

He ruffled her hair while enduring the sloppy kisses Mary Kate plastered on his cheek. Then he scooted down, depositing Mary Kate on the floor. Ashley immediately assaulted his other cheek with kisses.

"Now that's the kind of greeting a man could get used to," he said, laughing.

"Then maybe I should come over there, too," Lorelei said in a husky voice. "Except it wouldn't be your cheek I aimed for."

Her gaze did a slow slide up his body, touching on various body parts before settling on his lips. The heat blasted him again. He willed it not to reach his face but felt a blush rise from his neck. She grinned. *Darn it.*

He stood, pushing his glasses up his nose to give himself time to get under control. It wasn't enough time.

"Hello, Lorelei," he said. "What are you doing here?"

She turned off the music, thrust her lower lip out in a pretty pout, then sashayed across the room toward him.

"What kind of greeting is that? I'd suggest something more along the lines of, 'Hot damn. It's good to see you, babe.' "

"Hot damn," Mary Kate repeated.

"Damn," said Ashley.

"Don't swear, girls," Wade chastised, raising a scolding eyebrow at Lorelei. Even as he lifted it, he wondered when he'd become so uptight. "I don't call any women 'babe.' "

She walked toward him in such a way that all her attributes swayed. "Then can I call you 'babe'? Because that's what you are."

He swallowed, trying to get control of the heat rushing toward him as though released from a furnace. A cold shower seemed in order but running for the bathroom would be inappropriate.

"You haven't told me what you're doing here," he reminded her.

"I'm babysitting. I told the girl you hired she could go home. She seemed nice enough, but I wouldn't recommend that you call her again."

"Of course I'm not calling her again. She left the girls with you when she'd never seen you before."

"Cut her a break," Lorelei said. "She thought I was your girlfriend."

He felt the blood drain from his face.

"Oh, don't look like that. Even if I hadn't said so, she would have jumped to that conclusion because of all the presents I brought."

He arched an eyebrow. "Presents?"

"I was in Macy's and couldn't resist." If shopping made her this excited, he wondered what sex would do to her. Stop it, he scolded himself. "M.K., show your Daddy what I got you."

"Pretty dress," Mary Kate said, executing a pirouette. Ashley followed her sister's example, spinning round and round until the two girls twirled like tops.

"I got Ash a yellow one just like it, but she took it off almost immediately. She says she likes to be naked but I made her put on panties and a T-shirt."

"You shouldn't have bought them anything," Wade said. "It's not their birthday."

Lorelei laughed, showing even, white teeth. "If I had to wait until somebody's birthday to go shopping, I'd kill myself."

The twirling girls collapsed on the floor, laughing hysterically.

"They've been like this all night," Lorelei said. "They sure are spunky."

"What they are is overtired." Wade checked his watch. "It's more than an hour past their bedtime."

"Wow, they sure go to sleep early," Lorelei exclaimed. "It's barely past nine thirty."

He rubbed his brow. "You don't spend much time around kids, do you?"

He saw her defenses rise. Her back seemed to arch.

175

"I may not spend much time with children, but that doesn't mean I don't like them. Or that I'm not good with them. Or that I wouldn't date a man who had them. I'm willing to consider new things, different things. Unlike some people in this room."

Mary Kate got up, scrambled onto the overstuffed sofa and jumped up and down on it. Ashley gave a nearby chair the same treatment.

"Roo roo," Mary Kate yelled.

"Roo," echoed her sister.

Wade caught a jumping Mary Kate on the way up and held on tight as she squirmed in his arms. "Look, I need to get the girls to bed."

"I'll help," Lorelei declared. "After they're asleep, we can finish our conversation about how you should try new things."

"We had that conversation at the bowling alley."

"That was a lecture," she said, tossing her long blond hair. "You talked, I listened. I have some things to say, too."

"I have things to do," he said firmly.

He moved toward the chair but Ashley saw him coming and ran around the coffee table.

"Can't catch me, Daddy," she cried gleefully.

"As I've already said, I'll help," Lorelei said, lunging for Ashley. She caught her under the arms, lifted her into the air, and gave her belly a noisy kiss. The little girl giggled hysterically.

"Quieting them down would be helping," Wade said wryly.

Lorelei's giggle erupted from her like music. "Sorry," she said. "I'll do better."

"Again," Ashley demanded. "Again."

Lorelei gave his daughter's belly another raspberry kiss, which resulted in another bout of laughter.

"Correction," Lorelei said, smiling at him. "I'll do better starting now."

He tried not to smile back, the better not to encourage her, but he couldn't help himself.

She set a still-laughing Ashley down on the floor.

"Last one upstairs is a rotten egg," Lorelei shouted, kicking off her high heels and racing Ashley for the stairs.

"Let down, Daddy," Mary Kate said, pounding her small fists against his chest. Resigned to trying to put excitable kids to bed, he set her down so she could chase after Lorelei and her sister.

"Run, Daddy," Mary Kate called over her shoulder.

What the heck, he thought, before pantomiming a chase. He followed Mary Kate up the stairs, careful to stay a step behind her, resigned to being the rotten egg.

A solid hour later, Wade bent down to pick up the dainty high-heeled shoes that Lorelei had shed before racing the girls upstairs. He didn't usually find shoes sexy, but these were red as well as backless.

"I don't get it," Lorelei said after she'd taken the shoes from him. "Why do you want me to put on my shoes?"

"Because you're leaving." He leveled her with the stare he used at work when he wanted an order followed.

"Am not." She threw the shoes back down so they fell in a haphazard heap. "We agreed to finish that talk about how you're going to stop being such a stick-in-the-mud. Besides, I have a present for you."

"I didn't agree . . . ," he began. "I am not a stick-in-the . . . You got me a present?"

"A couple of them." She crossed the room, retrieved a Macy's bag from the sofa, and dug inside it. "I can return them if they don't fit, but I'm pretty sure they will. The salesman was about your size, though not as broad, so I made an educated guess." She pulled out two shirts and handed them to him. "How'd I do?"

She'd nailed the size but no way would he keep the shirts. "I can't accept these," he said, trying to hand them back.

She laced her fingers together and rested her joined hands under her chin. "No offense, babe, because you know I think you are one. But you wear ugly shirts. These babies are DKNY. The paisley poplin would look great with gray slacks. The squiggle print's pink so it'll go with anything. Trust me. You need these."

"I can pay for my own shirts—" he began.

"Don't worry about it. I put them on credit."

"And I can buy clothes for Mary Kate and Ashley when they need them."

"Don't tell me you're going to try to get me to take the dresses back, too," she said. Her face developed a pinched, hurt look. Darn it.

"Okay. The girls can keep the dresses but you're not paying for my shirts." The corners of her lips turned downward. "Not that I don't appreciate you buying them for me," he added. He glanced down at the two shirts and lied. "You have very good taste."

She sniffed. "I know."

"How about I keep the shirts and write you a check?" He located his checkbook and picked up a pen. "How much?"

She hesitated, then sighed. "A hundred fifty dollars."

"You paid seventy-five dollars apiece for these?"

"You've got to pay for quality," she said, sounding more hurt by the second. "Look, if you don't want the shirts, I'll take them back."

"I want them," he said, wondering if God would strike him down for lying. He wrote the check and handed it to her. She took it, folded it and slipped it into the back pocket of her very tight skirt, which outlined her very nicely shaped behind.

"I'm ready to have that talk now," she said.

"What talk?"

"The one about you being a stick-in-the-mud."

"I am not a—" he started, but she was no longer listening. She breezed into the family room, giving him no choice but to follow, and plopped down on his leather recliner. It figured she'd take over his favorite seat.

"Gosh, those girls of yours have such energy," she said. "The way they leapt from bed to bed even made me tired."

She yawned and stretched her arms above her head, the motion outlining her breasts in vivid detail. Wade stopped in the center of the room, well short of where temptation sat. When he crossed his arms over his chest, he noticed his shirt was soggy.

"That's not a usual part of their bedtime routine," he said. Neither was exuberantly splashing their father and each other as they took a bath.

"Routines are boring," Lorelei declared.

He thought of the toys strewn around the house, the grape-juice stain on the carpet, and the soiled clothing Lorelei had left in a pile in the sink.

"Young children need a routine," he stated.

She jumped to her feet and sharply saluted him. "Sir, yes sir."

His mouth twisted. "Are you mocking me?"

"Mocking you?" Her eyebrows rose. "I'm trying to get you to lighten up. Like you did upstairs for a half second or so at a time. It was fun, wasn't it?"

"I'm the one who'll pay for all that fun tomorrow morning when the girls are too tired to get out of bed for preschool."

"You're exaggerating," Lorelei said.

"Then you try getting them up tomorrow morning."

She gave him a suggestive grin. "Are you inviting me to stay overnight?"

"No." He thrust aside an image of her lying naked in his bed, beckoning him with an index finger that had its nail painted decadently red.

"Why not? We decided you needed to try new things."

"That's what you decided. I decided you're way too young for me."

"You can be such a fuddy-duddy," Lorelei said, closing the gap between them. Without her high heels, the top of her head didn't reach his chin. A blast of perfume hit him when she got close, making him want to sneeze. But he wanted to reach for her more.

"Look at how your arms are crossed over your chest. Which is a crying shame because it's such a very fine chest. I'm pretty good at body language and that tells me you're not open-minded." She threw up her hands. "You've totally closed yourself off to new possibilities."

He uncrossed his arms. Because he didn't trust his hands not to take what they wanted, he kept them at his side.

"There," he said, "are you satisfied?"

Her eyes sparkled. "Not even close."

His body hardened. "Look, Lorelei. I think you're a very attractive girl, but I'm not interested in a relationship with you."

"I'm a woman, not a girl," she corrected, then arched an eyebrow before deliberately staring at his crotch. The bulge in his pants was unmistakable. "And if you're not interested, then what's that all about?"

He briefly closed his eyes, trying to fight the over-powering attraction. "Do you have to say such outrageous things?"

"They're not outrageous. They're spontaneous. And everybody knows spontaneity is the spice of life."

She took a step closer to him and walked her long-nailed fingers up his chest until they reached his lips. Almost reverently, she traced the shape of them.

His body throbbed, his heart hammered and he felt a bead of sweat form on his upper lip. Her mischievous eyes, with their heavily mascaraed lashes, lifted to his.

"Go ahead, Wade," she whispered in a voice that sounded like sin and sex. "Be spontaneous and kiss me."

Lust hit him like an ocean wave during a storm. He

tried to hold it back but another wave of need followed. *Ah, heck.* How was he supposed to fight a tsunami?

He fastened a hand at the back of her blond head, lowered his mouth . . . and felt something tug at his pant leg.

His head's forward motion stopped a few inches from her lips.

"Daddy," a small voice said. "Wanna drink of water."

He abruptly let go of Lorelei and stepped back, as though guilty of a heinous crime. But Ashley's sleepy green eyes held no accusation. Say something, he told himself, but stood there like a big, dumb mute.

Lorelei crouched down to Ashley's level and smoothed his daughter's hair. "You've got rotten timing, Ash, but I'll get you a drink of water. Then you can go back upstairs."

"Want Daddy come with me," Ashley said on a plaintive note.

Lorelei looked about to protest but then she smiled and kissed the top of the little girl's head.

"A lot of us girls want your daddy tonight, honey," she said. "Tell you what, you can have him tonight. I'll take a rain check."

Her hot gaze met his over the top of his daughter's blond head, making promises he'd have no business taking her up on.

He broke eye contact and wiped at his brow. He needed to put some distance between them and to get a good night's sleep.

Maybe then he'd be strong enough to resist what he was still quite sure he shouldn't want.

Chapter Twenty

"Hey, Lorelei. You sure do look pretty this morning," Grady said, smothering his shock that his sister was at Palmer Construction headquarters before most of his office staff. And, miracle of miracles, she was working. Again.

Lorelei stood with her back to him at a tall, thin cabinet, a stack of manila folders balanced between her body and the crook of her elbow as though she were actually filing.

"Whatever you want, the answer's no," she said without turning around while she shoved a file folder into place.

"How do you know I want something?"

"Besides the fact that you complimented me while looking at the back of my head? Oh, let's see. How 'bout that sugary tone of voice?"

"I was shooting for buttery," he admitted.

She closed one file drawer and opened another, still

not looking at him. "I don't know what makes you think you can refuse to tell me what's going on between you and Mom and Dad one day, let alone call me self-absorbed—"

"I said you were a *little* self-absorbed and only because you forced me to," he interrupted.

"—and think you can waltz in here the next day and sweet-talk me so I'll do whatever you ask."

She crammed a couple more file folders in place before slamming the drawer with a bang and turning to face him.

"Because I'm not . . ." She stopped in midsentence, tilted her too-blond head, and pointed to the cardboard carrier in his right hand. "What do you have there?"

"I'll show you," Grady said, lifting the nearly weightless carrier onto a nearby desk. He talked in soothing tones as he bent down and reached inside for his new pet. "It's okay, girl. There's nothing to be afraid of."

When Gordo was free of the carrier, she blinked a few times and looked nervously around at her new surroundings. Grady picked up the little cat with one hand and held her out to his sister.

"Lorelei, meet Gordo," he said.

Lorelei made a soft noise, her expression turned tender, and the confrontation went out of her stance.

"You are so cute, I could just die," Lorelei told the cat, taking her from Grady and gathering her close. "Except what kind of name is Gordo for a cutie like you?"

"You really think she's cute?" Grady asked.

"Of course." Lorelei stared into the cat's aggressively homely face as she petted her. "And don't you dare let any man tell you differently. Do you hear me, Gordo?"

Grady figured he better ask his favor while the asking was good. "Then you'll take care of her for me today?"

Lorelei's head snapped up. "For you? You mean this is your cat? Since when do you have a cat?"

"Since this morning."

"But I thought you weren't home enough to justify getting a pet. And why a cat? With all those Westerns you watch, why not a little dogie?"

"Ha, ha," Grady said.

"I thought it was funny," Lorelei said. "So what gives?"

"Tori can't keep Gordo because her lease has a no-pets clause."

"Ah," Lorelei said, drawing out the syllable. "Tori. The plot thickens. Tell me more."

He shrugged. "There's not much more to tell. I've got to keep her because taking her back to the pound would be a death sentence. Nobody else would adopt a cat that looks like her."

An indentation appeared between Lorelei's eyebrows as she attempted to cover Gordo's ears.

"Don't say things like that in front of her, especially because they're not true. I'd adopt her in a second if Mandy wasn't allergic to cats," she said, referring to one of her three roommates. "But I wasn't asking about Gordo. I want to know more about you and Tori."

"Like what?"

"Men." Lorelei made a *tsk*ing sound. "You don't date anybody for, like, a year and then you ask a question like that. I want to know if she rings your bell, how serious you are, if I'll see her across the dinner table at Thanksgiving. Details, big brother, I want details."

No way would he tell Lorelei exactly how loudly Tori rang his bell, or how much he looked forward to having her ring it again, but she'd never shut up if he didn't say something.

"We're seeing each other," he said flatly. Hoping to stop her from asking more questions, he zigzagged over the linoleum floor and around cubicles to his office.

"Well, duh." Lorelei's voice came loud and clear from behind him. "I figured that out myself. But how seriously are you dating? I mean, like, is she your girlfriend or what?"

He'd have dismissed the notion as ludicrous as recently as a few days ago, but that had been before Tuesday night.

"I hope so," Grady said.

Lorelei beamed. "Oh, goody. I like her. I mean, the woman works in a department store. How cool is that? Can you ask her if she can get me a discount?"

Grady laid down his briefcase and came across his desk to open it. The papers jammed inside reminded him that the more successful his company became, the busier he got.

"No," he said.

"If you're going to be that way about it, I'll ask her myself," Lorelei said. "She has to be a softie if she came home from the pound with this cute little kitty."

"Which you'll keep an eye out for so I can get some work done." He nodded encouragingly toward the door as he took a seat behind his desk.

"Let's go and get you set up, sweetie," she said to Gordo, bringing the cat's scrunched-up face close to hers. To Grady, she said, "I'll need the keys to your SUV."

"For what?"

"The litter box, water bowl, and cat food you left there." She shook her head as understanding dawned. "You don't have any of those things, do you?"

"Don't look at me like that," he said, thinking he'd probably left those supplies behind when he slipped out of Tori's apartment at dawn. "I'm not used to cats."

"Obviously," she said, marching over to his desk and holding out her right hand palm up. He dug out his wallet and counted out a couple of bills.

"What? You don't want her to have *nice* things?" Lorelei asked, her hand still extended. He added more money.

He thought he'd finally gotten rid of her but then she paused at the mouth of his office. "By the way, you already had a call this morning. A Larry Schlichter."

His body went still. This was most likely the call he'd been waiting for since Pete Aiken had claimed somebody else at city hall wanted in on the action.

It made sense that somebody would be Schlichter, who was Seahaven's director of planning.

Aiken, the city clerk, could only peripherally affect which construction company got the community-center contract. Aiken had taken money to open the sealed bids that came to his office, thus making sure Grady submitted the low one.

But a low bid didn't guarantee a winner. Schlichter headed a committee that would review the bids and recommend one of them to city council at next week's regularly scheduled meeting.

Grady kept his voice casual. "Did Schlichter say what he wanted?"

"Nope. He didn't leave a number where he could be reached, either. He said you shouldn't call him, that he'd call you."

It seemed a lot to ask, especially because Grady's patience with Operation Citygate had worn thin. At the meeting with the FBI agent that morning, he'd argued that he should be the one to approach city officials rather than vice versa.

The agent hadn't gone for it, asking Grady to wait for city employees to solicit the bribes themselves so the FBI could build a stronger case. It could be that patience would pay off.

If Grady got evidence against Schlichter, he'd be one step farther up a ladder that would hopefully lead to the mayor. Then he could get his life back.

A life he hoped would include Tori.

Chapter Twenty-one

"I don't understand." Tori failed to keep the thick film of disappointment from coating her voice. "What am I doing here if the job has already been filled?"

Mayor Honoria Black leaned back in her sumptuous leather chair, which was inside a lavishly decorated office that must have cost the Seahaven taxpayers dearly. The carpeting was plush, the furniture mahogany, and the artwork on the walls originals.

"There will be other openings," the mayor said. "It never hurts to get that preliminary interview out of the way."

"But when I called yesterday, you gave the impression the job was mine for the asking," Tori reminded her.

"You must have heard me wrong," Mayor Black said smoothly. "Applicants must undergo a rigorous process before they can be considered for a city opening. You've only started it."

Tori fought disappointment, feeling silly for having believed her employment at city hall was both a done deal and the answer to her problems. Not only would she have been in prime position to prove Grady's integrity, but she would have been employed—no small feat for her.

"What exactly does the process entail?" she asked.

"Filling out an application and submitting a resume by the closing date of the job posting, to begin with. Secretarial positions, such as the one we just filled, require a typing test. And of course we ask for references and check them thoroughly."

"I see," Tori said, but she didn't.

If there wasn't a job opening at city hall, why was she there? With the standardized hiring process, she doubted this interview would suffice if a position became available.

"When do you forsee there being an opening?" Tori asked, smoothing the skirt of the chocolate-colored business suit that had seen her through too many unsuccessful job interviews.

"It's hard to say," Mayor Black said evasively, "but then I might get it into my mind to create one. That's the beauty of being the mayor. I can do anything I want."

"What would make you want to create a new position?" Tori asked.

"Let's just say I like to surround myself with good, loyal people." Honoria rocked in her chair. "That's why I'm glad for this chance for us to get better acquainted. All I really know about you is that you claim to have followed Grady around the golf course to get him to notice you."

Tori frowned, not liking the way that depiction made her sound. "That's not exactly the way it was."

"I knew it. I knew that story was bogus. So how exactly did you meet our young Mr. Palmer? A man as forceful as that, I bet he was the one who approached you."

Tori thought about the way he'd knocked on the window of her car, all but demanding she talk to him. "He did," she said. "He can be very persuasive when he wants something."

Honoria tilted her head. By no means could she be called a beauty, but Tori had to hand it to her hairdresser. A beautician with considerable skill had cut the mayor's short, dark hair to make the most of her coarse features.

"Isn't it funny that you should say that?" the mayor said. "I've often wondered that about Grady. I know he's a go-getter, but how far will he go to get what he wants?"

"I couldn't say," Tori said. "I don't know him well enough yet."

"When you do," Honoria said, leaning forward and lowering her voice, "you be sure to let me know."

Thirty minutes later, when the strange meeting with Honoria Black was history, Tori had a nagging feeling that the mayor had invited her into her office to pump her about Grady.

But that was ridiculous, given Tori's tenuous connection to the man. She felt her face flush when she thought back two nights ago to the way their bodies fit perfectly together.

Tenuous could be the wrong word, especially because she would have happily connected with him again if he'd been free last night.

She smiled as she replayed yesterday afternoon's telephone conversation in her head.

"I've barely been able to keep my mind on work thinking about what we did last night," Grady had claimed in a soft, low voice.

"Then come over tonight so we can do it again," she'd whispered, shocking herself but not him.

"I can't." Regret had been thick in his voice. "I have to work late on a bid package."

"Can't it wait?"

"Not with the deadline coming up fast. Hopefully I'll finish it up tonight. Believe me, I don't want to spend any more nights away from you than I have to."

She not only believed him, she believed *in* him. More than ever, she thought Grady one of those good men that were purportedly so hard to find.

But she'd failed in her mission to infiltrate city hall, thus blowing her chance to prove it.

She stopped walking and gazed around at the interior of the grand old building as it occurred to her that wasn't necessarily true.

She stood inside city hall at this very minute, with a very good excuse for being there. She needed to make the most of this opportunity, but how?

Ms. M had asked her to investigate Grady's dealings with city officials, and she'd meant to start with Pete Aiken. But she couldn't very well sidle up to somebody who knew the city clerk and say, "How 'bout that Pete Aiken?"

Or could she?

She lurked outside the city clerk's office, trying to get up her nerve. Five minutes ticked by while she loitered in the hall, rejecting one opening line after another.

She still hadn't moved when a small, round-faced woman with frizzy dark hair stepped out of the office and gave her a curious look.

"Hi," Tori said brightly.

The woman looked her up and down but didn't smile. "Can I help you with something?"

"Yes," Tori said, and belatedly realized the folly of her plan. She couldn't start firing questions at a woman who already seemed suspicious of her. But what legitimate reason could she give for skulking in the hall? "You can . . . tell me where the break room is. I'm . . . really thirsty."

"You work here?"

Tori shook her head. "Not yet. I was interviewing."

The tension seemed to leave the woman's body and she smiled at Tori. "So you got the dry mouth?"

"Excuse me?"

"From nerves. Job interviews do that to me, too," the woman said. "I'm due a break now. You can come with me.

"I'm Ann Dreher. I work in the city clerk's office as an administrative assistant," she told Tori as they walked the short distance to a small, empty room with tables and vending machines.

"Tori Whitley, wannabe administrative assistant in anybody's office," Tori said.

Ann laughed and left her side to get a bottle of orange juice from one of the machines. Tori smiled to herself as she fished some coins from the bottom of her purse and fed them into a soda machine. This PI business wasn't so hard after all.

She joined Ann at a circular table, trying to remember the chapter in *So, You Want to Be a PI* that dealt with interrogation.

Ah, yes. When trying to bleed information from an unsuspecting party, the conversation should flow seamlessly, the book suggested.

"That Pete Aiken," Tori said. "He's really something, isn't he?"

"You know Pete?"

Whoops. "Who doesn't?"

"Lots of people, I'd think." Ann sipped from her juice. "Why did you say he was really something?"

Who knew? Certainly not Tori. Time for an open-ended question. "You haven't noticed?"

"Of course I noticed. You can't miss those little holes. What I wonder is"—Ann leaned forward and whispered—"where he got the money to afford it. I thought the divorce pretty much wiped him out, not to mention the gambling."

Tori's antennae went up. Pete Aiken had a gambling problem? And now he was buying something with . . . holes?

"Tell me about it." Tori rolled her eyes and hoped Ann would take her literally. She didn't.

She waited a few moments but the other woman seemed more interested in drinking her juice than talking. Tori finally asked, "How much do you think it set him back?"

"I'd say a couple of thousand, at least."

"That much?"

"That's a drop in the bucket compared to what he's been spending on the new clothes and the personal trainer," she said. "But personally I think the cost is ridiculous."

"Yeah," Tori said, agreeing to she didn't know what, "considering it comes with holes."

Ann scrunched up her forehead. "What are you talking about?"

"What you're talking about," Tori answered.

"I'm talking about Pete's hair transplant."

"Me, too," Tori said, and thought fast. "You have to have a hole in your head to want one of those."

Tori left city hall ten minutes later feeling more like Calamity Jane than Jane Bond, but she had new information.

Pete Aiken had recently come into some money.

Of course, that could mean anything.

A rich relative could have willed him an inheritance, he could have reconciled with his wife and repooled their money, or the Publisher's Clearinghouse Sweepstakes could have come calling.

It didn't mean Grady had given the city clerk bribe money.

Ms. M said rumors about corruption swirled around city hall, but they were only rumors. Even if the city clerk had accepted a bribe, Tori couldn't make the leap that Grady had paid him off.

Yes, Grady supported the mayor and her questionable politics. Yes, he hung out with her supporters. Yes, the city had favored him with numerous contracts over the past nine months. And, yes, he was in line to build another, even more lucrative project.

But, at most, that was guilt by association. Just as the heated conversation at Mayor Black's party could have been about anything.

She checked her watch and saw that it was nearly time to meet Grady. Suddenly anxious to see him, she decided to head straight to his office instead of going home and changing.

Ms. M was right. She was a good judge of character.

A few hours in his presence would reassure her that he was who she thought he was: an upstanding businessman with nothing to hide.

Chapter Twenty-two

The instant Tori peered around the open door of Grady's office and spotted him sitting at his desk, she felt reassured.

His brow knitted in concentration and a pen in his left hand, Grady made notations on the papers strewn across his desk like the hard worker he was.

He'd already demonstrated his strong sense of family, his keen intellect, and his amazing ability to make love.

She blushed a little at the last thought but figured it showed insight into his character. If Grady wasn't a selfish lover, it followed that neither was he a selfish man.

Funny, she hadn't noticed before that he was a lefty. She supposed a better PI would have made a note of it, but then she observed things about him that other investigators wouldn't.

Like the golden streaks in his brown hair that

197

caused his tan to appear deeper and the way his upper teeth bit into that sensuous lower lip of his while he concentrated.

But Grady Palmer was much more than a handsome face. He was a good man who would never resort to bribery to get what he wanted.

Something so light its weight barely registered stepped on the toe of her high-heeled pump and she looked down to see Gordo staring back up at her.

"*Meow,*" the cat said.

Tori bent over to scoop the cat into her arms, earning grateful purrs from Gordo.

Grady finally looked up from his papers.

"Tori." His smile started at his lips and traveled to his eyes. Tori immediately felt as though she'd been transported back to the darkened bedroom where she and Grady had made love. "How long have you been standing there?"

"Long enough to tell that you need a break," she said, smiling back.

"Do I ever," he said, then grinned. "Shut the door."

She pulled it closed and started to step deeper into his office, but he held up a hand.

"No," he said, still grinning. "Don't move."

She stopped. "Why?"

"You'll see." He got to his feet and came around the desk.

"Now let me have Gordo," he said when he reached her.

She raised her brows quizzically but didn't comment as she handed over the cat, which he promptly set on the floor.

"There," he said, looking and sounding smug.

"Are you going to tell me what this is all about?" she asked.

"Better. I'll show you."

He pulled her into his arms and claimed her mouth with a mastery that made her knees buckle. It didn't matter. He held her as though he never intended to let her go, sweeping his tongue inside her mouth and turning on her internal generator.

Heat blasted her. Along with it came the certainty that this was where she belonged.

The doubts that had arisen at city hall vanished like the morning mist as he continued to pour himself into the kiss.

Grady had never been anything but open and honest. He was one of those straightforward types who was what he was. With Grady, she'd always know where she stood.

He wasn't the one with secrets. She was.

She clung to his shoulders when he broke off the kiss, afraid she'd fall if she didn't have help in supporting herself.

"Hope you didn't mind," he said, that openness shining through in his eyes. "This is the only spot in my office not visible to the masses."

She surveyed the small room, noticing that a large window took up part of the front wall.

She laid a hand on his cheek, feeling the beginning of his beard through his skin. "I definitely didn't mind. But I know somebody else who did."

Gordo alternately clawed at her leg, then his, emitting protesting *meows* that grew progressively louder.

"I'm surprised to see her in the office," Tori said.

Grady made a face. "I hope to get to the point where I can leave her alone but she refuses to be ignored."

"It's probably because it used to happen to her all the time," she said, lifting the cat once more. "But how can you pay attention to her when you're working?"

"Lorelei does that."

"That's right. Your sister works here. Why didn't I see her when I came in?"

"Quitting time's five o'clock. Lorelei's more into leaving early than working late." He frowned. "Although I've seen her here a couple of times lately after hours."

"Maybe she's changing."

"I don't know about that," he said. "Lorelei thinks she's perfect just the way she is. The working-late thing is probably an aberration."

"Speaking of working late, you don't have to, right? I thought we could make Gordo happy and stay in tonight instead of going out. We could go back to your place, get Chinese takeout and . . ."

Her voice trailed off when she noticed a decided lack of enthusiasm in his expression. "What is it?" she asked.

"You must not have gotten the message I left on your answering machine. I would have called your cell phone but I don't have the number."

"I've been out most of the day," she said, not wanting to take the time to explain that she'd been at city hall. She could tell him that later, after she found out what was going on. "What did the message say?"

"That I have to cancel for tonight."

Disappointment descended over her like a dark cloud. "But I thought you finished up the bid package last night."

"I did. Tonight I have a . . . business dinner."

The pause before he said "business dinner" was nearly imperceptible, but Tori picked up on it.

She looked into his eyes, only to find them shuttered. In a burst of clarity she knew that he hadn't told her everything.

"Isn't this kind of sudden?" she asked.

"These things sometimes crop up at the last minute," he said, but his answer sounded evasive.

His smile seemed tight when he added, "I'll make it up to you tomorrow."

"I'll hold you to that," she said, feeling her own smile waver.

She managed to keep her suspicions at bay until she reached her car, then she could no longer hold them back.

He'd said he had a business dinner, which on the surface seemed to indicate it had to do with his construction company. But what if the business were of the underhanded variety?

While at city hall, Tori had discovered the community-center bids were due tomorrow morning. If Grady were bribing city officials, the timing was certainly right.

No, Tori thought, shaking her head. Despite his relationship with Pete Aiken, Grady couldn't be on the wrong side of the law.

Too bad she didn't know for certain that he wasn't meeting with a city official, so she had hard information to back up her gut feeling.

"Wait a minute," she said aloud. "I can get the information. I'm a private eye."

She needed to at least attempt to discover who Grady was having dinner with tonight. The only way to do that with certainty was to follow him.

She chewed on the end of her thumb while she thought. She'd proven woefully inept at tailing a subject. Add the fact that Grady knew she drove a silver Beetle, and it spelled disaster. Unless . . .

She fished the silver disco ball from her purse, asked, "Should I do this?" and shook the little ball. Holding her breath, she turned it over.

Get it on, read the answer.

She picked up her cell phone and dialed.

"Sassenbury here."

"Eddie, it's Tori." She took a breath and rushed ahead. "Remember you said you'd be there for me if I needed help?"

"Sure do," Eddie said.

"I need you to help me follow somebody."

"No can do, cuz. I'm in the middle of something here."

"Tough. Because if you don't meet me in Seahaven at the corner of Sassafras and U.S. 1 in the next thirty minutes, I'm calling Ms. M and telling her we're giving back her retainer."

"You don't play fair," Eddie said.

"I'm in my Volkswagen," she said. "We don't have much time so I'll expect you here quick."

"But—"

"Ms. M gave me her cell phone number," Tori said.

"I'll be there," Eddie said.

When she hung up, Tori sat back against her seat and waited. So what if her conversation with Grady hadn't proved he had nothing to do with the shady dealings at city hall. Following him would.

She hoped.

Chapter Twenty-three

After he paid a nominal admission fee, Grady walked down the center of the 960-foot Lake Worth fishing pier. The salty sea breeze swept over him, but a funeral dirge played in his head and his steps were weighed down by disappointment.

He'd been right about Schlichter. The planning director had called back to set up a meeting, which could only mean he intended to solicit a bribe. Grady didn't know why he'd expected better from Schlichter. Just because he'd seemed like one of the good guys didn't mean he was.

After hearing through the grapevine that Tori had been at city hall today talking to the mayor, Grady even had renewed doubts about her.

He'd found himself searching his rearview mirror for her Volkswagen Beetle on the drive here. He hadn't seen it, which made him want to give her the benefit of the doubt, but her city hall connection still nagged at him.

Darkness had already descended on Lake Worth, which was in central Palm Beach County about an hour south of Seahaven, but the lighted pier remained open until midnight.

An old-timer with grizzled whiskers sat on a stool with his finger on his line and his eyes half closed. Ten feet from him a boy of about ten leaned on the railing, intently watching his bobbin for signs of fish biting while his father watched him.

"Catch anything tonight?" Grady asked the boy.

The boy's eyes didn't leave the gently lapping water of the Atlantic. "Not yet," he said before excitedly adding, "but I think I got one now."

The boy reeled in the line under the guidance of his father, groaning loudly when he pulled a clump of seaweed from the ocean. He removed the slimy mess, cast his line back into the water, and returned to his vigil.

Grady performed one of his own, scanning the pier for any sign of Larry Schlichter. The planning director's beard combined with his bald head and long gray ponytail should make him easy to pick out of a crowd.

When he didn't spot anyone fitting that description, Grady wondered if Schlichter had stood him up. He'd sounded nervous on the phone when he refused Grady's invitation to meet in his office.

Grady had grumbled, but finally agreed to meet at the pier. It amazed him that people like Schlichter, who expected phone lines and offices to be bugged, hadn't figured out the government had ears everywhere.

At the moment, the tiny recording device that doubled as the battery inside Grady's cell phone contained those ears. His FBI-issued pager was a microphone.

"Pssst. Palmer."

The summons came from a clean-shaven man in a dark-colored fishing hat who occupied a lonely section of the pier. He sat on a stool holding a pole with a hopelessly tangled line. He looked up at Grady from under the hat, revealing bushy gray eyebrows.

"Schlichter? Is that you? Where's the beard?"

"Shhhhh." Panic filled Larry Schlichter's face as his eyes swiveled from side to side. "Somebody might hear."

"I can barely hear you myself, Lar, with this wind blowing," Grady said, resting one elbow on the railing in feigned nonchalance.

In actuality, he was kicking himself for not pushing harder to meet in another location. Even though his equipment was top of the line, it might not pick up their conversation if the wind didn't die down.

"So what did you want to see me about?" Grady asked.

Schlichter sniffled, took a handkerchief from his pocket, and dabbed at his nose with an unsteady hand. "I'm sure you can guess," he said.

"Maybe I can, but I'd rather you tell me."

The Adam's apple in Schlichter's throat bobbed in stark relief when he swallowed. "How can I be sure you're not wearing a wire?"

It wasn't the first time a corrupt city official had broached the subject. Grady opened his arms wide and felt the wind cut through the cotton of his long-sleeved shirt. "If you want to frisk me, be my guest."

Schlichter shook his head. "I don't want to frisk you. And, for God's sake, put down your arms. You're drawing attention."

"Nobody's paying any attention to us, Lar. So suppose you tell me why you think I'd be wearing a wire."

Schlichter wiped a hand over his brow. "I don't know. I suppose because I've never done this sort of thing before."

This was like pulling teeth, but the FBI agent had cautioned Grady not to put words in the other man's mouth. "What sort of thing?"

Schlichter lowered his voice even more, but thankfully the wind had taken a break from its impression of a tornado. He leaned closer to the other man so the listening device could pick up his words.

"I know Pete Aiken is making sure you submit the low bid for the community center."

"Do you now," Grady said, crossing his arms over his chest.

"You've been around long enough to know a low bid isn't always enough to secure the job."

Grady set his mouth in a mutinous line but inside he was elated. He pictured himself as a fisherman and Larry Schlichter swimming around in the ocean, about to take his bait.

"I'm heading the committee that'll recommend to city council who should get the job," Schlichter said.

"Where are you going with this?" Grady didn't

have to fake anger. The thought of another corrupt official at city hall made it genuine.

"If you want the contract," Schlichter said, "you need me on your side."

The planning director was smarter than your run-of-the-mill corrupt official. He'd passed on the offer to frisk Grady, but still didn't trust him. Thus far he hadn't said anything incriminating.

"And how would I get you on my side?" Grady asked in a deceptively soft voice.

"The same way you got Pete on your side," Schlichter said and sniffed again.

"I already told Pete I didn't appreciate being hit up for more cash," Grady said through gritted teeth.

"Then you should have done your homework to find out who the real decision makers are at city hall." Schlichter reached for his handkerchief again, blew his nose again.

"So that's how it is," Grady said with disgust. "You need to feed your habit."

Schlichter's blue eyes flashed. "You don't know the first thing about me. I have a cold, not a habit."

"Then what's this all about?" Grady indicated the meeting at the remote pier with a sweep of his hand. "Why are you asking me for bribe money?"

When Schlichter didn't answer, Grady wondered if he'd gone too far. Schlichter already seemed suspicious. If he answered the question, it would be tantamount to admitting he was on the wrong side of the righteous.

"I'm tired of it, okay? I'm not stupid. I figured out

why your company keeps coming in with the low bid and confronted Pete. He wouldn't admit it but I could tell he was lying.

"Then I started looking around. City employees who aren't making any more money than me are driving around in Porsches, taking their boats out on the intracoastal, eating out every night. And I thought, what about me?"

"So you decided to collect some bribe money, starting with me?"

"Those are your words, not mine." Schlichter reverted back to cautious mode, but Grady thought he'd probably already said enough to damn himself.

"What if I don't pay?"

"You do whatever you think is best for your business," Schlichter said.

Grady reached into his back pocket and withdrew a wad of bills, which he handed to Schlichter.

The other man grabbed the money. "For God's sake, can't you be circumspect?"

He bent over, shielding the money with his body, while he surreptitiously counted it. Then he shook his head. "This isn't enough."

Grady reached into his opposite pocket where he kept the other half of the money. Together, it added up to a tidy sum.

"This is more than I paid Pete," he said, tapping the money against his palm. It was also all he was authorized to offer. "Take it or leave it."

"I'll take it," Schlichter said, snatching up the money.

"Of course you will," Grady muttered under his breath.

"What?" Schlichter asked.

"Nothing," Grady said. He turned on his heel and left without another word, feeling unaccountably disappointed that Larry Schlichter had done exactly what he expected him to do.

But of course he had. A greedy heart beat beneath that nice-guy facade, reinforcing Grady's belief that nobody was what they seemed. Maybe not even Tori.

He lifted his head and spotted a woman at the end of the pier walking quickly away from him. He couldn't see her hair color because of the baseball hat she wore but she was approximately the same height and weight as Tori.

Damn it.

"Tori," he shouted, but the woman didn't turn.

He broke into a run, his eyes trained on the woman's back, his footsteps pounding heavily on the wood. When he reached the stairs, he spotted her weaving between parked cars in the weakly lit parking lot. He tramped down the steps, taking them two by two.

"Hey, stop," he yelled, but the woman only moved faster.

He expected her to lead him to a silver Volkswagen Beetle, but she stopped beside a blue PT Cruiser, giving him time to close the gap between them.

She frantically dug in her purse as he approached, then swiveled in his direction with a small silver canister in her hand. *Mace.*

He closed his eyes, expecting the spray to hurt, but a wet cloud of something fragrant blasted him. Shielding his eyes with one hand, he peeked through his fingers. The woman looked nothing like Tori. Easily fifteen years older, she didn't even belong to the same race.

"I didn't mean to scare you," he began, but the woman wouldn't listen.

"Take one more step and I'll spray you again," she warned.

"But that's perfume," he said, wiping the stuff from his face.

"Then I'll scream. I swear I will."

He backed away with his hands in front of his face to show he meant no harm. "I'm sorry I frightened you. I thought you were someone else."

Keeping the perfume canister pointed at him, she scrambled inside her PT Cruiser and locked the doors.

He stood there, in the center of the dark parking lot, and grinned hugely. As the woman gunned the car and drove away, he gave her a jaunty wave.

She probably thought him a criminal, but he could live with that.

Because she hadn't been Tori.

From inside Eddie's car in a dark corner of the parking lot, Tori watched the woman in the baseball hat take a can of Mace from her purse and spray Grady.

She gasped and reached for the inner door handle. Eddie's hand clamped her wrist.

"Don't," Eddie warned. "Wait and see what happens."

"But he needs help!"

212

"Wait," Eddie repeated.

Grady put his hands in the air, no doubt to show the woman he was harmless, and backed away. He didn't act like a man who'd been Maced.

"What do you make of that?" Eddie asked as the woman scrambled into the car. "Do you recognize the woman?"

"No," she said, shaking her head. She'd gotten a good-enough look at the woman and felt sure she hadn't been one of the guests at the mayor's party.

"She wasn't the one Palmer met on the pier," supplied Eddie, who'd made it back to the car only seconds before Grady had chased the woman through the parking lot. "I couldn't get close enough to see much, but I'm sure it was a man."

The woman drove away with a screech of tires on pavement. Grady remained behind, standing in the middle of the parking lot, seemingly looking in their direction.

"Duck," Eddie ordered.

Tori ducked, bending low enough that nobody would be able to tell the car was occupied unless they got close.

They waited for long minutes. Tori hardly dared move, afraid even to breathe. At any second, she expected to hear the rap of his knuckles on the car window. The minutes stretched, but nothing happened.

She finally drew in a relieved lungful of breath and straightened. Grady—and his car—were gone.

"No," she cried, frantically looking around. But the now-empty lot stared her in the face. The truth was she'd failed. He'd cleared out while she was hid-

213

ing, leaving her no way to find out where he was headed next.

"What are you so uptight about?" Eddie asked. "We weren't going to follow him anyway."

"We weren't? Why not?"

"It's more important to determine who he met with. We'll wait here a while so you can get a look at the guy and see if you recognize him."

Eddie had positioned the car in such a way that they could see whoever entered or exited the pier. Because the entrance was lighted, she had a clear sight line.

"There he is," Eddie said after another ten minutes had passed, pointing out a man in a fishing hat carrying a pole. "Recognize him?"

"No," Tori said in relief, shaking her head. "Let's go."

Eddie ignored her, his eyes still on the man. Before she could prompt Eddie to leave again, the man dropped what looked to be his keys. When he stopped to bend over, his hat fell off, revealing a bald head and long gray hair in a ponytail.

She stiffened, because she'd talked to the man a few days before at Mayor Black's party. He'd worn a beard then, but she was sure it was the same man.

"What is it?" Eddie prompted. "Who is he?"

She searched her mind for his name. "It's Larry something or other. He's the city's planning director."

"Didn't you say the planning director was a major player in deciding who got that community-center bid?" he asked.

"I said he had some input," Tori said, deliberately

leaving out that the planning director headed the committee that made the recommendation to city council.

Eddie whistled long and low. Tori had told him some of the details of the case on the way over, and he'd obviously drawn his own conclusions.

"This looks bad for your boy Palmer, Tor," he said.

"I'm sure there's a logical explanation," she said.

"Then you need to find out what it is," Eddie said.

Chapter Twenty-four

Lorelei was not in a good mood.

Here she was at city hall, decked out in a new yellow minidress that made her figure look amazing, and the man she'd spent the last few nights fantasizing about had yet to arrive for work.

In a shocker, it seemed the ultraresponsible Wade Morrison was late.

Had she known this in advance, she wouldn't have pleaded with Grady to let her drop off Palmer Construction's bid for the community center contract and gotten her feelings hurt.

Although he'd finally relented, clearly her own brother doubted she was responsible enough to deliver a simple packet.

She'd nearly reached the exit when she realized she hadn't yet delivered the bid and backtracked to the city clerk's office.

"This is the bid from Palmer Construction," she

told the frizzy-haired young woman at the desk inside the office. "You'll notice I'm submitting it a full two hours before the deadline."

"I did notice that," said the woman, her smile turning to a puzzled frown.

"You should make a note of it," Lorelei said and went back the way she'd come.

Take that, Grady. And Wade, too, for that matter. He'd doubted she could help put his girls to bed. As though that took a rocket scientist, which she could become if she wanted.

She had the strength of will to get anything she wanted. That's why she'd come to city hall this morning in the first place.

She'd left Wade alone for more than twenty-four hours, which should be plenty of time for him to build up a craving for her. She certainly had one for him.

Darn the man for being late. She'd managed to get to work before ten. Why hadn't he?

She rounded the corner, her eyes downcast as she indulged in atypical brooding. The *thud-thud-thud* of rapid footsteps caused her to lift her chin.

Wade Morrison almost plowed straight into her. He put out an arm to steady her and her bad mood evaporated. Just like that.

Her shoulder was the only body part that he touched. But that was a start.

"Lorelei," he said in obvious surprise. "What are you doing here?"

Cute didn't begin to describe how he looked. True, his navy blue pants and unimaginative powder-blue shirt were pretty awful. And, yes, his shirt tail wasn't all the way tucked in. Not to mention his boring navy tie was askew and his hair had that just-out-of-bed quality. But she'd developed a thing for the rumpled look.

"I dropped off a bid, but only because I wanted an excuse to run into you," she said, smoothing her palms over his surprisingly wide shoulders. "Since we almost kissed, you're all I think about."

He blinked rapidly a few times, then quickly looked around. "Stop that, Lorelei. Anybody could walk by and see us."

He sounded flustered, which was so cute Lorelei could hardly stand it. A muscle jumped in his jaw, and she saw he had a faint smear of something blue there. She wet her thumb and rubbed it off.

"You're right," she told him, drawing back and snagging his hand. "We need someplace more private."

She spied a closed door. Pushing it open with one hand, she tugged on Wade's hand with the other. Within seconds, they were alone.

Wade cleared his throat. "This is the ladies' room."

"I know that, silly. Is there a better place to do something you don't want anyone else to see?"

She came flush against him, stood on tiptoes and tilted back her head only to get a view of his chin. Having none of that, she reached up to loop her arms around his neck and pull his head down.

She sensed resistance in every muscle. She kissed his lips anyway, only to find them tightly closed.

Ah, a challenge.

She was up to it, wrapping her arms around his

neck so that the softness of her body plastered against the hardness of his. She pressed open-mouthed kisses the length of his full mouth, thinking his lips were almost sinfully soft.

Long seconds passed before he groaned in the back of his throat and opened his mouth to give her tongue entrance. One hand held her head and the other cupped her bottom as he drew her closer and took over the kiss.

Bliss. That's what he tasted like underneath the minty tang of his toothpaste. She figured she better get used to the taste. He was so anal he'd probably slip out of bed to brush his teeth before morning sex.

She wouldn't mind as long as she was the woman in his bed. She'd have sex with him anytime, anywhere, under any circumstances. She rubbed her pelvis against his erection, wishing they were both naked.

One of his hands found her breast and liquid heat spread low in her stomach. "Let's do it," she said against his mouth. "Right now. Right here."

He raised his head, tearing his mouth away from hers so it was out of reach. Lines of strain bracketed his mouth. Beneath his fogged glasses, she thought his eyes were closed.

"I can't."

Sensuously she rubbed her body against him. "Why not?"

"Because . . ." His voice cracked and he started again. "Because I have a certain reputation to uphold. Because anybody could walk in on us."

"Nobody's going to walk in on us," Lorelei declared an instant before the door swung open.

Wade quickly sprang away from her, managing to

put space between them before a tall, big-boned woman strode into the bathroom with an almost regal air. They'd never been introduced but Lorelei immediately recognized Mayor Honoria Black.

"Hey, mayor," she said, strategically placing herself in front of the tenting of Wade's pants. "What's happening?"

Lorelei might have been invisible for all the attention the mayor paid her.

"Wade?" Her tone was sharp. "What are you doing in the ladies' room?"

"I, uh . . ."

He stammered like the good, rule-abiding man he was, too much of a goody-two-shoes to think on his feet.

"There was a palmetto bug in here," Lorelei interjected. "This man was kind enough to kill it for me."

Honoria Black's eyes narrowed. "I don't see a palmetto bug."

"Not now you don't," Lorelei said. "But you couldn't have missed it before. I'm surprised you didn't hear me scream when I spotted it. It was as big as a mouse, almost too monstrous to flush down the toilet."

"That's strange considering we have the building regularly sprayed."

Lorelei made her eyes go wide. "Then maybe you should think about switching exterminators."

"Maybe you should, mayor," Wade added weakly, then executed a sort of bow. "Now if you'll excuse me, I really should be . . . somewhere else."

After he left the ladies' room, Lorelei smiled dazzlingly at the mayor, then followed Wade into the hallway. She caught up to him in about ten steps. He didn't look at her, but kept on walking.

"So I was wrong," Lorelei said. "How was I supposed to know somebody would come into the ladies' room?"

"It's a public restroom, Lorelei, not a bedroom," he said through gritted teeth.

"Don't tell me you're angry," Lorelei said.

"Oh, no. I like getting caught necking in the restroom by my boss."

"She doesn't know we were necking. She thinks you were in there executing palmetto bugs."

"Like that was a believable story," he said.

"So what if it wasn't?"

He let out a short, disbelieving snort. "That was the mayor. She has the power to fire me."

"She can't fire you if she didn't see anything. Thanks to my smudge-proof lipstick, you don't even have any evidence on your face."

He shook his head and finally stopped walking. They were alone in the hall, which seemed cavernous.

"You don't get it. I'm a father. I have responsibilities. I have a reputation to uphold. I can't be ducking inside restrooms to neck with twenty-one-year-olds."

Lorelei's temper spiked. "My age isn't the issue."

"It might not be if you acted it."

Because his words held some truth, Lorelei's temper deflated. "Okay, maybe I asked for that. But look at it from my point of view. If you'd see me after hours, I wouldn't have to come around here during the day."

He blew out a breath, and she sensed he was weakening.

"See me tonight, Wade," she pleaded. "Please."

"I can't. I'm taking the girls out of town for the weekend to visit their grandparents in Tallahassee."

"Are you leaving tonight?"

"Tomorrow morning," he said, but it sounded like a reluctant admission. "But don't ask. Because I can't see you tonight, either."

"Why not?"

"Mary Kate and Ashley, for starters. Even if I wanted to take you out, I couldn't get a babysitter. Nobody who's ever babysat for them will do it again. You saw what happened with the last one."

"M.K. and Ash aren't bad kids. They're just mischievous," Lorelei said.

"Tell that to the director of their preschool," Wade muttered, "but I have a feeling she won't listen."

The sigh in his voice and the tight line of his lips alerted Lorelei that wasn't an idle comment. "What do you mean by that, Wade? Are the girls having problems at preschool?"

His sigh was audible. "That's why I'm late. I'd barely dropped them off this morning when I got a call on my cell phone from the assistant director. They'd gotten into the finger paints and were painting the other kids."

"That's what the blue spot on your jaw was," Lorelei commented.

"I drove back over there and helped her clean up but she wasn't happy. The director wasn't in today but her assistant called her and I have an appointment Monday morning. I think she's going to kick them out."

"Screw her, then." Lorelei felt compelled to restate her objection when she read disapproval on his face. "I mean, who needs her?"

"I do. If she tells me they can't come back, I'll be in one heck of a child-care bind."

"Then fight her." Lorelei put her hands on her hips. "She can't treat a pair of three-year-olds like juvenile delinquents."

Wade rubbed his forehead. "Unfortunately, she can. This wouldn't be the first preschool that has kicked them out."

"But M.K. and Ash are wonderful little girls."

He smiled at her with a tenderness she felt clean through to the center of her being. "I happen to agree, but we seem to hold the minority opinion."

"Then we'll convince them to see things our way," Lorelei said, gaining steam as her conviction took hold. "No way will we let some preschool big shot diss M.K. and Ash."

"Wait a minute," Wade said. "What do you mean by 'we'?"

"You and me," she said with heat. "When you meet with the director Monday morning, I'm coming with you."

Chapter Twenty-five

Grady fed another quarter into the parking meter outside the downtown Seahaven pub where he and Tori had eaten overstuffed roast beef sandwiches and washed them down with ale.

Tori nodded at a nearby sign stating the hours of enforcement for the meters as between nine A.M. and six P.M.

"Do you really think a cop would have ticketed you in the next ten minutes?" she asked when he rejoined her.

"No." He slung an arm around her shoulders and drew her delicious warmth against his body. "But it wouldn't be right not to pay."

"Good answer," she said, and he grinned at her.

She'd been asking him questions all night, not the multiple-choice variety like she had at the carnival, but every other kind imaginable.

"Do you always do the right thing?" she asked as he steered her toward the center of town.

"I try to," he said.

"You never told me whether you recycled everything or just glass and newspapers," she said, referring to a conversation she'd tried to start at dinner.

"You never told me why you dropped by city hall yesterday," he said as casually as he could, voicing the question that had been nagging at him for days.

Her eyebrows rose. "You heard about that?"

"I heard you had a meeting with the mayor."

"It wasn't a meeting," Tori said readily. "It was an interview. I thought she had a job opening, but it turned out she'd already filled the position."

He felt his body relax and realized he'd been holding himself rigid as he waited for her reply. Just as he'd hoped, she had a logical explanation. It seemed even more plausible because he knew she'd been searching for a job.

"It's just as well," he said. "You don't want to work at city hall anyway."

"I don't? Why not?"

He wanted to tell her about the whole sordid mess and his role in trying to clean it up, but he couldn't. Not with the FBI warning him they needed his complete secrecy.

"It's just not a good place to be," he said evasively, then nodded at their surroundings. "Now downtown Seahaven, that's a different story."

With architectural accents like dormer windows and steep rooftops on buildings that had been around for a hundred years, downtown Seahaven quietly seeped into the soul.

Crosswalk pavers and beautiful redwood park benches graced the street, improvements that the previous administration had approved. A red-and-white pole, reminiscent of bygone days, marked the front of an old-fashioned barbershop. A bakery window emblazoned with white cursive letters proclaimed the place BAKED TREASURES.

The restaurants and bars along the quiet streets seemed full but not packed, with traffic steady but not heavy.

"Did you know that I'd only been in Seahaven once before I moved here?" Tori asked. "My family drove through town when I was a little girl, but years later I still remembered it. My parents, though, they don't understand the allure."

"Did anyone besides your parents object to the move?" he asked, trying to sound casual.

"What do you mean?"

"That was a clumsy way of asking if you left some man behind."

"Yeah, I did. My former fiancé," she said matter-of-factly. "But he wasn't crushed about me leaving, if that's what you're asking."

He found he didn't like the notion of Tori engaged, but reminded himself she'd closed that chapter of her life. "What happened?"

"Nothing, really. That was the problem. Sumner—that's his name—is a nice guy. But there was no spark in our relationship. We started going out and drifted

227

along on inertia. But I didn't want to live the rest of my life in Sarasota being supported by a guy I liked but didn't love."

She grew silent, then asked. "How about you? Has there been any special woman in your life?"

"Not really. The women I date always seem to want something from me." He hadn't meant to state his conviction so baldly, but something about Tori inspired confidences.

"Do you think I want something from you?" she asked, her eyes serious, her mouth a troubled line.

He decided to make a joke of it. "Considering I'm planning to take you back to my place later, I sure hope so."

As he'd intended, she laughed. They passed a median graced with colorful impatiens, rounded a corner, and saw a line of patrons about twenty-deep waiting to get inside a redbrick building that housed the Seahaven movie theater.

"It looks like something out of the past," she commented.

"It's supposed to. The theater closed in the 1950s but two brothers reopened it earlier this year. They can't compete with first-run films, so they show classic stuff."

"Each month has a theme, right?"

"Uh-huh. Last month was films directed by Hitchcock. This month, it's classic Westerns."

She made a face, not sure she liked the sound of that, and squinted so she could make out the movie title on the marquee.

"*Stagecoach,*" she read. "Never heard of it."

"You never heard of the John Ford movie that launched John Wayne to stardom? Wayne is the Ringo Kid, one of the people on a stagecoach traveling in Indian territory. But that's all I'm going to say, because I don't want to ruin it for you."

"Oh, my gosh," she said and stopped walking. "You're a Western fan."

He shifted uncomfortably. "I wouldn't say that."

"You just gave the director, star, and plot line of a movie I never heard of. Admit it, you're a fan."

"Maybe a little," he said.

She clapped her hands. "I just figured out why Lorelei calls you Duke. It's because you like John Wayne."

"What's your point?"

"This is priceless," Tori said. "The point is that you are such a fraud, Grady Palmer. You're not nearly as cynical as you pretend to be. Nobody who likes Westerns is."

"How do you figure?"

"A Western is the ultimate morality play," she said. "The good guys always win. I took a film class in college and the professor theorized that's the secret to their popularity. They validate our sense of right and wrong."

"I don't know about that," he muttered, but without much conviction.

She smiled, thinking she had him figured out.

They took their place in line behind a handsome couple who looked to be in their fifties. The man was tall, with dark hair graying at the temples and a face that looked familiar. Almost as tall as the man, the attractive, fair-haired woman was his perfect foil.

The man nodded at Grady without smiling. "Palmer."

"Richardson," Grady replied, and Tori knew who the man was. She'd seen his face on campaign flyers.

"You're Forest Richardson," she said, more of a statement than a question.

"Why, yes, he is," the woman said, clearly pleased that Tori had recognized him. "And I'm Betty Richardson, his wife and unofficial campaign manager, telling you to be sure to vote for him in November."

"You don't need to say that to everyone we meet, Betty," her husband told her in a slightly embarrassed voice.

"There's nothing wrong with broadcasting that my husband is the best choice for mayor," Betty Richardson said.

"I agree," Tori said, finding the woman's devotion to her husband touching. "If you don't believe it, nobody will."

"Not everybody does believe it," Forest Richardson said obliquely, but it wasn't difficult to tell he referred to Grady.

"You do realize that Honoria Black will ruin our city with her prodevelopment stance?" Betty Richardson directed her question at Grady. "If she has her way, Seahaven will be like any other coastal city. Charmless. The little things we enjoy, like this movie theater, will be no more."

She made sense, Tori thought. Not for the first time,

she wondered why Grady supported Honoria Black. Tori's initial admiration for the mayor had given way to doubt that Honoria Black was the right person to guide Seahaven.

She couldn't imagine Mayor Black in downtown Seahaven, enjoying the simple charms of the city.

"Tell me something, Mr. Richardson, do you like Westerns?" Tori asked, after Grady had formally introduced her to the couple.

"Love 'em. It's the only place where the good guys always win," he said before it was his turn to pay for his tickets. After he did, he nodded at them. "Palmer. Nice meeting you, Miss Whitley."

A few minutes later, Tori and Grady took their seats in the small theater a few rows behind the Richardsons. The screen was huge, easily half again as large as the ones in standard movie theaters.

"I take it you and Forest Richardson aren't friends," Tori remarked after they were settled in their seats.

"We're barely acquaintances, but I run into him now and again," Grady said. "He knows I support Honoria."

"I liked him," Tori said.

"Of course you did," Grady replied. "He's running for mayor. He puts on his best face in public."

"I didn't think it was an act," she said. "I thought he seemed like a genuinely good guy."

"There is no such thing."

"You're forgetting that I'm on to you, Duke. You don't believe that any more than I do."

The previews came on, preventing further conversation, but she couldn't concentrate on the screen. Why couldn't Grady see that Forest Richardson and not Honoria Black had the good of Seahaven at heart?

Could it be because the almighty buck was more vital to him than the good of the city? Was making a profit so important that he'd pay for the privilege? Is that what he'd been doing on that pier with Larry Schlichter?

He put his arm around her, drawing her close. She breathed in his now-familiar scent and snuggled against him. Again her doubts receded as she settled back to watch John Wayne do the right thing.

Later, after they'd gotten back to his apartment, she excused herself, went into his bathroom, and shut the door. She sat on the closed toilet seat and took her disco ball from her purse.

"Don't fail me now," she whispered to the ball. "I need to know if I should trust him."

She turned the ball over and read, *My sources say split.*

She frowned.

"Can I trust him?" she asked more directly.

It's a bad scene, the ball replied.

Again, she shook the ball.

Whatever turns you on.

That was more like it, she thought, slipping the key-chain back into her purse. Grady turned her on.

She emerged from the bathroom and crossed the apartment until she stood only inches from him.

"Is everything all right?" he asked, concern for her showing in his blue eyes. "You were in there for a while."

"Everything's fine now," she said and kissed him.

He kissed her back, exactly the way she liked to be kissed. With wonder, passion, and barely restrained desire. The doubts fled from her again, carried away on a tide of intense emotion.

Much later, she lay wide awake in bed, listening to the soft sounds he made while he slept.

Other than Grady's closet love for Westerns, she hadn't uncovered any evidence today that proved she should trust him. But she would. She did.

Because she wanted to.

Chapter Twenty-six

Tori straightened from behind the counter, where she'd been stocking bottles of Lazenby foundation and moisturizer, and got a jolt.

Sky blue eyes outlined by navy blue liner gazed at her from not more than a foot away. Their bottle-blond owner rested both her elbows on the glass countertop, her dainty chin balanced on top of her hands.

"Hey, Tori," she said gaily, straightening to her full height, which was well shy of Tori's. "Remember me?"

"Of course I do," Tori said. "You're Grady's sister, Lorelei. You're the one who keeps telling me I have the power."

"Right." She looked pleased that Tori had remembered not only their meeting but their telephone conversation when she'd left a message at the office for Grady. "I'm glad that power thing is working out for one of us."

"How do you know it is?"

"Because you were with Grady last night."

"He told you about it?"

Lorelei laughed. "No. On the way back from the clubs last night, I was going to stop and talk to him about something. I changed my mind when I saw you going into his place."

"So he didn't tell you that we, uh, you know?"

"Slept together? Nope. You're the one who told me that. Just now, in fact."

Tori felt her face color.

"Don't be embarrassed," Lorelei said, laughing. "I'm glad you and my brother are getting it on."

"Me, too," Tori admitted. "Did you come here to talk about him?"

"Hell, no. I came because Grady said you were good with makeup." Hers was slathered on thick, hiding her pretty face. "Do you think you could make me look, oh, older? You know, so he can't dismiss me as some kid who doesn't know what she wants."

"So who can't dismiss you?"

Lorelei pressed her lips together, as though she'd said too much. But then she ran a hand through her blond hair and answered, "Wade Morrison, that's who."

"The tax assessor?"

"I know he wants me, Tori, but every time we start to get busy, he brings up the age thing. As though he's old enough to be my father or something, which he definitely is not. I want him to take me seriously."

"And you think new makeup will make that happen?"

"It's worth a try."

Tori tilted her head this way and that, critically examining Lorelei's fair coloring and fine bone structure, absently noting that she and Grady didn't resemble each other much at all.

"You'd look even prettier with different makeup, but I won't promise older." Tori tapped a finger against the side of her mouth. "Have you thought about coloring your hair?"

"I already do."

"I meant darker, not lighter," Tori said. "Society in general takes brunettes more seriously than blondes. When was the last time you heard a dumb brunette joke?"

"I can't say that I have," Lorelei said slowly.

"You'll want to wear your skirts a lot longer, too." Tori read panic in Lorelei's expression as she gazed down at her short, red micro-miniskirt. "When a woman's built like you, men tend to pay more attention to her body than her brain.

"Along those same lines," she continued before Lorelei could object, "have you thought about breast-reduction surgery?"

Both of Lorelei's hands flew protectively to her chest. "You can't be serious . . . ," she began, then her eyes cleared and she dropped her hands. "You aren't serious. You're trying to make a point."

"Did I succeed?"

"Only if you wanted me to realize that changing my appearance wouldn't accomplish anything but making me miserable."

"That about sums it up," Tori said. "This is only

my opinion, but a man who won't take you seriously solely because of the way you look isn't worth the trouble."

Lorelei nibbled on her lower lip and looked thoughtful. "I might have given Wade other reasons not to take me seriously."

"Then you have to change the way you act," Tori said.

"You could be on to something," Lorelei said, regarding her with new gravity. "Now I understand why my brother's head over heels. Thank you."

"You're welcome." Tori expected Lorelei to be on her way, but instead the other woman gave Tori a sheepish look.

"Do you really think I'd look prettier with different makeup?"

Tori nodded. "I really do. You tend to wear warm shades while cool shades would suit your fair coloring better."

"I want you to understand first of all that I wholeheartedly agree with what you said about appearances not being everything."

"Okay."

"But do you think you could do my makeup?" she asked with a little grimace. "I'm fighting the good fight here, and, hey, prettier can't hurt."

Tori laughed. "I sure can."

Fifteen minutes later, Tori used the powder on a contour brush to blend the edges of the pink-based blush line on Lorelei's cheeks.

"Remember when I said I didn't come here to talk about Grady?" Lorelei asked. "I changed my mind."

Tori put down the contour brush and picked up a small jar of eye-shadow primer. "Oh," she said vaguely. She liked Lorelei, but wasn't yet ready to publicly examine the details of her relationship with Grady.

"I need you to do me a favor, which in effect will be doing him a favor."

"Close your eyes," Tori ordered, and went to work applying the primer. When she finished, she used a fluff brush to apply a neutral base color to the entire eye area. "What do you need me to do?"

"Grady's birthday is next week, and my parents made reservations at Giovanni's. Do you know it?"

"The Italian restaurant on Main and Third." Tori added a medium neutral color in the crease of Lorelei's eyes and extended it up the brow bones. "It's one of my favorites."

"Ours, too," Lorelei said. "I need you to get Grady there at about seven on Tuesday."

Tori chose a smoky gray eye shadow and applied it over the medium neutral base. "No problem. But it's not much of a favor. I think it's sweet that your parents are trying to surprise him."

"That's the thing," Lorelei said. "It's not a surprise party."

Tori lined Lorelei's upper lids beginning at the outer corner of the eye and working toward the inner corner. Then she lined the lower lids, avoiding the lower inner lid so her eyes wouldn't look smaller. "I don't understand."

"My parents think Grady knows about it. He wouldn't return my mother's call after she phoned to invite him, so I called her back for him. I sort of told her he'd be there."

Tori remembered the way the woman at the carnival had insisted that Grady call his parents. And the way he'd deflected Tori's questions afterward.

"Is something wrong between Grady and your parents?"

"Something's very wrong, and it's eating me up inside," Lorelei said. "Grady and me, we've always had a great relationship with them. And now this. The worst part is nobody will tell me what it's about."

"And you think getting Grady and your parents together on his birthday will make things better?"

"They can't get worse. He won't even talk to them."

Tori grew silent as she brushed mascara on Lorelei's upper and lower lashes with a much lighter touch than Lorelei herself used. "I'll mention it but I can't promise he'll come when he finds out your parents will be there."

"Oh, but you can't tell him." Lorelei's eyes were pleading when she opened them. "If you do, I know for a fact he'll refuse to come."

Tori shook her head. "I don't know if keeping it a secret is the right thing to do, Lorelei."

"Of course it is. It's not right that there's this rift between them. Mom and Dad are ready to make up. Getting Grady to where they are could be all it takes."

Tori hesitated, wishing Grady had confided in her about his troubles with his parents so she could make a more informed decision.

"Please," Lorelei pleaded. "It's been almost a month. I don't know what else to do."

"He might be angry."

"Then he'll be angry at me, not you. I'll take the blame if things go wrong."

Tori put down the eye makeup brush and ran her hand through her hair. She simply couldn't make a decision this important without help.

"Could you excuse me for a minute?" she asked. Lorelei looked puzzled, but nodded.

Tori retrieved her purse from behind the makeup counter and reached inside for the miniature disco ball. She stood behind the counter, angling her body so that her back was to Lorelei.

"Should I bring Grady to the dinner?" she whispered to the disco ball, then shook.

"What's that?" a voice behind her asked.

Tori jumped, dropping her key chain in the process. Lorelei bent over, picked it up, and examined it.

"Cool," she said. "It's like a Magic 8 Ball, right? Here, let me ask if you should help me."

Lorelei gave the disco ball an enthusiastic shake, peered at the answer, and grinned. "Would you look at that. It says *Yes, definitely*."

The disco ball never answered in such bland terms, which meant Lorelei wasn't telling the truth. It also showed that she'd go to great lengths to see her brother reunited with her parents.

Tori made an instant decision. "If it means that much to you, I'll do it."

Lorelei threw her arms around Tori. "Thank you.

241

Thank you. It'll mean a lot to Grady and Mom and Dad, too. Just you watch."

"You're welcome," Tori said, still not sure she'd made the right decision. She took a step back. She'd yet to comb Lorelei's lashes, but the softer colors she'd used on the other woman already looked fantastic.

"Wade Morrison won't stand a chance when he sees you."

Lorelei grinned. "That's the idea."

Chapter Twenty-seven

Wade trudged up the sidewalk leading to the Wee Care Day Care Center, feeling more alone than he ever had in his life.

He'd read the writing on the paint-splattered chalkboard last week after Mary Kate and Ashley had gotten through with it.

Expelled, it said.

He fully expected that the director of the day-care center had already made her decision. This meeting was merely a formality.

He'd need to stay home with the girls until he figured out another arrangement.

This weekend while he was visiting his parents, who lived in a retirement community in his home town of Tallahassee, he'd briefly considered asking his mother to stay with him in Seahaven until he ironed out the problem.

He'd changed his mind when he noticed that his father, who was twenty years her senior, didn't get around as well as he used to. His arthritis had flared up, he needed surgery to correct cataracts, and his doctor had warned him to watch his weight.

Wade concluded that Dad needed Mom more than he and the girls did.

What the girls needed, he thought, was a woman who loved them without reservation.

Mary Kate and Ashley's mother didn't qualify. Oh, she loved them. But her patience wore thin after a few hours in their presence.

Asking her to care for the girls until he made other arrangements was not an option. On the rare occasions she exercised her visitation rights, she returned the twins well before the agreed-upon time.

Unfortunately Wade had exhausted his annual sick time on doctors' appointments, tummy aches, and sore throats.

He sighed. Even if it meant taking unpaid leave, he'd make it work out. He always did.

So why did he feel so alone today? He refused to attribute it to Lorelei Palmer's absence. For an instant there at city hall, when she'd offered to go to the meeting with him, his burden had seemed lighter. But she was so young and flighty he hadn't truly believed she'd show up.

The screech of brakes stopped him before he could enter the center. A red sports car with the top down and a blonde behind the wheel pulled into an empty space in the parking lot.

Lorelei got out of the car, waving and rushing toward him on her ridiculously high heels, her blond hair billowing behind her, her tight skirt preventing her from taking long steps.

His burden, incredibly, seemed to lighten.

"Sorry I'm late," she said. "Grady gives me such a hard time about leaving work that I had to wait to sneak out until he wasn't around."

She finger combed her hair, smacked her lips together, and smoothed her skirt. "How do I look?"

He'd thought Lorelei a beauty the instant he laid eyes on her, but today she looked positively gorgeous.

"Beautiful," he said before it occurred to him that he shouldn't encourage her.

She beamed, making him forget that encouraging her was a bad idea. "Really? Then I guess it was worth it."

"What was worth it?"

"Never mind about that. Let me take a look at you." She stood in front of him and gave him the critical once-over. "You'd look better out of those clothes than you do in them but you're probably hitting the right note for a meeting at a day-care center."

"I thought so," he said dryly, trying not to let on that he was amused.

"Your hair's falling into your face." Her fingers felt cool and smooth against his forehead when she reached up to smooth back his hair, making him wonder how they'd feel on other parts of his body.

His hair fell forward the moment she stopped touching it. "It always does that," he told her.

"Now if I could only get your hair to fall into my face," she said, her eyes twinkling. His body heated, not a good thing considering their destination.

"Lorelei," he began.

"I know that now is not the time," she interrupted, hooking her arm through his. "I know this is important, and I'm as ready as you are. Day-care gestapo, here we come."

"They might get uptight if you refer to them as the gestapo," he whispered to her as they entered the building together.

"Yeah, well, remember we're the good guys here. And we'll go to war if they dare try to toss M.K. and Ash out."

Wade mentally grimaced, wondering why he hadn't recognized the danger of bringing Lorelei with him before now. She was as unpredictable as the next card dealt in a game of five-card stud. Who knew what would come out of her mouth next?

A young woman with her hair in a long braid sat behind a bright yellow counter that effectively blocked passage to the rest of the center.

Beyond the counter, walls adorned with cutouts of rainbows, teddy bears, and cartoon characters led to classrooms of students who were divided depending upon their age.

"We're here to fight for the rights of children too young to stick up for themselves," Lorelei announced to the woman, whom Wade recognized as a part-time worker who helped out during the mornings.

The baffled woman looked to Wade for help.

"Good morning, Amy," he said. "I have an appointment with Donna Trent. This is Lorelei Palmer. She's with me."

"Of course," Amy said, her brow clearing. "Donna

said I should send you right in when you got here. She's in her office."

She nodded toward the office adjacent to the counter. The door was ajar but Wade rapped on it anyway, getting a portent of doom when an unsmiling Donna Trent gazed up at them.

The woman's warmth, which could light up her round face, had been one of the factors that helped Wade decide upon the center. She didn't have any of that warmth on display now.

"Come in and have a seat, Mr. Morrison," she said, flicking a glance at Lorelei. "And who are you?"

Lorelei stepped boldly into the office. "I'm Lorelei Palmer."

"She's a family friend," Wade said. "Feel free to say whatever you need to in front of her."

"I'm afraid it isn't good news," the director said, removing her reading glasses and carefully setting them on her desk. "Ashley and Mary Kate have been quite the handful lately."

"Well, of course they are," Lorelei declared. "They're three years old."

Donna Trent blew air from her nose. "Perhaps I didn't state that strongly enough. The twins have become a disruption."

"In what way?" Wade asked, although he feared he already knew. He'd heard the stories often enough from babysitters.

"You know about the finger-paint incident, of course," she said. "Lately Mary Kate has been throwing food at the other children at snack time. Ashley has been disrupting naps by skipping around the room

247

while singing jingles from commercials. I could go on but you probably get the idea."

"What would you like me to do about it?" Wade asked.

She tented her fingers and frowned. "I'm afraid it's too late for that. I hate to do this, but unfortunately I have to let Mary Kate and Ashley go."

Even though he'd expected as much, Wade felt himself deflate. He got ready to mount an argument against expulsion but Lorelei beat him to it.

"No," Lorelei said in a loud, clear voice.

"Excuse me?" Ms. Trent had delivered the bad news to him but now focused on Lorelei.

"No, you can't kick them out of day care," she said. "That's not acceptable."

Mrs. Trent's chin rose. "I'm the director of Wee Care. I decide what is acceptable."

"Then you need to revise your thinking. If you care as much as the name of the center says you do, you'll find another solution," Lorelei said with a full head of steam that made it impossible for anyone to interrupt. "It's unacceptable and unfeeling to kick M.K. and Ash out of your center just because they want attention."

Wade expected Mrs. Trent to lash back at Lorelei, but instead she looked thoughtful. "That's what you think the problem is? That they're trying to get attention?"

"Not just anybody's attention. Wade's attention," Lorelei said. "I've been thinking about this, and it's my theory that they believe on some level that he'll come to the center and take them home if they act up."

"That makes sense," Mrs. Trent said thoughtfully, "especially in light of their home situation."

Wade looked blankly from one woman to the other, feeling as though they spoke another language. "I don't understand."

"Didn't you say that your ex-wife has very little involvement with the children?" Mrs. Trent asked, and Wade nodded. "Ms. Palmer could be right. The twins could be dealing with abandonment issues, which manifest themselves as feelings of insecurity."

"So acting up is their way of making sure I return for them," he said, thinking that could explain the problems he'd had with babysitters.

"Exactly," Mrs. Trent said. "But that doesn't solve the problem of their disruptive behavior."

"Maybe it does," Lorelei interjected. "What if Wade stops in at the center on his lunch hour for a few weeks? That could be all the reassurance the girls need."

"It's a thought," Mrs. Trent said, picking up a pen and pointing it at him. "In the meantime, Mr. Morrison, you can reassure the girls by word and deed that you're always there for them."

"So they can stay." Lorelei made it a statement rather than a question.

"They can stay," Mrs. Trent agreed, "but it'll have to be on a wait-and-see basis. I have to consider the welfare of the other children in this center, too."

"I understand," Wade said, getting to his feet before she changed her mind. He reached across the desk and shook her hand. "Now that I have a handle on what the problem might be, I can deal with it."

After they checked in on the twins, who readily abandoned their bright-colored building blocks and launched themselves at their father, Wade walked Lorelei to her car.

"They seemed relieved when I told them I'd stop back at lunchtime," he remarked.

"See," Lorelei said smugly. "I told you so."

"But how did you figure that out?" he asked, shielding his glasses from the bright morning sun.

"Takes one to know one, I guess."

"What do you mean by that?"

She shrugged, a seemingly casual gesture that he knew wasn't. "You know my brother Grady, right? He was a model child. Good grades, good athlete, good behavior. He's eight years older than me but by the time I was in grade school I already knew I'd never stack up. So I got attention my own way."

"You acted up," he finished.

"I still do," she said before she stood on tiptoes, hooked her arms around his neck, and kissed him full on the mouth with a heat that rivaled that of the morning sun.

Then she winked at him and got in her car.

She had his undivided attention, but she hadn't needed to kiss him to get it. The meeting this morning had proved there was much about her to like and admire.

"Lorelei," he said before she could drive away. She gazed at him, and he met her eyes. "Thanks."

She blew him a dramatic kiss.

"For you, anything, anytime," she said, her eyes

gleaming. Before she drove away, she called, "Don't make me hunt you down, Wade Morrison. Call me and let me make good on my promise."

This time, he knew he would call.

Chapter Twenty-eight

Grady kept Tori's hand firmly in his when they got out of the SUV to walk the short two blocks to Giovanni's.

Although he'd rather have stayed in, with ready access to his bed or hers, he'd been open to her suggestion that they eat at the Italian restaurant.

"Can I ask you something, Duke?"

"You can ask me anything as long as you stop calling me Duke," he said pleasantly, although the nickname didn't bother him as much as it used to.

He liked old Westerns where the good guys came out on top. If Tori thought that made him a closet Pollyanna, so be it.

"But I like the nickname," she said, wrinkling up her nose. "It makes you seem like less of a curmudgeon."

"I'm not a curmudgeon."

"Only 'cause I won't let you be."

"What's the question?"

"Do you think the end justifies the means?"

He nearly stopped walking. Was this the prelude to a confession? Had he gotten it wrong after all when he'd gone with his heart and trusted her?

"Why do you ask?" he ventured. "What did you do?"

She looked guilty, telling him he was on the right path. "I know it's your birthday today," she confessed. "That's why I wanted us to go out."

He'd meant to ignore his birthday this year, considering the circumstances, but found he couldn't get annoyed.

"Lorelei told you," he guessed.

She nodded.

"So that's why we're going to Giovanni's."

She nodded again.

"I wish you'd told me before but I think it's nice that you want to take me out to dinner," he said as they reached the restaurant.

He opened the door and waited for her to precede him through it.

"That's only part of it," she said, sounding miserable.

"Then you can tell me the rest after dinner." He smiled at the vibrant, dark-haired woman in red who stood at the hostess stand and told her, "We have reservations for two under 'Whitley.' "

"Actually, the reservation's under 'Palmer,' " Tori corrected. "And it's for more than two."

The hairs at the back of Grady's neck stood at attention when the hostess checked something off in her book. She smiled pleasantly and gathered cheerful-looking red-and-white menus. "Right this way," she said.

"Would you give us a minute?" he asked the hostess before she could leave her stand.

She nodded her agreement and he took Tori's elbow, steering her into the empty waiting area at the entrance to the restaurant. "Who are we having dinner with?"

"If I tell you, you might not stay," Tori said.

"If you don't tell me, I'll definitely leave."

"Lorelei's here, and I'm pretty sure she brought her boyfriend and his twin girls."

"What boyfriend?"

"Wade Morrison. They've been seeing each other."

"What? But I told her to stay away from him. I told her he was bad news."

"She's all grown up now," Tori said. "She didn't listen."

"She damn well will listen to me," Grady said, turning to head back into the heart of the restaurant. Tori's hand on his arm detained him, reminding him of where they were.

He sighed. "I know. Now is neither the place nor the time."

"Now definitely isn't the time, but that's not it," Tori said. "Lorelei, Wade and his girls aren't the only people who came to celebrate your birthday. Your parents are here, too."

The news that his parents waited at the table took a temporary backseat to another, even harsher realization. Now he knew what she meant about the end justifying the means.

"You lied to me," he said. Again, he thought.

"I didn't lie. I just didn't tell you everything."

"A lie by omission is still a lie," he said.

"I meant well," she said quietly. "Lorelei did, too. She's sick about this rift with your parents and thought getting you together might help mend it."

"Lorelei doesn't know what she's talking about."

"That's because you won't tell her," Tori said. "She wants to help. For that matter, so do I. But neither of us can do anything if we don't know what's going on."

He nodded toward the exit of the restaurant. The corners of her mouth dipped in obvious disappointment but she preceded him outside, waiting beside the front of the restaurant for him to join her.

He indicated she should sit down at a wooden bench a storefront away and joined her when she did so.

"About a month ago, I needed a copy of my birth certificate," he said, trying to keep his voice flat. "Nobody was home at my parents' house so I let myself in with my key and went into Dad's office, thinking I might be able to find it myself. Instead I found my adoption papers."

Wade saw understanding dawn in Tori's eyes.

"Your parents never told you that you were adopted," she said. "They shouldn't have kept that from you."

"Damn right they shouldn't have. I turn twenty-nine today. You would have thought that sometime in the past twenty-nine years they would have mentioned it."

"That's why you're upset," she said.

"You'd be upset, too, if your entire life was a lie. All this time I thought they were my parents, and they're not."

Tori shook her head. "That's not true. They're your parents in every way that matters."

"Then why didn't they tell me the truth?"

"Have you discussed this with them?"

He shook his head vehemently. "I couldn't trust anything they told me. I can't stand being lied to. You know that."

"Sometimes people lie for the right reasons," she said softly. "Maybe they thought it would be best for you not to know."

"It wasn't," he said harshly.

"Okay, so they were wrong. But did it occur to you that they lied because they didn't want to lose your love?"

"You can't know that."

"Lorelei tells me that your mother cries over you. She wouldn't do that if she didn't care."

He raised his eyes skyward, for the first time taking into account how his estrangement from his parents might have affected them. He'd been so angry he hadn't considered they'd be hurt.

"It tears me up when my mother cries," he confessed.

"Then dry her tears, Grady," Tori said.

"You're saying I should forgive them?"

"That's what loving somebody's all about. Everybody makes mistakes. By punishing them for theirs, you're also hurting yourself."

He rubbed a hand over his face. "I've let it go on so long I'm not sure I can just walk back in that restaurant and let it end."

She reached for his hand, folding it in her smaller, softer one. He didn't know why that made him feel better, but it did. "You won't be alone," she said. "I'll be with you."

He nodded and, together, they stood.

Somehow, knowing she'd be at his side made all the difference.

"Are you okay?" Wade asked Lorelei later that night after they'd finally settled the girls in their side-by-side twin beds. "It's not every day you find out your brother was adopted."

Lorelei leaned her head back against the cushion of his sofa and turned to answer him. Not only had Grady and her parents taken a huge step toward mending their relationship at dinner, but they'd also broken their silence.

"It's wild," she said. "I love him every bit as much as I always did, but it explains a lot of things. Like his brown hair. His athleticism. The fact he's the only one in the family taller than five feet eight."

"I guess it'll take some getting used to," Wade said, smoothing the hair back from her face.

"I'll say. Grady still doesn't seem used to it."

"That's understandable. Most people find out they're adopted when they're kids," Wade said. "I can see why your brother felt betrayed."

"Me, too. But I think everything will be okay now," Lorelei said, knowing she spoke the truth. "Grady won't be able to hold a grudge. He pretends to be cynical, but inside where it matters he's a softie."

"Really?"

"Oh, yeah. The reason he's so tough on people is that he expects a lot from them. He has a highly developed sense of what's right and wrong."

"Then why is he doing so much business with the city?" Wade muttered, almost to himself.

"Excuse me?" she said.

"Nothing. I'm just trying to piece things together."

"He doesn't like me dating you," she confided, stroking his lean cheek to soften her words. "He warned me against you at the mayor's party. He said you weren't a good man."

"Is that so?"

"He must have got his wires crossed, because I know you are," she said, then kissed him shortly and sweetly on the lips. "For proof, all you have to do is look at how you are with M.K. and Ash."

"I haven't done a very good job there. I didn't realize their misbehavior was a cry for attention. I needed you to tell me that."

"You do, you know," Lorelei said.

"What?"

"Need me," she said. She removed his glasses and kissed him again, this time long, slow, and hot. She rubbed sensuously against him. "You not only need me sexually, you need me in your life. M.K. and Ash do, too. It's about time you admitted it."

"I admit it," he said, staring at her intently. She wondered if it was because he couldn't see clearly or because he finally did.

"You're not only saying that because you want sex, are you?"

He shook his head. "I meant I want you in my life, Lorelei."

"That's what I want, too," she said softly.

He got up and extended his right hand. She took it, letting him pull her to her feet. "That doesn't mean I don't want sex, too."

She laughed. "I thought we couldn't make love with the girls in the house."

"The girls are deep sleepers, and there's a lock on my bedroom door," he said.

She pretended to think about it, but really, what was there to think about? She wanted this man. She even believed she loved him, although she'd be quiet about that. She couldn't risk sending him into hiding once again.

"Okay, I'll make love to you," she said, as though it had been his idea all along, "but I'll leave before the girls get up in the morning. It wouldn't be right for them to see me."

"Since when did you get to be so responsible?" he asked, drawing her close.

"Since I met you," she said, and preceded to spend the next few hours showing him exactly how exciting her new responsible self could be.

Chapter Twenty-nine

Tori watched in fascination as her friend Crystal dug into her Chocolate Seduction with undisguised relish.

"Mmmmm," Crystal said when she'd barely finished chewing the piece of chocolate-glazed, double-fudge cake. "The food here is to die for. I can't believe I never heard of this place before."

Neither had Tori until Grady pointed it out on the way back from the carnival. Tucked between a barbershop and a dry cleaner in an obscure strip shopping center, the restaurant gave new meaning to the term "out-of-the-way."

Crystal took another bite of cake and demolished it as quickly as the last.

"This cake alone was worth the hassle I had to go through to get a night out. Not that being waited on and spending time with you isn't enough. But this . . . this is better than sex."

"I doubt that," Tori said before she could stop herself.

Crystal raised her fork in the air. "Girlfriend, do tell. I can't believe we got through dinner without you mentioning you had a man."

Tori could believe it. Crystal had been at her entertaining best talking about her not-yet-potty-trained sons, her husband's quest to become a stand-up comic, and the cast of characters at the Roseate Spoonbill.

"It's kind of new," Tori said.

"Oh, my gosh," Crystal exclaimed. "Is this the multiple-choice guy from the other night? Did he pass the question about the position of the toilet seat?"

"He passed every question, even the one about cats."

"You don't mean he actually likes your homely little rat-cat?"

"Better. My landlady wouldn't let me keep Gordo, so Grady took her. She's living with him now."

"There's only one explanation for that," Crystal said, shaking her head. "He has it bad for you, girl."

"Maybe not as bad as I have it for him," Tori confided. "I think I'm in love."

"So where is Loverboy now?"

Tori got ready to reiterate what Grady had told her about working late, but the words never reached her mouth.

Because Grady, looking tall and handsome in a cream-colored shirt and brown slacks that accentuated his coloring, walked into the restaurant.

"There," Tori breathed.

"Excuse me. What did that mean? Are you paying attention? What are you looking at anyway?" Crystal's back was to the front door and she twisted in her seat.

"Turn around," Tori said, fastening a hand on her friend's arm. "I don't want him to see me."

Crystal threw her free hand up in the air. "Who?"

"Grady," Tori said as she watched him say something to the hostess and glance over the sea of diners. She quickly picked up a menu that was still on the table, opened it, and hid behind it, à la the mysterious Ms. M the first time they'd met.

She peeked over the top of the menu and watched Grady thread his way to a back table with a sense of purpose. He didn't look her way once.

Crystal's index finger appeared at the top of the menu, pushing it down so Tori's face was once again out in the open.

"I take it that hunk who just walked in here is Loverboy and he told you he'd be somewhere else tonight?"

"He said he'd be working."

"Then go over there and give him a piece of your mind for lying to you," Crystal declared.

Tori shook her head, trying to ignore her breaking heart. A girlfriend would be in her rights to confront him. A private eye wouldn't. She technically still worked for Ms. M, which meant she should have checked Grady's story about working late instead of taking it as gospel.

"I can't do that. I need to know who he's meeting," Tori said. Tables stretched the length of the long, thin restaurant. Grady sat somewhere behind her, at a table she couldn't see. "Can you tell who he's with, Crystal?"

"If it's a woman, I'll go over there and slug him for you," Crystal said, craning her neck to do as Tori asked. She frowned. "It's a man. He's middle-aged. I'd guess early forties. Dyed black hair. Lots of gel."

The description sounded familiar, but Tori couldn't mentally match it with anyone she knew. "Can you see what they're doing?"

"Talking, it seems like. No, wait a minute. That lying hunk you're dating just took something out of his pocket. It looks like . . . an envelope. He's giving it to the hair-gel guy."

Tori's heart seemed to stop beating. It sounded like a classic bribe. The city council meeting that would determine which construction company got the contract to build the community center was tomorrow night.

Everything inside Tori rebelled at the notion of Grady paying off city officials to win the contract. There had to be another explanation.

"What's happening now?" she asked Crystal.

"Hair-gel guy's getting up. And coming this way. Quick, the menu," Crystal said, then hid her face behind it. Tori didn't turn. She didn't need to because the man Grady had met would come into view within seconds.

She offered up a silent prayer. *Please don't let it be*

someone from city hall. Then she waited for the man to pass their table.

"Why am I hiding behind this menu?" Crystal asked a few seconds after he passed. "If I don't know that man, he certainly doesn't know me."

Her words hardly registered because the man had all of Tori's attention. His slacks were different, but she recognized his black silk shirt as the one he'd worn at the mayor's party. She still had the business card he'd given her somewhere at home.

Hair-gel guy was Ned Weimer, the mayor's chief of staff.

Grady wiped his damp palms on his slacks, ignoring the cup of coffee he'd ordered from the waitress.

His stomach churned, making the thought of drinking anything, even a glass of water, seem impossible.

The exchange with Ned Weimer had gone as well as could be hoped, but it had still left him feeling dirty.

Now that Tori was in his life, he wanted more than ever for the city hall investigation, and his part in it, to be over.

Taking into account that he had the mayor's chief of staff on tape accepting a bribe, he could see a light at the end of the tunnel. But he couldn't help thinking the light signaled a train coming.

Thrusting the negative thought aside, as Tori would no doubt advise, he took a bill from his wallet and threw it on the table.

It had been a full five minutes since Weimer had left, plenty of time for the other man to have cleared out.

He rose, intending to walk out of the restaurant as quickly as he'd come into it, but the back of a woman's head stopped him. Her hair was an unusual shade of rich auburn, and she wore it loose around her shoulders. The same way Tori did.

His heart pounding, he approached the table. The freckled redhead sitting across from the woman with the auburn hair stared daggers at him, but she wasn't the one who mattered.

"Tori," he ventured, hoping he was mistaken.

The woman turned and he found himself staring at his lover. The lover he never should have trusted. Especially after he'd discovered the tête-à-tête she'd had with the mayor at city hall.

"Are you following me?" he asked in an accusing voice.

"Following you? We were through eating dinner before you got here." The redhead answered for Tori, who looked as though she'd been struck.

Grady knew with instant clarity that Tori had seen him with Weimer and pieced two and two together. Judging by her expression, she'd come up with an answer of five.

"What are you doing here anyway when you said you'd be working?" the redhead continued when neither he nor Tori spoke.

At the woman's raised voice, other diners turned to stare. Not good. Grady bent at the waist, imploring Tori in a soft voice, "Can I talk to you in private? Outside the restaurant?"

"Don't go with him, Tor," her friend advised. "A

man like him probably knows how to sweet-talk a woman."

Tori hesitated.

"Please," Grady added.

Tori nodded once, then laid a hand on the other woman's arm before she could erupt. "I need to do this, Crystal. It'll only take a few minutes."

The restaurant was not only small but full, making the parking lot the only place they could hold a private conversation.

Grady thought of a half-dozen openings but discarded them all, not wanting to tip his hand if he were mistaken about the conclusions she'd reached.

He'd parked near the front of the lot, not far from where they stopped. Before he could begin talking, he heard a frantic scratching on his car window. It was Gordo, who'd clearly recognized Tori.

Figuring he needed all the help he could get, he opened the door and picked up the little cat, who practically crawled over him to get to Tori.

"She cries if I leave her alone too long," he confided.

"If you're trying to soften me up, it's not working," Tori said as she cradled the cat against her chest. "Because that's the last time I'll trust a cat as a judge of character."

"Excuse me?"

"So you like cats? So what? It could be an act."

"It's not an act," he denied.

Her lower lip trembled when she gazed at him, but her eyes turned granite hard. "I know you paid Ned Weimer a bribe."

Damn, he thought, how was he supposed to refute what was essentially the truth?

He could tell her about his part in Operation City-gate, but that would be laying it all on the line. He'd have to trust her implicitly, with no more room for doubt.

"Don't worry. I won't turn you in," she said, sounding infinitely sad. "But I can't continue seeing you, either."

"Why not?" he asked, needing to know.

"Because you're not the man I thought you were," she said, handing over Gordo, who started to cry. When she reached out to touch his cheek, the hardness had gone out of her eyes. Now they just looked miserable. "Good-bye, Grady."

"Wait," he said before she could walk out of his life. "I can explain."

"Nothing you say will make a difference," she said, backing up a step.

"Please, wait. I can't talk freely until I shut this off." He pulled his cell phone from his breast pocket and turned it off. "There. Now I'll explain everything."

She stopped retreating. "Why did you have to turn off your cell phone before you could talk?"

He took a deep breath, then plunged ahead. "Because I don't want it to record what I have to say."

"Your cell phone's a recorder?"

"Not the cell phone itself, but the battery inside," he corrected, then indicated the pager clipped to his belt. "That's a microphone."

While she digested the information, he gently took her by the shoulders, gazed deeply into her eyes, and trusted.

"I am the man you think I am," he said. "But I'm also part of an FBI sting operation to clean up city hall."

Tori sat next to Grady on a sofa in her apartment, with Gordo asleep on her lap, hardly able to digest the story he'd been telling her for the past thirty minutes.

After his declaration in the parking lot, she'd gone back inside the restaurant and told a concerned and protesting Crystal she'd catch a ride back to town with Grady.

He'd told her a little in the car, but saved the bulk of the story for when they were alone—with only Gordo to overhear—in her apartment.

"So you won't really go to any lengths to secure a contract?" she asked while stroking the little cat.

"Far from it," he said. "Larger contracts mean more staff and bigger responsibilities. Palmer Construction started as a small family business, and I'm happy to keep it that way."

"And you don't really wholeheartedly support Mayor Black and her progrowth movement?"

"On the contrary, I'm planning to vote for Forest Richardson if it gets that far. Now that we have the mayor's chief of staff on tape accepting a bribe, I'm kind of hoping the queen will fall."

"This is incredible," she said. "Like something out of a movie. You know what this makes you? A hero."

He quickly shook his head. "I'm far from a hero. I'm just an ordinary guy trying to do the right thing."

She picked up Gordo from her lap, set the cat down on the other side of the sofa, and turned toward Grady. She took his face in her hands and gazed into his eyes.

"Don't ever let anyone say you're ordinary," she said, pressing a light kiss to his soft lips. "It takes an extraordinary person to do what you've done."

"Then you'll forgive me for lying to you?" he asked with a rueful grin. "I didn't want to but I had no choice. I couldn't tell you everything until I trusted you."

She froze as the meaning of his words penetrated the haze she'd been navigating since his confession earlier that evening.

He'd trusted her with a secret that federal agents had warned him not to share, a secret that could spell grave consequences if it got out to the wrong people, and yet she continued to deceive him.

She had to make her own confession, had to tell him that she'd been hired to spy on him. She'd do it while protecting her client's identity, not that she knew who Ms. M was.

"Tori?" Concern touched the blue of Grady's eyes. "Is something wrong?"

"There's something I need to tell you," she said, the words escaping in a husky purr.

"I have something to tell you first, but I want you to know I've never said this to any other woman. Except, of course, Lorelei and my mother." He laughed a little. "And would you believe it? I'm not even nervous.

Do you know why? Because it's so right. You're so right."

"But—"

"Shhhh." He touched two fingers to her lips, and his hard features softened. "Let me finish. I love you, Tori Whitley."

Tears spilled from her eyes.

He deserved the truth but she couldn't bear to ruin this beautiful moment. Her motives for lying were not nearly as altruistic as his had been.

How could she make him understand that he meant more to her than any investigation when, in fact, she still worked for the client?

The bottom line was that she couldn't tell him, not until she resigned and returned the money she hadn't spent. In time, she'd give it all back.

"Tori," he said, tenderly touching the spot on her cheek where tears streamed. "Why are you crying?"

Touched by his concern, she smiled at him through her tears, vowing that she'd make it up to him. Tomorrow.

"I'm crying because I'm happy," she said, which was at least partially true. "And because I love you, too."

A sudden rush of emotion came over his face, so bright it had to be joy. He took her into his arms and kissed her, the heat and beauty of the moment banishing all thoughts from Tori's head except one.

After she informed Ms. M and Eddie that she was off the case, she'd tell Grady everything.

Tomorrow.

Chapter Thirty

The sensation of delicate fingertips dancing over the skin of his bare chest tugged at Grady, trying to pull him from a sated sleep.

He smiled without opening his eyes, which still felt heavy with fatigue from how little sleep he and Tori had gotten the night before.

They'd had much better things to do.

The fingertips tickled his skin, dragging him the rest of the way from sleep. He wouldn't mind being awakened this way every morning for the rest of his life.

"Meow."

His eyes popped open to find a pair of slitted blue cat eyes staring back at him. Gordo's eyes. Tiny paws, instead of enchanted fingertips, perched on his chest.

"No offense, but I was expecting someone else," he said, lifting Gordo and setting her down on Tori's side of the bed.

But Tori was gone.

Momentary panic gripped him, then vanished when he got a whiff of pancakes cooking. Blueberry, if he wasn't mistaken.

Tori was making breakfast.

For a moment, he'd feared that she'd bolted. Crazy, considering they'd had great sex the night before in her bed, but he couldn't help thinking the concern was legitimate.

Beneath the thick veil of happiness, something had been bothering her last night. Something she hadn't felt comfortable sharing with him.

It's always daylight before the dark, he thought, but thrust the thought from his mind.

That was the old Grady. The new one believed in miracles. Tori had told him she loved him, hadn't she?

He checked the time on the alarm clock. Eight o'clock. Later than he usually got to the office, but he'd arrive earlier than most of his employees if he made it in by nine.

He sat up in bed and stretched, aware of the cat's eyes on him.

"So you think I should put some clothes on before I go into the kitchen? It ever occur to you that modesty can be a sin instead of a virtue?"

The cat continued to stare.

"All right, already," he said, reaching to the floor for the boxer shorts and pants he'd discarded last night.

His hand encountered something else under the lip of the bed. A paperback book. Curious, he picked it up.

The cover was red with the black silhouette of a

man in a trench coat, a bowler hat on his head, a cigar dangling from his lips. The title of the book was *So, You Want to Be a PI*.

Everything inside him went cold.

He'd believed Tori to be a private investigator in the early days of their relationship, but he'd slowly discarded the notion as he got to know her. Could he have been wrong?

He placed the book on her nightstand, cautioning himself against jumping to conclusions.

Tori could be reading the book for pleasure. PIs and the way they operated interested plenty of people. Stories about them riddled the fiction shelves at bookstores, not to mention the television screen.

He slowly pulled on his underwear and pants and shrugged into his shirt. All the time the book stayed in his line of vision, taunting him.

He wanted to trust Tori, but a little voice nagged at him: The sweeter is the wine, the sharper is the berry.

He shut out the voice. Everything happening at city hall had made him paranoid. Tori didn't investigate cases. She did makeup.

Resolutely ignoring the book, he went into the kitchen. Dressed in nothing but an oversized T-shirt that reached the top of her thighs, Tori stood with her back to him. Her long legs were bare, making him remember how they'd wrapped around him the night before when she'd moaned his name. She flipped over a bubbling hot pancake with a spatula.

"Oh, rats," she said and held up the spatula. Part of

the pancake dripped from it, and he couldn't help but laugh.

"It's not funny," she said, sending him a woeful look over her shoulder. "I wanted to make you a nice breakfast, but I can't cook any better than I can do most things."

He circled her waist from behind, drawing her close so he could drop a kiss in her hair. "On the contrary, you do some things very well."

She laughed and swatted away his wandering hand. "If you distract me any more, we'll have charred pancake pieces for breakfast instead of just pancake pieces."

A few minutes later, he sat across the breakfast table from her chewing on some truly awful pancakes. She glanced up at him between bites, smiling as though she were truly happy.

Nah, he thought when the book crept once more into his subconscious. She couldn't be a PI hired to unearth his secrets. She loved him. He could see it in her eyes, feel it in her touch. But the skeptic inside him couldn't leave it alone.

"Tori, that stuff I told you last night about what I'm doing for the FBI, nobody else can know about it," he said.

She nodded but didn't reply, which could well have been because her mouth was full of hard-to-swallow pancakes.

"Indictments are set to come out soon, and nothing can get in the way," he continued. "I've been jumping at shadows lately, which was why I was so suspicious of you when we first met. I thought somebody at city hall hired you to follow me."

He watched her carefully for a reaction, but her face remained blank.

"Why would they do that?" she asked.

"To find out if I'm as corrupt as I seem. People in government positions sometimes get paranoid about bribing the wrong people. Bribe an honest man, and it could spell trouble. Especially if that honest man has the FBI's ear, like I do."

Something that looked like alarm leaped into her eyes but it vanished so quickly he thought he might have imagined it. Talk about being paranoid. He was the paranoid one.

"I understand," she said.

Not *You can count on me to keep quiet.* Or *Of course nobody hired me to follow you.* Just *I understand.*

It became obvious after a moment that she didn't intend to expand on her reply. Having somehow managed to finish the pancakes, he put down his fork and pushed his chair back from the table.

"I'd love to stay, but I've got to get home and take a shower before Gordo and me can go into the office," he said.

He picked up the cat, wondering if he imagined the sudden tension in the room. But he sensed that anxiety in the kiss she gave him at the door. He identified warmth and affection, too, causing him to doubt his perceptions. She could have been holding herself rigidly because she feared crushing Gordo.

Cursing his suspicious nature, he headed for his car. Her voice stopped him before he reached it. "Grady, wait!"

He turned, dreading what she might tell him.

Still wearing only the nightshirt with her feet bare, Tori rushed to catch up to him. Her full breasts bounced slightly as she ran, calling attention to her braless state.

He glanced around. Some of her neighbors, getting into their cars to leave for work, stared. An older man with a mustache took his glasses from his breast pocket and put them on, the better to see the show.

Uncaring if the man saw *him* in a state of undress, Grady unbuttoned his shirt and draped it over her shoulders, pulling the lapels closed. The sun wasn't yet hot enough to scorch but it felt warm on his shoulders as he looked down at her pinched features.

He was right. Something was wrong.

"You must have something important to tell me if you came out here dressed like this," he said, keeping his voice light. "What is it?"

"Grady, I—" She stopped.

His muscles tensed. Fearing the worst, he prompted, "What?"

Her mouth worked but no sound escaped. Her heart seemed to be in her eyes. She closed them, opened them again, and finally spoke. "I just wanted to tell you that I love you," she said softly.

"I love you, too," he said.

That was the truth. He did love her. But he was no longer sure that he trusted her.

* * *

Tori stood in the parking lot watching Grady drive away. Gordo had climbed onto his lap and had her pint-sized paws pressed against the window. She stared out at Tori in what looked like sympathy.

"Did you have that cat in your apartment all night?" Mrs. Grumley suddenly appeared at her side, her hands on her hips as she sent Tori her best glare. "And why are you dressed like that? I could have you arrested for public indecency."

"Try it, and I'll find out who owns this building and tell them how you harass the tenants," Tori snapped, surprising herself as much as she had Mrs. Grumley.

She gingerly walked back to her apartment, conscious of the rapidly heating pavement under her bare feet. The retreat fell short in the dignity department, but it couldn't be helped.

She didn't have time to worry about the cantankerous landlady, not with her mind filled with the things Grady had told her.

Back inside her apartment, she stood in the middle of her living room, worrying that snooping into Grady's affairs had put him into terrible jeopardy.

His belief that somebody at city hall might be having him investigated was not only rational but possible. That somebody could even be Ms. M.

What did Tori know about the other woman except that she had an exquisite sense of style and understood how to wear makeup?

Last night Tori had silently vowed to resign from the case at the first opportunity, but she couldn't quit until she determined that Ms. M meant Grady no harm.

To do that, she needed to uncover the identity of her

mysterious client. As usual, she didn't have a clue how to proceed. But Eddie would.

She prayed it wasn't too late to set things right.

Whether her cousin liked it or not, he was going to help her.

Chapter Thirty-one

Tori didn't creep when she entered the darkened bedroom. Why bother with the sun already high in the sky and the day approaching the noon hour?

Sunlight streamed through an opening in one of the slitted miniblinds, casting enough light for her to make out the sleeping man in the bed. He lay on his back, snoring gently with his mouth open.

She approached with her weapon and raised it before letting it hover momentarily above his face. Then she lowered it, wiggling her wrist back and forth as she did so.

The snore turned into a sneeze, and his hands flailed in the air, swatting at the weapon as he came instantly awake.

"I'd say good morning, Eddie, if it weren't nearly noon," Tori said.

"Tori?" Her cousin sounded confused. "What are you doing here?"

"Waking you up with a feather duster," she said, examining the object curiously. "Although I can't imagine why a self-avowed slob like you needs a feather duster."

"I dust with it, okay?" Eddie said grumpily. "I don't mind clutter but I don't like dust."

"I don't like being kept in the dark." Tori moved to the windows and opened the blinds so the Florida sun streamed in.

Eddie winced and shielded his eyes. "Hell, Tori," he said. "Did you have to do that?"

She pinpointed the exact second he realized his chest was bare by the frantic speed at which he pulled the covers to his chin. "Could you give a guy a break? I'm naked here."

"It's your fault I'm here. You weren't in the office, and you didn't answer your phones."

"I turned them off so I could get some shut-eye," Eddie said, rubbing a hand over his unshaven jaw. "I was on stakeout last night."

"Poor you," she said without sympathy.

"How'd you get in anyway?" Eddie asked, then brightened slightly. "Hey, you must be getting the hang of things if you broke in without me hearing you."

"Your spare key was under your doormat," she said. "Shouldn't you know better as a private investigator?"

"What is this? Give-Eddie-a-hard-time day?" Eddie asked. "What do I have to do to get you to scram?"

"Tell me who Ms. M is."

Eddie shook his head. "We've already had this conversation. How the hell am I supposed to know who she is? She wouldn't tell me."

"Why didn't you demand to know?"

"I already told you. She's paying us a lot of money."

"But don't PIs have standards?"

He made a *b-rap* sound with his lips. "Just 'cause I can't bother with all those rules doesn't mean I don't have standards. Hell, you're not even legit."

"What do you mean?"

"You don't have a PI license so I should have registered you as my intern, but who has time for that?"

"You should have made time."

"I hired you to save time, cuz."

"But by cutting corners, you could have put Grady in danger. What if our client wants to hurt him?"

"So that's what this is all about." His eyes narrowed. "You've got a thing for the subject. I thought as much that night we followed him."

"I'm not up for a lecture from you, Eddie," Tori said tightly. "Just answer the question."

"About Ms. M wanting to hurt the subject? Aw, come on. You've seen her. She's an old lady, well preserved but still an old lady."

"There's more than one way to harm somebody," Tori said. "I want to know who she is and what her motives are."

"Like I said, I don't know," Eddie said.

Flattery, Tori figured, could get her somewhere. "A private investigator as good as you must have ways of finding out."

"Of course I have ways."

"Then tell me what they are."

Eddie sighed. "If I tell you how I'd go about finding out, will you promise to go away and leave me alone?"

"I promise," Tori said readily.

"Tell her you won't give her any information until you have her real name and motive for investigating him," Eddie said. "That's it. Good-bye."

"But that's too simple," Tori said. "Don't I need to follow her or have her license plate run or—"

"You've been watching too many movies, Tor. Sometimes the simplest way is the best. Set up a meeting and ask her."

Tori waited impatiently on a park bench between the monkey bars and a man-made lake.

Ms. M had been agreeable to meeting but had insisted upon picking the place. She'd specified not only the county park, but an exact location within the park.

"You don't need me to tell you that details are important when you're on a case, Jane," she'd said.

Tori wished Ms. M would have anticipated the tiny detail that the bench she'd chosen was in full sun. With the temperature hovering near eighty, Tori would have roasted if she hadn't chosen a summery ensemble of a blue-jean miniskirt, sandals, and a short-sleeved cotton shirt.

It seemed everybody in the park had dressed for warm weather—one leggy little girl even wore a bathing suit—except the woman striding across the grassy open area straight for the bench.

Her outfit consisted of a black blouse, black pants, and oversized black sunglasses. The high heels of her black shoes sank into the earth as she walked.

Who on earth would dress like that to come to a park? Tori thought an instant before she recognized the woman.

Ah, of course. Ms. M.

"Isn't this the perfect place for a clandestine meeting?" Ms. M asked in a stage whisper when she reached her. "Who's going to pay attention to two women meeting in a park?"

Oblivious to the stares she still attracted, she sat down on the bench and angled her body toward Tori's. "Fill me in. I've been dying to find out what you have for me."

Would she use that information to ruin Grady? Tori didn't think so but she couldn't take the chance.

"That's why I wanted to meet," Tori said. "I can't tell you anything until I know who you are and why you wanted Grady investigated."

"Impossible." Ms. M swept the air with the flat of her hand. "That's not how the deal works."

"You had the deal with Eddie, not with me," Tori said. "I won't take the chance that you're conspiring against Grady."

"I love intrigue and conspiracy as much as the next woman, Jane," Ms. M said, "but what are you talking about?"

"Let me rephrase. How do I know you don't intend to use what I've found out about Grady against him?"

Tori couldn't read the expression in Ms. M's eyes because of the dark glasses, but she did see the other woman's mouth twist. "Why would I do that?"

"You tell me," Tori said. "It would help if I knew why you wanted him investigated."

"I already told you. I need to find out if he's a good man," Ms. M said evasively.

"But what you actually want is for him to be a

bad man, isn't it? Then you'll use his goodness against him."

"I'm not following you."

"Yet you were perfectly willing to hire me to follow him," Tori said. "I can't let you harm Grady, Ms. M."

"Harm him! I have no intention of harming him. And why do you keep calling him Grady? Aren't you PIs supposed to refer to the people you have under investigation as 'subjects'?"

"That's not the point," Tori said.

"Oh, yes it is. I think I've figured it out. I knew you'd made contact with the subject, but I didn't realize it was close contact." Ms. M slipped off her sunglasses and looked Tori straight in the eyes. Hers were the exact color of Grady's, Tori realized. "You've fallen in love with him, haven't you?"

Tori glanced away, not wanting Ms. M to read the truth on her face. "How I feel about Grady is immaterial."

"I wouldn't say that," Ms. M said thoughtfully. "I hired you to investigate the subject's character. I doubt you'd have fallen in love with him if he weren't a good man."

Tori panicked. Grady had warned her that corrupt Seahaven officials trusted him only because they thought he was dishonest. "I didn't say that. Maybe he's a bad man."

"Nonsense," Ms. M said. "I sensed when we first met that you were as good a judge of character as I am. So you've already given me the essential piece of information I sought."

"If you use it to hurt him," Tori said with clenched teeth, "I'll hunt you down."

"Such dramatics." She put a hand to her breast, then lowered her voice. "All right. To put your mind at ease, I'll tell you what you want to know. My name is Margo Lazenby."

Her last name struck an immediate chord. The jars of makeup and beauty supplies Tori sold every weekend, not to mention the ones she used daily, had *Lazenby* written in bold script across the front of them.

The popularity of the company's line of cosmetics was so great that Lazenby had recently branched into perfume. Frasier's department store had gotten the new scent in last week. The perfume was called Margo, after the founder and CEO of the company.

"Margo" started with *M,* thus the nickname "Ms. M."

"As in the cosmetics company?" Tori asked, then continued before she could answer. "That's why you asked what brand of makeup I used. You have a vested interest in Lazenby products."

"Shhhh." Ms. M put a finger to her lips, looking worriedly around. "We must never, ever use real names. You must continue to call me Ms. M, but you are right. And believe me, I've had my people working on improving our line of eye makeup. My goal is to get you and others like you to switch over from Revlon."

"But I don't understand," Tori began.

"If one of my company's products needs improvement, I'm determined to see it improves," she declared.

287

Darlene Gardner

"Not about the makeup," Tori clarified. "I don't understand about Grady. Why did you want him investigated?"

"If I tell you, I'll expect a report on your findings by the close of business tomorrow."

"You'll have it along with my resignation," Tori said, silently vowing to protect Grady by leaving out his role in Operation Citygate. If indictments were imminent, Ms. M would have the whole story soon enough anyway. "I can't continue to lie to him."

"Fair enough. I wanted to know what kind of person Grady Palmer is because . . ." Ms. M paused, exhibiting her flair for the dramatic. ". . . he's my grandson."

Chapter Thirty-two

Betrayal weighed down on Grady like a lead overcoat as he watched the woman who'd met with Tori get into her gold Mercedes and drive away from the park.

With gently wrinkled skin and flawlessly styled hair that spoke of a life of privilege, the woman looked to be no older than sixty. Her figure was superb for a woman of her age but oddly clad all in black.

Something about the cast of her features seemed familiar, although Grady was quite sure he had never seen her before in his life.

He knew her name, though: Margo Lazenby.

His FBI contact had gotten it through DMV records minutes after Grady called in the license-plate number of her expensive, highly polished car. But Margo Lazenby's wasn't the only name the agent had turned up in the past few hours.

The other belonged to Eddie Sassenbury, a licensed

private investigator who lived in a cookie-cutter house in an affordable section of Boca Raton.

Tori had led him to both Lazenby and Sassenbury.

The knowledge that he'd been right about Tori felt like a sword to his soul. He almost wished he could go back to that morning, before he'd spotted the paperback on the floor near her bed. Then surely his hunch that she was hiding something wouldn't have turned into a compulsion to follow her.

Being right, he thought, was vastly overrated.

Making himself move, he got out of the car. He could see Tori in the distance, still sitting on the park bench where she'd met with Margo Lazenby. Her right hand was on her forehead, her eyes downcast.

She looked up when he got within about twenty feet. Even from that distance, he read shock and guilt so vivid it could have been written on her face in red marker.

"Grady, what are you doing here?" she asked, getting to her feet. Her light-yellow shirt and casual skirt made her look like the picture of innocence, but he knew better.

"You're the private eye, you tell me," he said roughly. Her face went pale, but he couldn't let that sway him. "Don't bother to deny it. I know you're working for Eddie Sassenbury."

Her eyes appeared haunted when they met his. "You followed me."

"Just returning the favor."

"But why?"

"Does the title *So, You Want to Be a PI* ring any bells?"

"I can explain," she said, sounding almost desperate. "Eddie's my cousin. He's the private investigator, not me. He was shorthanded and talked me into helping him. It was never supposed to go this far."

"It was unlucky for me that it did."

She swallowed, grimacing as though in pain. "I deserved that."

"You deserve a hell of a lot worse," he bit out. "Tell me what your assignment was."

She blinked, looked away at the shimmering lake in the distance and then back at him.

"I was supposed to find out as much about you as I could," she finally said. "Eddie said I should do some research, then follow you around and write down my impressions. He made it sound simple but then you confronted me and it got complicated."

The knowledge that he'd been nothing more than an assignment to Tori burned the pit of his stomach. His impulse was to walk away from her and try to never look back, but he couldn't leave until he had more information.

"I need to know how much you told Margo Lazenby," he said, hardening his features so she wouldn't see the hurt beneath the surface.

"You know who she is?"

"I know she's the CEO of Lazenby Cosmetics and that she wants to build her new headquarters in Seahaven," he said. "That won't happen without zoning changes, which gives her a vested interest in Honoria Black being re-elected mayor."

"You've got it wrong," she said. "Mrs. Lazenby didn't hire Sassenbury Investigations because of

Honoria. She hired us to find out about you because . . ."

She didn't finish her sentence, which fueled his anger. "What's the matter?" he asked harshly. "Run out of lies?"

"I wasn't going to lie," she shot back. "I just wasn't sure I should tell you."

"Tell me what?" he demanded.

"That Margo Lazenby is your grandmother," she retorted.

His heart clutched. But even through the shock of the revelation, he knew in his gut that it was the truth. Margo Lazenby's features had seemed familiar because he saw a masculine version of them every day when he looked in the mirror.

"Even if that's true," he said through the thickness in his throat, "that doesn't mean she has my best interests at heart."

"Didn't you hear what I just said? She's your grandmother!"

"So what? She could still be mixed up in the corruption at city hall. Thanks to you, she's probably telling everybody about the sting operation now."

"You think I told her about your part in that?" She was a good enough actress that she sounded incredulous.

"Didn't you?"

"No! I asked her to meet so I could let her know I wasn't going to tell her anything."

"You expect me to believe that?"

"It's the truth. After what you said this morning, I needed to find out why she wanted you investigated."

"Like you didn't already know."

"I didn't," she said. "My cousin Eddie never asked. He just took her money and assigned me the case. I'm not blameless. I should have refused to help, but I didn't know enough about private investigation to realize we should have had her reasons up front. Please, Grady. You've got to believe I'd never do anything to hurt you."

He felt as though hands were around his neck, squeezing the hope from him, so he could hardly muster the will to form words. "And here I thought you were paid to follow me and compile information for a client."

She bit her lip, unable to deny it.

"Just tell me this, Tori, was sleeping with me part of the assignment?"

"I slept with you because I fell in love with you!" she cried, grabbing the front of his shirt. "I know I should have told you about the investigation before now, but that's the truth."

"You sure as hell should have told me before last night."

"I was going to," she said. "But then everything was so perfect that I didn't want to ruin it. So I made up my mind to resign from the case first. But I couldn't do that until I made sure I hadn't put you in danger."

"Now why am I having such a hard time believing that?"

"I'll tell you why," she said as tears streamed down her face. "Because you're protecting yourself from getting hurt. You want so badly for the world to be a place where the good guys prevail that you're afraid to believe in anything. You won't see with your heart. You only use your eyes."

"So now you're a psychologist," he said contemptuously, prying her fingers from the front of his shirt. "You don't have any right to psychoanalyze me, not after what you did."

"I'm starting to think the worst thing I did was fall in love with a man as intractable as you."

"You just keep right on lying, don't you? The next thing I know, you'll be telling me it's not your fault because chronic lying is a disease."

"That's a terrible thing to say."

"I'm not feeling very charitable." He crossed his arms over his chest to keep the ache at bay. "I get that way when I find out the woman I thought I loved has betrayed me."

"Are you saying you don't love me anymore?"

The sun blazed down on her, throwing her tear-streaked face into stark focus. The tortured emotion stamped on her features looked genuine, but he'd already fallen for her act once. He didn't intend to be taken for a fool a second time.

He started to confirm that he no longer loved her but found he couldn't be as hypocritical as she was.

"I'm saying that I never want to see you again," he said, and walked out of her life, resolutely trying to ignore the ache in his chest.

Chapter Thirty-three

Fifteen minutes after the Seahaven City Council convened for its bimonthly meeting, Grady entered the building that served as the center of operations for Lazenby Cosmetics.

Photos of beautiful models wearing Lazenby products adorned the walls. *Wear our products,* their gorgeous smiling faces seemed to say, *and you'll look this way, too.*

Grady determinedly thrust aside the thought that Tori was more beautiful than any of them and focused on his surroundings.

One word—LAZENBY—was bolded, scrawled on the front wood panel of the reception desk. Behind it sat a receptionist with shockingly short black hair, who was as stunning as any of the models in the photos. She looked up expectantly.

"Grady Palmer to see Margo Lazenby," he announced.

She examined a pad in front of her, then gave him a bland smile. "I'm sorry, Mr. Palmer, but Mrs. Lazenby doesn't see anyone without an appointment."

At the receptionist's cool, polite professionalism, Grady's estimation of Margo Lazenby raised a notch. She knew enough to let a beautiful woman be the first thing visitors to Lazenby Cosmetics saw, but she'd made sure that woman had a brain.

"I respect that," he said, "but could you please let her know that I'm here anyway."

"Certainly, sir," she said.

Grady waited while she called upstairs. She nodded as she listened to what was being said on the other end of the line, hung up, and smiled at Grady once more.

"If you'll wait by the elevator, Mr. Palmer, Mrs. Lazenby's assistant will be down shortly to escort you upstairs."

He waited, which is what his contact at the FBI had wanted him to do before he contacted Margo Lazenby. Grady had postponed the confrontation, but only until after the council meeting had started.

He understood that the FBI's case would be seriously weakened if the Seahaven City Council didn't award Palmer Construction the contract to build the community center. But it was too late now for Margo Lazenby to alert city officials to choose another company.

Of course, if Tori had passed on the information about Operation Citygate, the FBI's case could already be sunk. He swallowed hard at the thought, not wanting to believe she'd betrayed him but unable to give her the benefit of the doubt.

Whatever happened, Grady's role in the sting operation was finally coming to an end. The government had failed to gather any evidence incriminating Honoria Black, but the FBI planned to ask the grand jury for indictments tomorrow.

The elevator door slid open, revealing a man who looked like he'd been spit polished. His hair was black and as shiny as his pointed black dress shoes. Although it was just past five o'clock, his thin, angular face was devoid of even the hint of a shadow. His double-breasted suit, which was obviously expensive, engulfed his thin body.

"I'm Quincy Franklin, assistant to Mrs. Lazenby," he said in a nasal voice more irritating than chalk on a blackboard. "Aunt Margo has entrusted me to see you upstairs, but then she entrusts me with many things."

He kept his skinny index finger pressed on the elevator button as Grady entered the car, surreptitiously checking his reflection in the mirrored paneling.

The elevator had barely risen from the first floor when he presented first the right side of his profile and then the left. "What do you think?"

Grady backed up a step. "Think of what?"

"My makeup. I'm trying to convince Aunt Margo to market cosmetics specifically for men. We could call the line either Lazenby for Men or, better yet, La*men*by. Get it?"

Grady made a noncommittal noise.

"I told Aunt Margo that more men wear makeup than she might think, to hide blemishes or when they're having a bad-face day." He lowered his voice to a whisper. "I think she's weakening."

The elevator stopped at the upper floor, which consisted of another reception counter and more photos of gorgeous women with stunning cheekbones and amazing eyes. If Quincy Franklin manned this station, then Grady needed to revise his previous impression about Margo Lazenby's brilliance in surrounding herself with good people.

"Be sure to mention to Aunt Margo that you'd buy the Lamenby products," he told Grady before he opened the door to the inner suite.

Margo Lazenby waited for him off to the side of her desk in a leather sofa in a buttery lemon color. She'd changed from her black ensemble to a sapphire-blue dress that called attention to her eyes, which were as blue as his own.

"Aunt Margo, Mr. Palmer is here," Quincy Franklin announced. "And he has something to tell you about Lamenby. He thinks it's a fantastic idea, which isn't surprising because—"

"Thank you, Quincy," she interrupted as she put down her martini glass on a gleaming end table and stood. "You may go now."

"But—"

"I said that will be all, Quincy," she said without looking at him, those strangely familiar blue eyes fastened on Grady.

The click of the door announced her assistant's departure, leaving Grady alone with the woman who claimed to be his grandmother.

"I'm Margo Lazenby." She came across the room and took his hand, holding it while she examined his face. "And I hope like hell you don't really think men should wear makeup."

Grady almost smiled. Almost, but not quite. "No, I don't."

"Thank the heavens." She released his hand and dramatically wiped a hand over her brow. "Would you like a martini? I don't usually drink before six, but your visit has come as quite a shock."

"No, thank you," he said.

She indicated a leather chair that matched her sofa. "Have a seat, then, and tell me what brings you here."

She walked back to the sofa, but he held his ground.

"I want to know why you hired Tori Whitley to investigate me," he said, his voice snagging on Tori's name. How long, he wondered, would her deception hurt?

Margo waited until she was settled and the martini was once again in her hand before saying, "You're assertive. I like that. Jane—that's what I like to call Tori—says you're also honest and trustworthy, but I must say I'm disappointed in her for telling you my name."

"She didn't tell me," he said, compelled to protect her and angry at himself because of that. "I followed her today and had your license plate run."

"You're clever, too. You don't know how much that gladdens me. Quincy's a boob, which is why I'm glad you met him."

"I don't see how that concerns me."

"It will help you understand why I wanted to make contact with you."

"I don't follow."

"Sit down and I'll tell you."

"I'd rather stand."

"Very well," she said, and took a sip of her drink. "A few months ago, I had a heart-attack scare. It turned out to be heartburn, but it got me to thinking about my mortality. I can pass for sixty, but I'm seventy-one. If I died tomorrow, Quincy would inherit my company."

"What does that have to do with me?"

"Oh, come now. We've already established that you're a bright man. Surely you know that I'm your grandmother."

Hearing her state their relationship aloud jolted him, but Grady strived not to show it. "So you say."

"So I know, and so do you. We look alike. Quincy's related to me by marriage. You're related by blood."

"Where are you going with this?"

"I'll get to that in due time." She crossed one elegant leg over the other. "Your mother's name was Melanie. She was my only child, and I wanted the best of everything for her. She was smart but defiant and very beautiful. Lazenby was already a force in the cosmetics industry, and I was grooming her to eventually take over the company. Then she got pregnant with you."

Grady stiffened, not sure he wanted to hear the story but unable to object.

"Melanie was dating a man I disliked. I thought he had no ambition or drive. She said she loved him but she caved soon enough when I told her I'd cut her off if she didn't give you up for adoption. I stipulated she couldn't tell her boyfriend about you."

She stated the facts without emotion. Grady winced. "How could you do something like that?"

"I thought it was for the best at the time, but now I see I preyed on Melanie's weakness." Margo sighed, and Grady saw that she wasn't as unemotional about the terrible thing she'd done as she appeared. "She was a child of privilege. She couldn't bear the thought of doing without."

"What happened to her?"

"That's the ironic thing. About five years after you were born, she was dating a wealthy Boca entrepreneur I approved of without reservation. He was rich, handsome, and ambitious. I didn't know he was also reckless until he crashed his private plane with my daughter as a passenger."

A lump formed in Grady's throat, and he walked to the armchair and sank into it. After a moment, he managed to ask, "Why look me up now? Why not then?"

"I was still under the delusion that I'd done the right thing. And I still had my husband. Harry didn't have a head for business, but I loved him. And he loved me."

Her eyes filled with tears, and she wiped moisture from under them with the pad of her thumb before gathering herself once again.

"After Harry died two years ago, it occurred to me that I was all alone. Harry and Melanie were gone, and I effectively sent you away before you were born. But you were out there somewhere. All I needed to do was find you.

"I got your name and address without much trouble. But I'm a cautious woman. Before I let you into my life, and possibly my will, I wanted to know what kind of man you were. That's why I hired Sassenbury Investigations."

"I don't want your money."

"I wouldn't give it to you if you did. But there's plenty of time to talk about that later. For now, I'm wondering if you'd give me something else: your companionship. And, maybe one day, your forgiveness."

He considered her request. "After what you did, why should I agree to that?"

"Because like it or not, you have Lazenby blood. It's not a connection you can sever that easily."

"I'll have to think about it," Grady said, rising and turning to walk away. Margo's voice stopped him when he'd nearly reached the door.

"Don't you want to know who your father is?"

His blood seemed to freeze. He turned, trying to keep his expression neutral. "I figured you'd lost touch with him after all these years."

"Oh, no. He's still in the area. In Seahaven, in fact. It turned out I was wrong about him not having the potential to make something of himself. He's very successful."

"Who is he?" Grady asked.

"His name is Forest Richardson. You may have heard of him. He's running for mayor against Honoria Black."

302

Chapter Thirty-four

Wade looked both ways before crossing the street in front of city hall, stuffing the red envelope deeper into his pocket so nobody else would see it.

When he reached the sidewalk, he walked as close to the buildings as he dared. Still, he felt conspicuous.

The other people who had attended the city council meeting spilled out of the building and into their cars. His destination was the Seahaven Hotel.

That's where the bold, slanted writing on the scented pink paper inside the red envelope had directed him.

Meet me, was all it had said, followed by Lorelei's signature and the red-lipstick imprint of her mouth.

Something else had been inside the envelope, too: the key to room 233 of the Seahaven Hotel.

"Hey, Morrison."

He didn't want to stop and turn around, but he did.

Ned Weimer quickly closed in on him, patting his gelled hair, his small eyes darting right and left.

"Remember that thing we talked about last week?" he asked, which could only be an oblique reference to his request that Wade significantly cut a businessman's tax bill in exchange for cash. "Do you think we could apply it to a couple of other businesses?"

Wanting to be rid of the other man, Wade said, "I don't see why not, but could we talk about it another time?"

"Yes, of course. I'll be in touch," he said and scurried off, not even asking where Wade was headed.

He'd probably aroused the curiosity of others, though. A young boy of about twelve, whom Lorelei had probably found outside on the street, had burst into the meeting at about the time the council had awarded Palmer Construction the community-center contract.

In a high, shrill voice, the boy asked somebody near the door to point out Wade Morrison. Then he'd blundered down the center of the room and asked the man in the aisle seat to pass the red envelope down to Wade.

The cheeky kid had even winked.

The last time Lorelei had been in city hall, Wade had instructed her to be more discreet. Her method of delivering the envelope didn't qualify.

The note didn't even make sense. It read like a come on, but that couldn't be. Lorelei had offered to pick up the twins at day care, which she should have done more than an hour ago.

Mary Kate and Ashley had to be with her. Not only would nobody else in Seahaven consent to baby-sit them, but Wade wouldn't trust the twins to a sitter he hadn't screened first.

So why had Lorelei arranged to have him meet her and the girls in room 233 of the Seahaven Hotel?

The hotel paid homage to days gone by, with an ornate crystal chandelier, wood-paneled walls, and early twentieth-century furniture.

Wade didn't stop to admire the surroundings, quickly striding through the lobby and taking the stairs to the first floor.

He was slightly out of breath when he reached Room 233 and took out the key. He expected to open the door to the excited chatter of his children but instead he heard music. Something young and modern.

Lorelei stepped into view, wearing stiletto heels and a backless black dress that looked amazing on her. Her eyes danced while his darted around the room, searching for Ashley and Mary Kate.

"Hey, there, handsome," she said. "I see you got my note."

The mention of the note temporarily distracted him from the absence of his daughters.

He removed the red envelope from his pocket.

"I thought we talked about being discreet, Lorelei," he said. "Everybody at the meeting saw that boy give me this."

"My bad," she said, covering her mouth with slender fingers topped with decadent red nails and managing to sound not the least bit repentant. "Once I pour you a glass of champagne, I know you'll forgive me."

She wiggled over to a stand on which sat a bottle of champagne wedged in a bucket of ice. Wade recognized the label of an expensive brand as she popped the cork.

"How can you afford that?" he asked.

"The same way I afforded the room," she said, laughing. "My credit card."

She poured two glasses and brought one over to him, holding it out like the temptress she was. She lowered her lashes and peered up at him through them, causing his body to pay attention.

He didn't want the champagne. He wanted to sweep the glasses aside, tear off her clothes, and make love to her until morning.

By the teasing gleam in her eyes, she knew that. He knew she wouldn't stop him, that in fact it was what she wanted, too.

But he couldn't surrender to temptation. One of them had to be the responsible party here. Despite her insistence that she slip out of his house at dawn when they'd made love in his bed, she'd proven time and again that it sure as heck wouldn't be her.

"Where are the girls?" he asked in a voice that sounded husky despite his best attempt to speak normally.

She walked those long-nailed fingers up his chest until they reached his lips.

"They're at your house," she said, her eyes focused on his lips.

"With a sitter?"

She nodded, silently giving him the green light to do what they both knew he wanted to do.

But that was the very thing he couldn't do.

"Darn it, Lorelei," he said, stepping out of her reach. "How could you have been so irresponsible?"

She looked confused. "Irresponsible? Exactly how was I irresponsible?"

"For starters, you told me you'd pick up the girls."

"I did pick them up," she said, but he didn't give her time to expand on the statement.

"You were supposed to look after them until I got home, but instead you passed them off to who knows who."

"I know who if you'd shut up for a minute so I could tell you."

"What does it matter? We both know you shouldn't have left them. You have to check out the babysitters you use, Lorelei. You can't just trust the girls to anybody who comes along just because you want to have a good time."

"That's what you think I did," she said, her eyes steely. "Passed the girls off to somebody I didn't even know so I could have a good time."

"That's what I know you did."

"Go on," she said. "I want to hear the rest. You said the girls were only for starters."

She crossed her arms over her chest. Her lips thinned, her breasts heaved and her eyes glinted. He ignored the signs that she was getting good and irate. He was the only one with the right to be angry.

"We've already talked about the red envelope, so let's discuss this room." He indicated their luxurious surroundings. "If you had to put it on credit, you can't afford it."

"So you don't think a special occasion merits a special setting?"

"What special occasion?"

"I was going to tell you I love you, you idiot," Lorelei said, striding over to the bucket and setting down her glass of champagne.

She loved him? Something that had been dormant inside Wade for a very long time flared to life, brightening the room. But only for a second, because Lorelei didn't look loving. Anger bubbled from her like boiling water.

"Good thing I found out what you really think of me." She blinked her eyes, which had started to tear. "You don't give me enough credit. I'd never foist off M.K. and Ash the way you say I did."

"Then where are they?"

"With my mother," she said. "Remember how she and the girls hit it off at Grady's birthday dinner? She called me on my cell just after I picked them up and wanted to know what the deal was between me and you. When I told her, she offered to watch the girls so we could have some time alone."

A sick feeling gripped Wade when he recalled the unfair accusations he'd thrown at her. He massaged his forehead, which had begun to throb.

"I'm sorry, Lorelei," he said. "I shouldn't have said those things."

"You shouldn't have thought them," she said. "Maybe I haven't been the most responsible person in

308

the world up to this point. But that changed when I met you and M.K. and Ash. Haven't you been paying attention at all?"

"I said I was sorry."

"Sorry doesn't cut it, not when you insist on thinking of me as some irresponsible kid," she said. "I'm not a kid. I'm a woman."

"I know," he said, coming forward and trying to take her into his arms. She shrugged him off.

"I don't think we should see each other anymore," she said.

"What?" Panic rose in him. "That's crazy. I apologized."

"I don't think you mean it. I think you look at me and see your ex-wife. But I'm not like her. I'd never leave M.K. and Ash like she did. I didn't give birth to them but I already love them.'"

"That's another reason you shouldn't break up with me," he said, desperate to make her change her mind about not seeing him anymore.

"What's the first?"

"You love me," he said. "You said so."

Her chin lifted. "Yeah, well, I changed my mind."

"You can't change your mind about something like that," he protested.

"Just watch me." She brushed by him and headed for the door. "Tell M.K. and Ash I'll stop by the day-care center to visit. I still love *them*."

She emphasized the last word, then banged out of the hotel room, leaving him alone with the champagne and absolutely nothing to celebrate.

Chapter Thirty-five

Lorelei sneaked into work late. Again. But this time she did it by design.

True to her word, she'd stopped by the day-care center that morning to spend a few minutes with M.K. and Ash.

Because she hadn't wanted to risk running into the jerk who had broken her heart and caused her to cry away half a night's sleep, she hadn't showed up at the center until ten.

She'd stayed longer than she'd planned, first because she couldn't tear herself away from the twins and then because their teacher needed help cutting out paper dolls.

To top all that off, Donna Trent, the director, had wanted to run a very interesting proposition by her. The proposal had intrigued Lorelei so much, in fact, that she'd said yes on the spot.

No sooner had she gotten into her car than her cell

phone had rung. One of the clerks at city hall, with whom she'd gotten friendly, had called to tell her the news spreading like wildfire through the city.

It seemed the longtime rumors of corruption at city hall were more than fiction.

A federal grand jury had convened that morning and word was that a good number of important city hall types would soon be indicted. Her friend mentioned by name city clerk Pete Aiken, planning director Larry Schlichter, and chief of staff Ned Weimer.

All of the distractions added up to Lorelei arriving at the office not only late, but seriously late. Another few minutes and it'd be lunchtime.

She planned to quietly creep to her desk, then act as though she'd been there for hours. Considering the commotion that was sure to accompany the imminent issuing of indictments, that shouldn't be difficult.

Except Lorelei never imagined the commotion would be taking place at Palmer Construction.

Muffled shouts came from somewhere in the building, loud enough that Lorelei recognized the voices.

Grady . . . and the heartbreaking jerk.

She followed the ruckus to her brother's office door, which was closed but didn't afford much privacy because of the glass window that took up part of the front wall.

She gaped at the sight of her brother and her jerk standing about six inches apart, making angry hand gestures and yapping at each other.

Her jerk was giving as good, or possibly better, than

he got, which was surprising considering his geek tendencies.

If she hadn't been so angry and hurt, she might have found his new tough-guy persona sexy. But even then she'd have been forced to intervene because he looked like he might pop Grady one in the nose.

Unsurprised to find the door cracked—really, the decibel level was earsplitting—she burst into the office.

Neither man noticed her arrival.

"I mean it. You stay away from my sister," Grady shouted.

"Standing right here," Lorelei said, but Wade's response drowned out her words.

"That's not up to you. It's up to Lorelei."

"Darn right it is," she said. This time Grady's shout swallowed her voice.

"I know what's best for my sister, and you aren't it."

Lorelei clapped her hands together three times, the way M.K. and Ash's day-care providers did when they needed to restore order.

The men turned toward her in unison, and the shouting stopped abruptly.

"What in the world is going on here?" she asked, addressing her brother. She wasn't ready to look at Wade, even if he was wearing the pink squiggle-print DKNY shirt she'd bought him.

"I told Morrison to get out, but he won't leave," Grady said in a heated tone.

"And I told him I wasn't going anywhere until I talked to you," Wade said.

Lorelei made herself look at Wade. With that wayward strand of dark hair in his face and his mouth set in a determined line beneath his geek glasses, he looked so damned good she wanted to hit him. Her throat grew thick, but she made her vocal cords work.

"I can't believe you actually thought talking to me here would be a good idea," she said, trying to sound sassy.

"You wouldn't come to your door last night and you won't return my calls." Wade sounded exasperated. "What else was I supposed to do?"

"Leave her alone," Grady answered.

Lorelei ignored Grady and kept her expression carefully irritable as she continued to address Wade. "What makes you think I want to talk to you?"

"I don't need you to talk," Wade said. "I need you to listen."

"She doesn't have to listen to you," Grady interjected. "Lorelei, tell this guy to keep away from you. He's in trouble, and I don't want him dragging you into it."

The serious tone in her brother's voice alarmed Lorelei. "What do you mean he's in trouble?"

"You've probably heard by now that indictments are being handed out this afternoon," Grady said. "My guess is that Morrison here will get one."

"He will not," Lorelei said at the same time that Wade expressed his own protest.

"Don't listen to him, Lorelei. I tell you, he's mixed up in the corruption at city hall," Grady said.

"Look who's talking," Wade retorted. "You've given out so much bribe money it's a wonder you're not bankrupt."

Lorelei clapped again, appalled at the testosterone running rampant in the room.

"Quiet, both of you," she said in her most authoritative voice. She strode to the door and pulled it shut, probably disappointing the eavesdroppers in the outer office.

"First of all, Grady is one of the most honest people I know," she said to Wade. "If it's true that he's been giving out bribes, then he's working for the government. Nothing else makes sense."

"How did you—?" Grady began.

She swung her eyes to her brother. "Don't interrupt, Grady. I'm not through talking. I have a few things to say to you, too. Wade is not going to be indicted. He's every bit as good a man as you are."

"You can't know that," Grady scoffed. "You only met the guy a few weeks ago."

"Don't argue with me, Grady Palmer. When I say I know something, I know it. And I know this like I know how to breathe."

"But how do you know it?" Grady persisted.

"I know it in here," she said, thumping her heart. "When you love somebody, you've got to take that leap of faith."

Complete silence greeted her declaration. Grady's eyes grew so round she might have laughed had she been in a more jovial mood. She slowly shifted her gaze to Wade.

A smile had started to spread across the face that she fully expected to see filled with contrition, because she wasn't going to forgive him if he didn't grovel enough.

"I thought you changed your mind about loving me," Wade reminded her.

She shook her index finger at him. "If you pull another stunt like you did last night, I'll change it back again."

"I still don't trust him," Grady said.

"That's your problem, Grady. You don't trust anyone." Lorelei nodded toward a still-smiling Wade. "Clear up his confusion, Wade. Tell him why you won't be indicted."

"Because I've been providing the government with the names of every person who has offered me a bribe to lower their tax bills."

"Now it all makes sense," Grady said, sounding like he was talking to himself. "That's why they weren't keen on me approaching you. They knew I'd be wasting my time."

"What are you talking about?" Wade asked. "Who is 'they'?"

"The FBI," Grady said. "I've been using their money to bribe city officials."

"I told you so," Lorelei said, turning to give Wade a smug look. "I told you Grady was working for Uncle Sam."

"But how did you know that?" Grady asked.

"What other explanation could there be?" Lorelei answered rhetorically, then thought about her brother's rationale for asking the question. "I'm not stupid, you know."

"Just irresponsible," Grady muttered under his breath.

"Take that back."

Those very words tapped against the backs of Lorelei's teeth, but Wade spoke them. That was a curious development, considering the accusations he'd thrown at her the night before.

"I can't take it back," Grady said. "I love Lorelei, but responsibility is not one of her virtues. Take today, for example. She's three hours late for work."

"Then she must have a good reason," Wade said and crossed his arms over his chest. He nodded toward Lorelei. "Tell him what it is, Lorelei."

"I was at Wee Care. That's the day-care center where Wade's twin girls go to school. The director offered me a job, and I've decided to take it," she told Grady.

"You? Work at a day-care center?" Grady's disbelief seemed to radiate from him in waves. "Has anyone ever left you alone with a child before?"

"I've trusted her with my daughters," Wade said before Lorelei could take offense. "She's wonderful with them. The children at the day-care center will be lucky to have her."

"Thank you," Lorelei said, smiling at him.

"You're welcome," Wade said, smiling back.

"Grady," Lorelei said without breaking eye contact with Wade, "don't you have somewhere you need to be?"

"This is my office," he reminded her.

"Let me put it another way," Lorelei said. "Get out of here, Grady."

"If you hadn't quit, I'd fire you," Grady groused, but mercifully he left.

Before Wade could completely close the gap be-

317

tween them, Lorelei placed a restraining hand on his chest.

"Not so fast, buster," she said. "You came here to talk to me. So talk."

"I acted like an idiot last night," he said, looking so cute she could just eat him up. Or lick him. Yes, licking him would be better.

"So far, so good," Lorelei said encouragingly. "Go on."

"When I met you, it seemed like all you wanted to do was have fun, and I didn't know how to handle that." Behind his glasses, his eyes were earnest. "I didn't know how to handle you."

"So you tried to keep me away by claiming I was too young and irresponsible?"

"That's about the sum of it," he said, sounding disappointed with himself, as well he should be. "Somewhere along the line, with the responsibility of raising the girls, I forgot how to have fun."

"I don't have any problem with being your good-time girl," she said, making her eyebrows waggle, "but I should point out that I'm starting to get a handle on that responsibility thing."

"I've noticed," he said.

"You darn well better have noticed," Lorelei said. "I'm getting better at it every day. I even cut up one of my credit cards today."

"How many do you have left?"

"Two."

He made a face.

"Hey, I didn't say I was perfectly responsible," Lorelei said with spirit. "I said I was improving."

"I can help you with that," he said.

"Only if you let me help you have fun."

A corner of his mouth quirked. "So you forgive me?"

"That depends on why you want me to forgive you."

He frowned. "Because I love you."

She smacked him once on the chest. "Ya think you could have told me that before now?"

He gently massaged the spot she'd assaulted. "Careful, or I might change my mind about loving you."

"You better not if you know what's good for you," she said, then started to drag his mouth down to hers.

"You're good for me," he said, making her smile.

But at the last instant, before their lips could meet, he stiffened.

"What's wrong?" she breathed.

"The window," he said. "Everybody will see us kissing."

"So what?"

"So your brother might come in here and punch me in the nose."

"If he does, I'll punch him back for you."

His mouth was so close to hers that she felt his smile against her lips, felt the breath from his laugh, saw his glasses begin to fog.

"You're right," he said. "So what?"

And then the ultraresponsible, megaconservative Wade Morrison kissed her in full view of anyone who happened to look their way.

It was the start, Lorelei thought as her love for him rose up and spilled into her kiss, of something beautiful.

Chapter Thirty-six

Gordo clawed at Grady's leg until he decided that continuing to ignore her would be hazardous to the material of his pants.

"All right, already," he said, bending over to pick up the cat. He tried to put her on his lap but Gordo had other ideas.

She placed her front paws on his desk, struggling to pull herself onto it. Then she plopped down on a stack of papers, rested her head on her paws, and stared at him.

"You think I don't know you disapprove of the way I handled things with Tori?" he asked. "It's tearing me up inside, too, but this is her fault."

Gordo's stare seemed to turn to a glare.

"Don't look at me that way," he said. "She's the one who can't be trusted. You know that, right?"

The cat, of course, didn't respond.

Grady put his arms on his desk and dropped his

head into the cradle they made. He still had it bad for Tori if he'd resorted to explaining himself to a cat, but that was tough. He had to get over her.

He determinedly raised his head and noticed that Gordo had settled on his copy of the community-center bid. He'd normally shoo the cat from his papers, but he wouldn't need that anymore.

The contract the city had awarded would surely be nullified, if it hadn't been already. Palmer Construction couldn't go ahead with the development of the center when the bid process had been blatantly unfair.

Because his company had won the contract, questions already abounded about what role Grady may have played in the sweep the FBI had made of city hall that afternoon.

The truth would soon come out but Grady didn't feel comfortable announcing his part in Operation Citygate, not when all the indicted parties had yet to surrender to federal authorities.

To escape the curious, he'd spent the day in his office, ignoring the phone.

The intercom on his desk buzzed, followed by Lorelei's voice. His sister must have finally returned from the long lunch she'd taken with Wade Morrison.

She'd gone with his permission even though she'd put in about zero minutes of actual work since the day had officially begun at nine.

But he couldn't get too upset about that. It wasn't every day a man realized his sister had grown up and become a responsible citizen.

"Grady, someone is here to see you," Lorelei said.

Tori, Grady thought. Tori had come to ask him to reconsider her apology.

"I told him you weren't seeing anybody today, but he says this is personal," Lorelei continued, eliminating the possibility that his visitor was Tori. "He says his name is Forest Richardson."

The air left Grady's lungs.

"Grady, did you hear me?" Lorelei asked when he didn't respond. "I said Forest Richardson is here to see you."

"I heard you." Grady could breathe again, which meant he could speak. He fervently wished he could also get through the upcoming meeting, which he both looked forward to and dreaded. "Send him in."

Grady had run into Forest Richardson a dozen times over the past few years but felt as though he were seeing the other man for the first time when he entered the office.

Richardson stared, and Grady stared back.

About as tall as Grady himself, Richardson had thick, graying hair that might have once been the same color as Grady's, but his facial features were broader. The way he carried himself was the same, though. Shoulders back, head high, chin tilted.

He didn't sit down, and Grady didn't rise.

Richardson nodded at Gordo, who had stopped staring at Grady long enough to gawk at Richardson. "There's a white rat on your desk."

"Cat," Grady corrected. "She's sitting on her tail."

"Yours?"

Grady nodded. "It's a long story."

"Maybe you'll tell it to me one day," he said, then paused. "I heard a remarkable story just this morning from Margo Lazenby. She called me out of the blue to say her daughter Melanie gave up a baby for adoption twenty-nine years ago."

"She told me the same story, but she added a couple of twists that were pretty unbelievable," Grady said, watching the other man carefully. "One of them was that the man who got her daughter pregnant never knew a thing about it."

"Then she must not have told you how she sent Melanie away, allegedly to boarding school. Or how she pressured her not to have anything else to do with the father of the baby."

"She told me some of it," Grady said, then paused. "I'm wrestling with how much I should believe."

"Believe all of it," Richardson said. "It's all true."

His stare was direct, his eyes honest, but doubt still niggled in the back of Grady's mind. "We should take a DNA test to find out for certain," he said.

"I don't need a test but I'll provide a sample if you want. I'll do anything if it means you and I can have a relationship."

"Why?" Grady asked suspiciously.

"Believe this, too. I was happy about Margo's news. After I got over the shock, of course." Richardson smiled a little. "I always wanted a son or a daughter, but Betty and I couldn't have children of our own. Hearing about you was like a miracle."

Grady swallowed, because the other man—his *father*—seemed sincere. It seemed incredible that, up until a few days ago when he'd mended his relationship with the parents who raised him, he felt as though he had no fathers. Now he had two. But old, skeptical habits died hard.

"About that relationship," Grady said, forcing himself to take things slowly, "I'd like to hold off until we know for sure."

Richardson's mouth drooped and his eyes grew sad, but then he nodded. "I've waited twenty-nine years. I can wait a couple of more weeks."

The phone rang. Grady ignored it, knowing Lorelei or his other secretary would pick it up.

"It's been a crazy day," he said.

"I heard."

His response held no censure but Grady felt compelled to explain. "I know some are saying that I'm as guilty as the people who were indicted today. I want you to know that's not true."

"I know that," Richardson said mildly.

Grady blinked, because he hadn't expected the response. "How do you know that?"

"You're my son," he said simply and walked out of the office.

Grady was still puzzling over Richardson's reply a few hours later after he dropped a protesting Gordo off at home and arrived in West Palm Beach.

He checked the address to make sure he was at the right place—a branch office of the Southern District of Florida's U.S. attorney's office—then paid scant attention to his surroundings as he entered the building.

After Grady's vocal support of Honoria Black for mayor, Forest Richardson could have been excused for believing Grady was a guilty player in Operation Citygate.

But instead Richardson had taken that leap of faith and believed, just like Lorelei had when Grady wrongly accused Wade Morrison of accepting kickbacks, just like Grady hadn't when Tori asked him to trust her.

"Grady, my man." FBI Special Agent Hector Rodriquez immediately appeared to shake Grady's hand. Their face-to-face meetings had been infrequent over their nine months of working together, but Hector was much more than a voice on the phone. Because nobody else had known about Grady's part in the sting operation, Hector had become confidant and friend. "The shit has done hit the fan, and we couldn't have made it fly without you."

Grady smiled at the other man's giddiness. The agent wasn't anything like the serious, dour-faced FBI agents portrayed in film and fiction.

"That's an image I could have done without," Grady said.

"As long as you can't do without some celebratory alcohol, I'm cool with it," Hector said, referring to his invitation for Grady to join him for a drink. "Give me a couple of minutes to finish up and then we can go get happy."

"I'd be happier if we had managed to get the goods on Mayor Black," Grady said. "Any indication yet whether one of the others will turn on her?"

"We don't need anyone to rat on her," Hector said.

"Why not?"

Hector's face broke into a huge grin. "You haven't heard, have you?"

"Heard what?"

"I could fill you in but it'll be more fun to let Honoria tell you."

Grady glanced around the emptying office building, but saw no sign of the mayor. "You're not making sense, Hector."

The agent nodded to an empty office at the back of the room. "Go sit in that office and give me a minute. It'll make wonderful sense soon enough."

Grady didn't have to wait more than five minutes before Hector appeared with an audiotape and a tape recorder.

"This is a copy," he said, waving the audio tape at Grady. "The U.S. attorney needed the original to present as evidence tomorrow when he convenes a special session of the federal grand jury."

"I thought that happened today."

"It did, but he wants one more indictment."

Hector cracked his gum and popped the tape into the recorder, obviously enjoying himself.

"Ready for this?" he asked, his finger on the PLAY button.

"Would you play it already?" Grady said impatiently.

"Gladly," Hector said and hit PLAY.

Grady instantly recognized Honoria Black's deep, almost masculine voice.

"City Hall doesn't have any openings, but as I told you before, that's not a problem. I can create a job for you and call it temporary. When a permanent position becomes available, I'll move you into it."

Grady wondered if he were listening to a jobs-for-cash scheme. He'd heard of another corrupt administration that fattened its coffers that way. But how had Hector gotten this tape?

"Did you bug the mayor's office?" Grady asked.

Hector put a finger to his lips. "Shut up or you'll miss the good part."

"I'm the mayor," Honoria Black said on the tape, probably in response to a question Grady had missed by interrupting. "I can do anything I want."

"But you must want something in return," came the reply.

Grady recognized the second voice, too. It belonged to Tori. He gripped his thigh with the hand that rested on it so hard that his knuckles whitened. He scarcely breathed as he listened to their exchange.

"That's the way of the world," the mayor said. "I scratch your back, you scratch mine. What I want you to do isn't so hard. I'll even bump your salary up a grade or two if you're successful."

"What exactly is it that you want me to do?" Tori asked as though she were eager—*eager*—to comply.

"You're probably aware that some of my top people were indicted today," the mayor said. "Grady bribed all three of them. We believe he's planning to testify against them. And that, my dear, is where you come in."

"I don't understand."

"I know you and Grady had a bad breakup. Here's your chance to get back at him."

The tape contained only a few seconds of silence

after her declaration, but to Grady it felt like an eternity.

"Get back at him how?" Tori asked.

"I need you to say that Grady threatened the members of my administration, coercing them to take the money and give him the contract he wanted."

"Threatened? How?"

"The usual way. Exposure. My city clerk is cheating on his girlfriend. My planning director has a drug problem. And my chief of staff doesn't want anyone to know he's gay."

"So you're saying that Grady found out these things and used them to pressure your employees to give him what he wanted?"

"You catch on fast," the mayor said. "What do you say? Will you do it?"

"Yes," Tori said.

Hector switched off the tape, oblivious to its effect on Grady. Shock had rendered his body immobile but his mind whirled.

"What do you think of that?" Hector asked with undisguised glee.

"I don't believe it," Grady said.

"I can hardly believe it, either. But it's legit. We got the mayor on tape, soliciting false testimony in exchange for employment. She's going down." He pointed his index finger in the air and then shot it to the floor.

"I didn't mean I don't believe that you got Mayor Black. I mean I don't believe that Tori sold me out," Grady said slowly, choosing his words carefully, meaning every one.

"Sold you out? What are you talking about, man?"

"What Tori said on the tape, about agreeing to lie about me, there has to be an explanation." Grady's conviction grew stronger as he talked. "Tori must have known you'd bugged Mayor Black's office. She must have been playing an angle."

"Back up a minute." Hector's black eyebrows drew together to form a line that reminded Grady vaguely of a caterpillar. "Didn't you learn anything in all these months of working with me? No judge would allow us to put a bug in the mayor's office. Hell, that conversation didn't even take place at city hall. They were in the lobby of some hotel."

"Then where was the bug?"

"In Tori's purse," Hector said. "The minute the mayor called and asked her to meet, she phoned our office and offered to tape the conversation. She said she had a feeling the mayor was up to no good."

"So it was just like I said," Grady said, his voice thick with emotion and wonder. "Tori didn't betray me."

"Damn right she didn't," Hector said. "That girl of yours is no traitor. She's a hero. She's the one who brought down the mayor."

Chapter Thirty-seven

"Okay, disco ball. The last time I came to you for advice, I had to ask the question three times before you got the answer right. Let's shoot for a better percentage than that."

Crossing the index and middle fingers of her left hand for luck, Tori held the tiny silver ball between the corresponding fingers of her right hand and shook.

"Should I go after Grady and make him believe I love him?"

Her breath was stalled in her throat when she turned over the ball and read, *No way, Jose.*

"What?" The word exploded from her. "What kind of rotten answer is that?"

Shaking her head in disgust, she manipulated the silver ball until it came free of the key chain.

"You know what, dude, you're not hip anymore," she said, tossing the ball in a perfect arc so it fell into her kitchen trash can. "With the answers you've been giving lately, I don't need you."

She didn't care what the ball advised. She'd make Grady listen to her, even if she had to tie him to a chair first.

So she'd messed up. Everybody did. But that didn't mean she didn't love him. Or that he couldn't trust her.

"You better not have that rat in there," Mrs. Grumley called to her when she emerged from her apartment into the gathering dusk. "All I need is one more reason, and you're out of here."

Tori's spine straightened and she tramped up to the older woman.

"I don't care what you do. You know why?" Tori didn't wait for Mrs. Grumley's reply. "Because I know what I want and it's not to live here. Do you hear that? I don't *want* to live here anymore."

"Yes, you do," Mrs. Grumley said. "You're terrified at the thought of me throwing you out."

"Not anymore. I'm tired of dealing with you. So there," she said, barely resisting the urge to stick out her tongue.

Mrs. Grumley's lower lip trembled. "That wasn't a very nice thing to say."

"You haven't been nice to me."

"That's different. I'm an old lady. I'm allowed to be mean. But you're young. You need to respect your elders. Besides, if you leave, who will I pick on?"

"You enjoy picking on me?"

"Picking on people is what I do," Mrs. Grumley said. "You're an easy target, because you never stick up for yourself."

"That stops now," Tori said defiantly. "Because from now on, I'm going after what I want."

She'd been a ditherer all her life, but this time she was absolutely certain of what she wanted.

She wanted Grady.

She couldn't pinpoint the exact time she'd realized it, perhaps because the knowledge had come to her gradually. Or possibly because she'd wanted him from the start.

But she'd been aware of how she felt when Mayor Black had tried to get her to sully his reputation. She'd smiled and nodded, all the while wanting to throttle the mayor for daring to try to hurt him.

She'd silently vowed then and there that she'd make Grady believe she loved him. She'd teach him how to trust. Asking the disco ball its advice had been a formality.

Thirty minutes later, she stood at Grady's front door repeatedly ringing the doorbell. Nobody answered, but signs indicated that Grady was home. A light shone in the back of the house, and she heard voices. Loud, raised voices.

Her stomach flip-flopped, and her blood ran as cold as chilled water from a refrigerator dispenser.

The FBI had handed out indictments in Operation Citygate earlier today, but the indicted parties had until tomorrow to surrender.

One of them could be inside Grady's house right now, trying to carry out a vendetta.

Her heart hammered in concert with her fruitless banging on the door. She strained to hear what was going on inside the house. The voices seemed to grow in volume but she couldn't make out what they were saying.

"Please, oh, please," she pleaded, her eyes lifted to the sky. "Please let Grady be okay."

She ran around the side of the house, her tennis shoes sinking into earth damp from one of the afternoon rainstorms that were so prevalent in Florida.

Grady's backyard was small, with a screened-in porch taking up most of the available area. She yanked on the patio door, surprised to find it unlocked.

The voices sounded even louder at the back of the house. Rushing to the rear door, she pounded on it and called Grady's name. Nobody answered.

"Where would he keep a key?" she asked aloud, trying to think over the pounding of her heart.

Standing on tiptoes, she ran her shaking fingertips along the door ledge. Then she stooped down and lifted the doormat. She would have checked under the flowerpot if there were one.

"Damn it," she said.

She thought about calling 9-1-1 only to realize she'd left her phone in her car. And she'd been forced to park a couple of blocks away. She'd have to waste precious minutes retrieving it unless she could figure out a way to break into the house.

A broom rested against the wall nearest to her. She reached for it, turned it over, and rammed the window. Glass shattered, and she reached inside to unlock the door and push it open.

She rushed into his house, saw a flash of something at her feet, and screamed.

"*Meow,*" the something said.

"Gordo," she exclaimed, her heart beating so hard she thought it might have punctured her chest wall. "Where's Grady? Is he in trouble?"

The voices had grown louder than ever, but she noticed something strange. One of them talked about an 80 percent chance of precipitation and the balmy weather they were enjoying. Another laughed and said something about life in the tropics.

Groaning, she realized the voices originated from the clock radio on Grady's kitchen counter.

She shut off the radio, feeling silly for having overreacted, and only now realizing that she'd invaded his privacy. Again.

Her heart had only begun to slow when she heard a key turn in the front door.

Where was Tori? Grady wondered as he entered his house. Since listening to the tape of her and Honoria Black, he'd been desperate to find her.

He'd managed to down only one happy-hour drink before his patience had run out and he'd gone to her apartment. She hadn't been there, but her landlady had, pleading with him to talk Tori out of leaving.

The possible meaning of the landlady's request had nagged at him during the drive back to his place. Was Tori planning to leave Seahaven? To leave him? After the way he'd doubted her, he wouldn't blame her.

He kicked off his shoes, ran a hand over the back of his neck, and stood stock still.

Somebody was inside the house.

He knew it as surely as he knew Gordo would have greeted him if that weren't the case.

He grew quiet, not daring to move, and listened.

The floor in the kitchen creaked.

An oversized yellow-and-red golf umbrella rested against the wall nearest the door. He grabbed it and moved stealthily toward the back of the house. Taking a deep breath for courage, he burst into the kitchen with the umbrella raised.

A woman screamed, backed up against the stove, and grimaced. But not just any woman. Tori, her reddish brown hair tumbled around her shoulders, looking as lovely as she had the first time he'd seen her. He lowered the umbrella.

"I know this looks bad, but I can explain," she said, talking fast. "I heard voices and came around back to investigate when nobody answered the doorbell. I couldn't get in so I broke the glass on your door so I could—"

"I believe you," he interrupted, but she kept on talking.

"—check on you, but the voices were coming from the radio. And then I heard you at the door and thought that maybe if I snuck out the back and came around the front then you'd believe—"

She suddenly stopped talking, tilted her head quizzically, and stared at him. "Did you say you believed me?"

He nodded, and she looked puzzled.

"You don't think I'm here to snoop on you?"

"Nope," he said.

"But you've got to admit it looks bad, you finding me inside your house."

"Tori, I said I believe you," Grady repeated, then

scratched his head bec——
was thinking. For all he knew, she ——
about loving him. "Aw, hell. I'm going to ——
straight out and say it. I don't want you to leave Seahaven."

"Who said anything about me leaving Seahaven?"

"Mrs. Grumley. She wants you to stay."

"Why?"

"Hell if I know."

"I don't mean why does Mrs. Grumley want me to
stay. She explained that already." She paused, and a
crease appeared between her eyebrows. "I meant why
do you believe me?"

"I heard the tape with you and Mayor Black."

"Aaah," she said, managing to put a wealth of sad-
ness in the single syllable. "Special Agent Rodriquez
told you what I did."

"That's just it," Grady said, shaking his head. "He
didn't tell me until after I'd already listened to the
tape. Before then, I did like you asked. I listened with
my heart rather than my ears."

Her eyes filled with tears and her voice sounded
husky when she said, "I said you should see with your
heart rather than your eyes."

"Same thing," Grady said, covering his heart with
his right hand. "Because when I heard that tape, my
heart knew you wouldn't betray me."

"Of course I wouldn't." Some of her tears
brimmed over, and she wiped them from her cheeks.
"I love you."

"And I love you," he said, his heart full of her.

They met each other halfway, careful not to step on

...e thing to
...m. "I never lied

...his neck, pulling his willing
...s. She put her heart in her kiss,
...t him know once and forever that she
w... ...ly what she seemed: the woman who loved
hi...

Neither of them could speak for a moment when they finally surfaced for air, but then Grady managed to laugh.

"It's a good thing I believe you. Otherwise, I'd think you said all that because of Margo's plan."

"Margo Lazenby? You met with her? And you believe she's your grandmother?"

"She's quite persistent, my grandmother is, which you probably already know," he said. "She tracked down my cell phone number when she couldn't get in touch with you. I had a call from her about an hour ago, asking if I knew where you were."

Tori frowned. "Why would she want to talk to me? I've already resigned from the case."

"It has nothing to do with the case," he said. "It has to do with Lazenby Cosmetics. She said it came to her in a flash this afternoon that you would be the perfect choice to help her run the cosmetics company. She says you have flair and style."

Tori's mouth dropped open, because here it was. Finally. The perfect job. The road to independence. The

338